Finally the dark clouds parted and the blue skies appeared; the Allies were at last winning the war. Then came Victory night when it seemed as if all London had gone wild and they had a big street party. Annie still sat outside her house, but her limbs had stiffened so she made little attempt to go far. They all danced a knees-up, and even Sheila wore a coloured paper hat . The horror of the blitz and the buzz bombs was soon forgotten.

They had lit a big bonfire and weird shadowy figures careered around it but Annie sat dreaming of those who would never return. 'Well, fank God I've lived to see this day,' she said, albeit sadly.

Also by Lena Kennedy

MAGGIE
NELLY KELLY
AUTUMN ALLEY
LADY PENELOPE
LIZZIE
SUSAN
LILY, MY LOVELY

LENA KENNEDY

Down Our Street

Futura

A Futura Book

Copyright © Lena Kennedy 1986

First published in Great Britain in 1986
by Macdonald & Co (Publishers) Ltd
London & Sydney

This edition published in 1987 by Futura Publications

ISBN 0 7088 3273 3

Reproduced, printed and bound in Great Britain by
Hazell Watson & Viney Limited,
Member of the BPCC Group,
Aylesbury, Bucks

Futura Publications
A Division of
Macdonald & Co (Publishers) Ltd
Greater London House
Hampstead Road
London NW1 7QX
A BPCC plc Company

This story is dedicated to the slum street where I was brought up. It was called Witham Street, part of a poor area between East and North London, a small street that is no longer there.

I can still see in my mind's eye the shop on the corner run by the rosy-cheeked Mrs Appleby; the coal shed around the corner from where I humped a shopping bag full of coals every other day after school. I can taste the ha'p'orth of cracklings from Coren fish and chip shop in Hyde Road, the pie and mash, pease pudding and faggots – we never went short of food if we had a penny to spend, though that was not very often.

This book is for the little gang of mischievous boys that roamed our street – Dinny, Georgie, Nobby and Tony. One got the George medal for bravery in the Second World War but lost it to Long & Dowty's (the pawn broker) because he was Hearts of Oak. Some were lost in the war but others are still strong fine men who made good lives for themselves.

It's for the girls with whom I played endless games of hopscotch and skipping – Ninny, Eadie, Maudie and the Davis sisters.

We fought and made up, played out till dark in the street, which was the only place left to play as there was no room in our overcrowded houses. We were all poor, no one had many possessions yet our little community survived, until that big bomb razed it to the ground leaving us just with sad and fond memories. So to Witham Street I dedicate this story and I know all of you who write in and tell me of your memories will welcome it.

Lena Kennedy

Chapter One

Hopping

The Flanagans lived in a typical small back street of London's East End and theirs was the biggest family in the street.

'Twelve times Annie Flanagan's been in child bed,' old Gran, the midwife, remarked the last time. 'Annie's no bother. They just pops out on their own by now, they does.'

Indeed, childbearing was no trouble to Annie. After each child was born she would be up the next day and off to her job around the corner in the coal yard after handing the new baby to one of her daughters. Nowadays it was Sheila, who was thirteen and had not yet left school. She would often be seen parading up and down the street with a large cumbersome old pram in which two children sat at one end and the new baby was tucked in at the other. Around Sheila's skirt, several little ones hung on as she walked along the pavement, this tall, thin, ungainly girl who took on her responsibilities without a grumble. It was quite a burden for a girl of her age but she had had to take care of her little brothers and sisters since her elder sister Emily had started work in a blouse factory.

Sheila accepted her role with good will and cheerfulness. And while her daughter took charge of the brood, Annie Flanagan would be hard at work. With her mop of black curly hair swept up in a bun and her face so blackened by coal dust that only her bright blue eyes were visible, Annie would shovel lumps of coal onto a large set of scales to weigh them for her customers. These customers of hers were mostly young children. Coal was very necessary but extremely expensive so it was only bought at the yard in small amounts. Annie would dole it out into shopping bags – seven pounds or fourteen pounds at a time – and then it would take all the strength of two skinny little kids to lug it home.

Annie Flanagan was always bright and cheerful as she set about her work, for this was her livelihood and she enjoyed it. Her boss was a man called Jack Davies. He owned the business and was usually out all day with his horse and cart delivering coal to those better-off customers who could afford a whole sackful. He would roam around the streets yelling, 'Coal! Coal!' in a loud voice which echoed around the neighbourhoods. Sitting with him in the cart would be one of the Flanagan boys ready to help with a delivery or hold the horse's head to stop it bolting.

If one Flanagan boy left the job on Jack Davies' cart for a better job elsewhere there was always another Flanagan boy ready to take over. It was much the same with the wood chopping after school. One small Flanagan lad would sit on the cold stone floor of the back yard chopping wood up into thin sticks. After tying the sticks into bundles, he would take them to the local shop to sell for firewood.

When it came to part-time jobs – big or small – the Flanagans had a monopoly. No one else got a look in. And inevitably that caused some resentment in the street and harsh words were often muttered. 'Money-grabbing buggers, those Flanagans,' someone would say, and others would nod their heads in agreement.

But the Flanagans didn't care. Like most big families they clung together and looked after each other. Their small two-roomed house was the same size as all the others in the street and it was a wonder how they all managed to sleep in there, let alone eat. But that was always a secret, for outsiders were not encouraged into Annie's house. Every little Flanagan was up early in the morning and off to some kind of work before school or after school. Each one had his or her part to play; and every year Annie produced another little worker to add to this family workforce of hers.

Her husband, Dan Flanagan, worked at the docks. His was not a regular job but he had good luck as a casual worker and seldom missed a day. Every day the casual labourers went down to the dock and waited in a gang to sign on as the ships came in for unloading. Dan was a big man with a red face and a thick bull neck, and he always managed to push his way past the other fellows when it came to getting a day's work. Then in the evenings he would arrive home to be greeted by his mob of kids. The sides of his coat would bulge out from the loot he had managed to scrounge that day and secrete away in hidden pockets. If anyone had suggested to Dan that he was not honest they would have got a bunch of fives. What he had in his pockets was considered by him to be genuine perks of the job. Bottles of spirits were swapped with the butcher for legs of lamb; the grocer's bill at Appleby's was paid for with a couple of large tins of bully beef and there was always at least one little Flanagan urchin knocking at the neighbours' doors trying to flog some article of clothing or other.

Such was the Flanagans' way of survival. Theirs was a big untidy nest but it was a cosy one too, and kept warm and dry by the business spirit of all the members of the family.

When Annie began to carry her thirteenth child, nobody was surprised. Nor were they amazed that Annie shovelled up and weighed out the coal almost to the last day of her pregnancy, singing in her strong Irish voice or returning the jibes in her humorous way. 'Ah well, 'tis the grace of God,' she'd say. 'I'll hope for another girl this time. Got eight boys, so I might be lucky.'

Once a year when the coal yard was slack, Annie took her whole family for a holiday to the hop fields for three weeks.

'Gives the kids a bit of a holiday,' she always remarked, and some might have whispered that it helped her to save a few pounds as well.

So every August the Flanagan family made a general exodus from our street. They all went, except those who had to work – Dan and the two older boys, Joe and young Dan and, this year, Emily. But Sheila, Nancy, Letty and the other six little brothers all went off early one morning with Annie, wide with her pregnancy. Letty pushed the big pram full of toddlers while Sheila pushed another pram full of luggage and household equipment. The street folk would get up early on these occasions to peer out between the curtains to watch the Flanagans go. Each little child carried a packed bag and they all laughed and chatted and waved goodbye as if they were going on a world cruise. The smiles on their faces showed that they could not have been happier. On they marched, through the pale morning mist, all the way to London Bridge Station to board the train, the 'hopper special' bound for Kent, where the Flanagans had a regular pitch down at the hop fields.

It was a long train journey to Kent, taking five hours from London Bridge, but invariably the Flanagan family would arrive at the little Kentish station in good spirits ready to pile into the farmer's cart which was waiting ready to transport them all off to the hop fields.

Like the rest of the hop pickers they were given an old tin hut to live in for their stay. While the small kids shrieked with wonder and excitement as they ran through the farm's green meadows and pointed and yelled at the cows and sheep, Annie and her older girls would set about making their hut as comfortable as possible. There was an old wood stove in one corner but otherwise no furniture at all. In no time the mattress covers were pulled out of the suitcase and stuffed with sweet-smelling hay collected from the farmer. The old stove was packed with wood and lit so that soon it was hot enough for the kettle to be put on to boil. For their essential privacy, old lace curtains were hung up at the window, and the larder was well stocked with their provisions – tea, sugar and plenty of tinned milk.

After a supper of mackerel brought with them from London, the Flanagans would go to say hello to their neighbours in the other huts around. Every August it was the same. Many people came every year, so there were plenty of old friends to see and memories to recall. Someone lit a camp fire and the adults sat around it sharing bottles of beer while the children played outside until bedtime.

The next morning it was an early start for everyone to get a good pitch to work from sun up to sun down, stripping down the hops from their vines and dropping them into the hop bins. Everyone joined in. Whole families worked together each getting paid for the quota of hops they picked. Whatever the weather in wind, rain, heat or cold they all worked with a will and a lively spirit. Cockney songs passed along the lines of pickers; rude jokes were shared during the midday meal which was eaten hurriedly beside the hop bins. Lavatory facilities were provided at the edge of the field but they were rarely used. Most people went behind the heaps of empty vines so as not to lose precious time from the pulling and the picking of the hops.

The very small children all played together. These little mobs of London kids would go off scrumping apples and picking berries wherever they liked, leaving gates open and tramping over crops and becoming a general nuisance to the farmers. But the kids didn't care; this was their annual holiday from which they returned suntanned, healthy and happy, though occasionally a little lousy, since the washing facilities were not particularly good.

Typically, Annie who had been hopping for the past ten years, had it all well organized. A big tin bath was hidden under the hut. Every Friday night it was pulled out, placed beside the camp fire, and filled with water. In it, protesting loudly, the small kids were washed and scrubbed until their skin shone, and then their hair was denitted with a small-tooth comb. Annie's children were always immaculatly clean by the end of it.

On Sundays no one worked. This was the time to wander in the woods and stop and paddle in the cool streams. It was the time to take in the strange countryside that was so different from their usual world, to look at the birds and the deer, the fish in the stream and to listen to the wind as it raced through the trees, rustling the leaves and causing great trunks to sway. Everyone always liked it in Kent but no one was ever sorry to return to the grime of the city they loved. For they felt more at home in London than in the Kent country-side.

Annie Flanagan and her brood were well known to be the hardest workers on the farm and they had always made plenty of money by the time the three weeks were up. When it was time to return to the smoke, Annie was always happy to be going back with her fine healthy brood and the pram packed with huge hopping apples and the toddlers perched on top.

Fond farewells were exchanged amongst the hop pickers. 'See you next year,' they all called to each other. Some seemed a little sad but at least they knew they could look forward to seeing their new and old friends the next summer.

This year Annie was very heavy and her footsteps slow as they walked to the country station. The farmer's cart that had collected them did not take them back to the station.

'Reckon yer'll make it, Annie?' someone asked with great concern.

'Yus,' Annie replied confidently. 'I'll get 'ome in time.'

But back at London Bridge Station she said wearily, 'Come on, girls, let's get the bus. The boys can walk it and push the prams 'ome.'

So with her three daughters, Sheila, Nancy and Letty, Annie boarded the bus and made tracks for their East End home. She sat on the seat moving restlessly, and then she gave a big yell and clutched her belly.

'Stop the bus!' cried someone. 'This woman's having a baby!'

All the other astonished passengers got off to catch another bus and the kids were turfed off while a kind woman who knew what she was doing went to Annie's aid.

The ambulance arrived much too late. By the time it came, Annie was sitting up nursing her baby, but the ambulance men still insisted on taking them both to Bart's Hospital.

Sheila, Nancy and Letty trekked home together. 'Muvver had our baby on the bleedin' bus,' cried Sheila to a neighbour in the street.

'Oh, my Gawd!' the neighbour cried. 'What she have?'

'A girl,' said Letty. 'Goin' to call her Amy, after Amy Johnson.'

'Well, I never,' said the neighbour, and Annie Flanagan giving birth on a bus was the talk of the district for days. The *Star* and the *Standard* newsboys ran around yelling: 'Late night final. Baby born on London bus.' And the Flanagans even made it into the Sunday papers with a picture of the whole family standing outside their small house with Annie seated on a chair with the new baby on her lap. And the baby, Amy, was from then on known as 'our Amy, the one who got herself in the newspapers'.

Later, Annie said to Gran, the old midwife, 'Sorry, gel, I never made it for yer. I was so showed up with all them people looking on. I swear I'll have no more kids. I don't care where old Dan sticks it but it won't be up me.'

And Annie kept her word, for this little girl was the last of her brood. The baby of the family she remained and our Amy was generally spoilt by everyone. Not only had her arrival into the world brought a little notoriety to our street, but she was also a beautiful, pleasant baby with lots of golden curls, so who could not dote on her?

Annie went back to her job in the coal yard and did not fall pregnant again. As her large family grew up extra money was brought into the household. They now had lino in the passage and all the way up the stairs, and a pair of pretty new curtains in the front room. Emily, now courting, would sit in that front room on Sundays, kissing and cuddling with a nice young man, while her little brothers and the other street urchins would peer in through the window giggling and nudging each other as they spied on the young lovers.

And so life went on down our street much as it always had, even when times were hard for most people. The huge Flanagan family weathered the storm of the Depression and survived quite well in comparison to other poor families in the street. Perhaps it was their flair for enterprise and their unity that protected them.

In two years Annie was three times made a grandmother. First, Emily, who was now married and lived just round the corner, gave birth, and her baby was first to inherit Amy's pram. Then Annie's second son, young Dan, who now lived on the south side of London, became a father when his wife had produced one child and then another in quick succession. Nothing disturbed or bothered Annie. The kids left home, married and produced children; it was all in the way of life. No one got a posh wedding and very little time was taken off work for any sort of celebration. In 1938 her eldest son, Joe, joined up for the army.

Annie was quite stout now that she had finished childbearing and would puff out her cheeks as she lifted the huge coal shovel to fill the scales. But on Saturday nights, she scrubbed the coal dust from between the lines on her face, put on a white blouse and went to meet her husband Dan in the pub on the corner. Sometimes they would come home shouting and quarrelling and the whole street would listen. And sometimes they just sang uproariously and in harmony all the cheery Cockney songs, adding to the general belief that the

Flanagans were one great big happy family. Perhaps some were aware that war was in the air but none had a clue that it would change the pattern of life down our street and everywhere else, for that matter.

When Joe came home on leave from the army one day, Annie was pleased that he looked very smart and had two stripes. But Joe was not concerned with his appearance.

'Mother,' he said, 'you should think seriously of moving this lot out of London, because when the war comes it will be London that will get it.'

'What bleedin' war?' asked Annie in surprise. 'I never 'eard o' no war.'

Dan said, ' 'Ush yer mouff, boy. Don't come 'ome 'ere scarin' yer muvver and the kids.'

And Joe could see that there was little point in saying more.

Amy was now five and skipped and jumped along beside the pram and played ball in the road with the other kids. There was no problem with parked cars because it was a dead-end street, and so mobs of children played out in the road in perfect safety. At the other end was the Regent's Canal where the boys swam during the school holidays or fished for tiddlers.

One night big Dan came down the road looking a trifle weary. Half way down the street, he suddenly fell face downwards. All the kids milled around him not knowing what to do, until Charlie, the knock-up man, rushed out of his house and picked Dan up by the arms. Then he supported Dan's head which had lolled forward. Dan's face was bluish.

Little Amy took one look at her dad and then ran crying for Annie.

No one could revive Dan. He was taken to the local hospital in an ambulance but the bad news came back that Dan's heart had just given out. He was forty-five years old.

There followed the sad days of mourning and then the funeral. All the little girls wore homemade black-and-white checked dresses, and the boys wore black ties and had black squares sewn on their jackets. The neighbours were very kind; it was a shame to see this big Flanagan family so subdued. Yet the very next day after the funeral Annie went to the coal yard, and Siddy joined Jack Davies on the coal cart, Billy ran the paper stand, and Wally chopped the wood. So life went on. Annie's brood learned to survive the hard way. Only Amy was fussed and spoilt more than ever before. With her lovely blonde hair and her fat little legs, she would skip, jump and run, gathering compliments wherever she went. She was a charming, lively child, and well-loved by all.

That August the neighbours asked, 'Will you still go 'oppin', Annie?'

'Course I will,' replied Annie who yearned for the smell of the wood smoke and the happy company of the other hop-pickers. And indeed they went down to Kent, but that year they had travelled in style. Billy had learned to drive and had bought an old van which he used to do part-time removal jobs. So this year at the beginning of August they all piled in the van and off they went to the Kent hopfields. Thus Annie, her children and her grandchildren headed down to the old familiar hopping hut amid the glories of rural Kent, to the camp fire, the booze, the happy campers and hard work. Annie still wore a black dress but that was the only sign of her widowhood. The lines on her face had deepened but still the bright blue eyes looked out shrewdly onto the world, as amid her brood she began to pick the heavy, sweet-smelling hops at a terrific rate never ceasing to work until the sun went down.

Amy was not one for working hard and she spent most of the day playing with a tiny mongrel puppy that Wally had obtained for her. The dog was black and white and known as Spot because of the black patch over one eye.

No one in the hop field cared about what was going on away from it – that the world was in turmoil, and that

Chamberlain was visiting Hitler. No one was bothered. There was always peace and beauty down there in Kent. The huge ripe apples dropped from the trees and the children played in the sweet meadowlands. Life could not have been pleasanter.

But one rather chilly evening just before dark, a light mist rose from the road. A large car came down those country lanes rather too speedily. It was driven by a lady, a member of the local gentry, who had drunk rather too many sherries at a neighbour's drink's party. She was in a hurry to get home before her husband started getting angry. He did not like to attend these social occasions she loved so much and he tolerated his wife's attendance at them on the understanding that his own timetable was never put out. He liked to eat at 7.30 sharp every night.

This lady drove on, deep in thought and not paying attention enough to be able to brake as a little black-and-white dog rushed out from the hedgerow and ran across the road. She put her foot on the brake then but as the car went into a skid, she heard a great thud and saw a small figure, a child, being flung into the air.

The car had hit a tree and stopped. The woman was dazed and sat bewildered in her seat as blurred figures stood around the car, shouting and shaking their fists at her. Above their curses, she thought she could hear a child crying and gasping for help. Then as she was pulled from the car, she realized that the child was trapped between the wheels.

It was only when the fire brigade came that they were able to cut the young girl free. Then little Amy, unconscious, and badly injured, was placed with tender care in the ambulance and with her mother beside her, was taken to the Maidstone Hospital.

Annie sat in that hospital corridor for days, waiting and hoping for good news. On the fourth day she was told that Amy would live but that she had bad injuries and would need a lot of special care.

Annie sank to her knees. 'Oh, dear Lord,' she prayed, 'thank you.'

Amy was in that hospital for six months. Annie visited her twice a week every week. They had shorn off Amy's lovely curls. She had a deep scar on her forehead; her poor little legs had been broken and were in splints. But after the six months Annie brought her home to care for her. And as always, the other members of the family rallied round, taking it in turns to accompany Amy to the London Hospital for therapy as an out-patient.

It was nearly hopping time again before Amy recovered. She was no longer the little sunshine girl everyone had loved. She was often cross and querulous and got thoroughly spoilt.

The lady driver of the car had felt deeply ashamed of what had happened and offered Annie some compensation. But Annie had pride. 'No,' she had retorted. 'Just pay the horspital expenses, that's all I want from you.' She almost spat the words out. For she knew that her daughter would bear those scars for the rest of her life.

Chapter Two

The Blitz

It was the beginning of September 1939. The sun shone down the street and Annie stood in Mrs Appleby's little shop on the corner, her hands folded under the big sacking apron which she usually wore when she went hopping.

Mrs Appleby's moon face was more solemn than usual as she loaded Annie's purchases into the shopping bag for her. 'News ain't so good, is it, Annie?'

'No, it ain't,' replied Annie crossly. 'Bloody farmer don't want us dahn 'oppin' this year. He told Billy that the soldiers is goin' to do it.'

'It means one thing,' replied Mrs Appleby, 'that we definitely will have a war. It's not all propaganda, yer knows.'

'Well,' said Annie, ramming the rest of her packets in the bag, 'I won't be buyin' so much if I ain't goin' dahn 'oppin'. Won't need ter stock up on tea an' sugar.'

'Yer might as well, Annie,' replied Mrs Appleby. ' 'Cos it's all goin' ter be rationed, that's what they say.'

'I'll believe that when I sees it,' grumbled Annie. 'And I'll still save a few bob on yer bills.' With that, Annie stomped out of the dim, dusty shop into the bright sunshine. Standing on the corner of the street she yelled in a loud voice. 'Emily! Emily! Come over for a cuppa, and bring the baby. Want ter tell yer somefink.'

Annie's daughter Emily put her bedraggled head out of her

top window and yelled back. 'All right, Muvver. I'll just finish makin' the bed an' I'll be o'er. Put the ke'le on.'

Five minutes later, they were sitting in Annie's untidy cramped kitchen drinking tea. On her lap Emily held a chubby child who gnawed at a huge crust of bread. Emily looked like a younger version of her mother, with the same black hair and wide hips.

'I dunno what the world's a comin' to,' grumbled Annie. 'No 'oppin' this year and that old cow next door 'ad a face like a kike 'cause I didn't stock up on me provisions like I usually does.' Annie's big face was distorted with rage as her wide mouth worked angrily and her odd upper teeth gnawed at her bottom lip.

Emily said, 'We're goin' t'have a war, Muvver, there's more t'worry abaht than yer bleedin' 'oppin'.'

'And that ain't all,' declared Annie. 'Ol' Jack says he ain't openin' up the coal yard next season. Somefink abaht it ain't bein' worff it, and the guvment's takin' 'im over. I can't understand it.' Annie was quite indignant that her little world was being changed in ways and for reasons she couldn't understand. She was very upset.

'All I 'opes is that my Fred don't get called up,' muttered Emily. ' 'E might be, 'cos 'e's bin in the Terrys, yer know, an' they says that they will be the first ter go.'

'Ger away,' cried Annie, 'they got plenty o' soldiers. What abaht all the lads from this street? Only 'ad to ger in a bit o' trouble wiff the law and they was shoved in the army.'

Emily sighed and picked up her baby. 'I'll go 'ome an' listen to the wireless,' she said in a depressed voice.

'Lotter good that'll do yer,' said Annie, who never listened to it. 'It'd be better if yer cleaned up that bleedin' 'ouse o' yours.'

'Oh, shurrup,' cried Emily, her eyes full of tears. It never did any good to argue with her mother.

But Annie put on her cardigan. 'It's gettin' cold. I'll go and get the kids from school,' she muttered to herself. Then off she went down that familiar street towards the big council school to wait for the younger members of her family to come out at four o'clock. She realized how strange she was feeling; she hadn't felt like this since the day poor Dan had collapsed and died. She stared dismally at the spot outside Charlie Nelson's house where Dan had lain and drawn his last breath. She passed the big factory beside the canal where the workers seemed to be working hard at something or other. There were lots of sandbags all piled up; they seemed to be preparing a deep shelter. A shelter was what Annie would be needing before the end of the month, but she was a long way from realizing that. Annie never read newspapers, and seldom listened to the relay wireless that rang out from almost every house in the street except hers. Absorbed in her own world, the world of horror, bloodshed and partings had not become real to her, not yet.

The kids dashed out of school full of the news of the day. 'If there's war, we got to get evacuated,' said Nancy.

'Wot the bleedin' 'ell is that?' demanded Annie.

The little boys hopped up and down and ran around, yelling, 'I'm an airyplane, bang! bang!'

'Oh,' said Annie, ' 'ere yer are, go an' get some chips. I ain't cooking tonight. Might go an' 'ave a glass o' stout. I'm fed up wiff all this bloody talk o' war. C'mon, Amy, my luv, come and wait wiff me.'

Outside, Annie grasped hold of Amy's hand. But Amy, whose scarred forehead and stiff leg made her different from the other children, put out her tongue and snapped, 'No, I ain't! I'm going with Nancy to the chip shop.'

With a deep sigh, Annie let go of Amy's hand and went over to the pub. It was not open yet, and would not be until five. Annie felt quite fed up. It had really been a rotten day, but there were many, many more to come.

It happened on Sunday morning the next week. The relay

wireless, which was very loud, was being operated from a shop across the main road. For a small sum each week it was then relayed into the houses. The announcer was saying in a deep voice that the prime minister was about to make a special announcement. Everyone stood around waiting. The boys on the corner gathered round the nearest house and stood listening, caps perched on the back of their heads, chokers around their necks. The kids stopped playing and old folk stood by their front doors. There was a silent air of expectancy throughout the whole street, as if the words of doom were to be spoken.

'We are now at war with Germany,' the prime minister's voice declared with such a feeling of finality.

The silence remained in the air for a second or two, and then there was a loud buzz as everyone began to mill about talking.

One old man muttered, 'Wot's all the fuss? Lived frew two wars, I 'ave, an' wiff enuff brahn ale I'll live frew anuvver.'

But one old lady looked very worried. 'Oh, dear, the poor kids,' she wailed.

It was then that the eerie sound of the siren started up, at exactly eleven o'clock. Everyone looked astounded and then rushed hither and thither for a few moments before moving more quickly towards the new shelter which Annie had seen earlier being built underneath the factory.

Annie gathered her brood together and took them back inside her house. 'Nuffink to be frightened of,' she said. 'It's only practice.'

Ten minutes later the all-clear sounded and Emily came rushing back from the shelter with her children. 'Oh, Muvver,' she gasped, 'why didn't yer take cover?'

'Wot for?' asked Annie calmly. 'Was only a false alarm.'

'Well, it might not 'ave bin,' cried Emily in exasperation. 'I tell yer wot, I ain't stayin' 'ere. I'll get 'vacuated, me and my kids.'

'Please yerself,' returned Annie, 'but I ain't leavin' me house, not for 'alf a dozen bleedin' 'itlers.'

The day the kids came out of school with their notices to be evacuated, Annie was still arguing. 'Wot the bloody 'ell for? We ain't had no air raid,' she reasoned.

But Emily, who was always very sensible, said, 'Look, Muvver, it's compulsory for the kids, and you can go as well, if you like.'

'No, fanks,' said Annie, 'if I can't go 'oppin', I ain't goin' nowhere else.'

Nancy, however, was very practical. 'Get our fings together, Mum, 'cause we gotter be outside the school in the morning if we are going.'

'Won't it be nice,?' Letty said. 'It'll be real country where we are goin'.'

'Do what yer like,' declared Annie, plonking herself down in an easy chair. 'Yer always bloody well do, but I warns yer, yer will all be glad to get back 'ome again.'

The next morning, well scrubbed and quite tidy, the younger Flanagan children stood ready to go. Labels hung about their necks detailing their names and address; gas masks hung over their shoulders; and sandwich boxes swung by their sides.

Annie looked sulky and folded her arms obstinately. But Nancy kissed her and prepared to marshal the little group out of the front door.

Amy clung to Nancy's hand.

'Oh, not Amy!' cried Annie in despair.

'There's no reason why yer can't come, Muvver,' said Nancy, who was very adult in her way, 'other muvvers are goin'.'

Annie's lips clamped down hard. 'Write to me,' she said. 'I betcher will be 'ome next week,' she added.

As Nancy marched the little family out of the house Annie sat in her chair, too upset even to cry.

There was great excitement outside the school that morning. Everyone was saying goodbye. The mums were tearful and the kids were all playing up and enjoying the attention focused on them. It was such a momentous day when the kids were evacuated from our street.

And after they had gone, taken off in a bus to the railway station, an eerie silence hung in the air. The street was abandoned, deserted, the pavements were clean and tidy, and just a few straggly dogs and cats snuffled about searching mournfully for their little owners.

Annie sat in her tiny kitchen feeling quite dejected. Her arms were crossed and her brow knitted in a sullen expression. That is how she looked when Sheila came home from work. Then Billy popped in and Siddy arrived back from his last day working on the coal cart. He was black with dust. 'Muvver,' he said, 'where's the 'ot water? I wanna wash.'

Sheila had sat down very weary as usual. 'Wot we got for tea, Mum?' she asked.

'Get any Woodbines from Appleby's today, Mum?' asked Billy.

Annie shook her big mournful head, let out a sob, and then burst into tears with loud Irish howls. 'The kids 'ave bin 'vacuated and Emily and her kids have gorn wiff 'em too. What'm I goin' ter do?'

Her remaining children rushed to comfort her. Sidney kissed her and hugged her tight leaving a black mark on her blouse. Sheila clung round her neck and wept. 'Cheer up, Mum,' she said, 'I'll go an' get us some fags.'

Annie wiped her eyes and blew her nose. 'Oh, come on,' she said. 'Let's get the supper ready, life has ter go on.'

Soon the fire was burning bright and the kettle singing on the hob. Annie sliced up the big ham she had been keeping for the weekend, while Sheila fried chips. Soon the family, though somewhat reduced in size, was sitting around that great table once more.

Things began to happen very quickly over the next two weeks. First, Joe's wife wrote to say that Joe was in France, and then Emily's husband got called up. Billy volunteered for the Army Transport and young Dan was going into the Air Force. Annie could hold on to her family no longer. Before Christmas that year, her brood had gradually dispersed, leaving poor Annie feeling very alone and somewhat confused about what was happening.

Sheila clung close. She changed her job to sewing army uniforms and always came home after work each evening to keep Annie company. But when Sheila's boyfriend, Stan, got called up, she was very upset.

Only young Sidney seemed indifferent to what was going on. The war had lost him his job on the coal cart. The horse and cart had been sold and his boss had gone off to the country. Siddy now hung about on the corner with a small group of youths. Only those unfit for the services or too lazy to work were left, for most of the lads in the street had gone. Siddy signed on the dole and hung around all day. He lay in bed in the morning and stayed out half the night.

'Gerrup, you lazy sod!' Annie would charge into the communal bedroom in the mornings and bellow at him. To lie in bed late was a crime.

'Wot's wrong wiff Sidney?' she asked Sheila. 'Why's 'e loafin' around when there's good money to be made on war work?'

Fair, gentle Sheila would try to explain. 'Muvver, he don't believe in it.'

'Don't believe in wot?' Annie would ask querulously.

'In war, Mum. He doesn't fink people should kill each other.'

'Don't fink wot? Why, if 'is Dad were 'ere he'd ger a good 'iding, he would.'

'But, Mum, Siddy is really sincere. He had no intention of

fighting in this war. He says it's against his own working class. He has got principles.'

Annie could hardly believe her ears. 'Well! I never 'eard such nonsense! He don't 'ave ter go in the army if he's scared. Why can't 'e work in the factory, or somefink?'

'Oh, Mum, leave him alone,' Sheila begged, eager not to allow any rows to start.

Annie could not understand and was most disgruntled by her son's behaviour. But Siddy did not care. He wore a striped suit and a big wide hat. He spent a lot of time with his many pals and was seldom ever at home.

'Now where's that sod?' Annie would demand.

Gentle Sheila, sitting quietly knitting socks for the soldiers, would look at her anxiously. 'Mum, you have driven him out. All I hope is that he don't get into trouble.'

'What trouble?' exclaimed Annie. 'Ain't we all got enough trouble?'

And trouble had indeed begun, for each night it was a general exodus over to the shelter for Annie and Sheila since Hitler had begun his bombing of London. Even Annie realized that it was better to be in the safety of that deep shelter than under the flimsy kitchen table. She and Sheila went over every night and also often in the day when the daylight raids began. Sheila clung close and lovingly to her mum, and wrote long letters to her boyfriend until he went missing at Dunkirk. Then she became even more withdrawn and extremely nervous of the bombs. And so Annie Flanagan with that one last daughter, sat out the early days of the war in London, often wondering if she would ever see the rest of her family again.

Chapter Three

Evacuation

On that September morning in 1939, when the long crowded train pulled slowly out of Victoria Station and puffed its way down south, it had several hundred children aboard. The East End had been emptied of its child population, and these children were now being transported off to rural areas away from the expected forthcoming blitz.

The kids leaned out of the windows waving wildly and shouting goodbye to everyone in great excitement. To most, it was a great adventure. They sang raucous street songs such as, 'Let's all go dahn 'oppin',' with memories of happier days. A few tears were shed but were soon forgotten.

Nancy sat with Amy on her lap and pointed at the cows in the field through the train window.

Amy looked unhappy. 'Why didn't Mum come wiff us, Nancy?' Her voice sounded depressed. 'She will get killed when the bombs drop.'

'Oh, you mustn't say that, darlin',' cried Nancy, hugging her close.

Nancy was not yet fourteen and a very pretty girl. Her auburn hair hung down her back in rippling waves; she had long slim legs, a small waist and sleepy brown eyes. She was already becoming a lovely young woman, and here she was on her way to an unknown destination with a family of little brothers and sisters in her charge. But she was used to

27

minding the children; like her elder sisters, she had done this from a very early age.

An anxious Letty sat facing Nancy, occasionally sniffing or rubbing her nose. She was dark and a little highly strung. Next to her was Lily, who was dark, sturdy and very self-possessed. 'I wonder how the boys are,' Lily said. Boys and girls had been segregated on the train and kept in their original school classes to make it easier when separating them.

'We must try and find them when the train stops,' said Nancy. 'You know how mischievous they are.'

The train rolled on through the English countryside towards the southwest coast, but at a junction just outside a station, the train was split in two. While the first half continued on, the back half went off up to the Midlands, taking Annie Flanagan's little boys with it. They were to disappear for quite a few years.

Nancy was very worried when she realized that the boys had gone but a kind schoolteacher calmed her down and explained that there had been too many children for the small village that they were heading for, so they had sent half in another direction.

It was nightfall when the train finally stopped at a small station on the borders of Devon and Dorset. That first night away from home, the travel-weary children huddled down together under grey army blankets on the floor of the village hall, munching their sandwiches and sipping mugs of steaming cocoa. Some began to cry for their mothers, while others were simply too excited to sleep. The billeting officer, a young woman with a nice smile, spent the whole night going around and consoling them.

In the very early morning when the cock crowed and the Devon shores were lit up by the rising sun, the children were roused and told to stand up straight on the stage.

'We don't leave each other,' whispered Nancy firmly. 'Hold

hands tight, Letty and Lily, and I'll hold on to Amy's.' The four girls' faces were white and fearful.

Gradually the hall began to empty as nicely dressed folk came in to look at the children and take them away to their homes. One woman was directed towards the Flanagan girls. She smiled at them and then went out again.

'We are like a lot of bloody monkeys in a cage. I want to go 'ome,' snivelled Letty.

Nancy grimaced. 'Shurrup. I am tryin' to get someone who will 'ave all of us. I've told the obliging lady but she finks it's doubtful.'

Amy sat on the edge of the stage dangling her thin odd legs and each time anyone looked in her direction she put her tongue out at them or sometimes put her thumb to her nose and banged her heels against the stage to make a noise like a big drum.

'Stop it, Amy!' Nancy cried, 'Behave or no one will 'ave us.'

A very nice lady in a nurse's uniform came and stood beside her. 'What's your name?' Her voice was soft and musical. She had a fresh face full of freckles and a lovely smile.

'Nancy,' she replied quietly. 'And these are my sisters,' she added, pointing to Letty, Lily and Amy.

The woman cast an amused glance at the other girls. 'You can come to me if you want,' she said, 'but I can't have the other children, I'm afraid. I have to go out to work.'

'Oh, I'll look after them,' cried Nancy. 'No trouble, I always have done.'

'Well, bring that sister,' she said, indicating Letty, 'but I'm afraid we'll have to find a place nearby for the smaller ones.'

Nancy was at a loss. But because she did not know what else to do, she agreed. 'Be a good girl,' she whispered to Amy. 'I'll see you every day.'

But Amy wasn't having any of it. She started to scream and

cry out. 'I want my sister!' she shouted, and began to jump up and down noisily.

As Letty and Nancy disappeared, the billeting officer tried to cope with Amy. 'Now come, dear, you have got your other sister, and you're to go with this nice lady who doesn't live far away.' She pointed to a jolly fat woman who stood by the door waiting for Amy and Lily.

After many tears and much to do, the girls all settled into their various billets. Amy was very crestfallen at having been separated from Nancy and she clung frantically to Lily who was a little bewildered herself. But the jolly fat woman took them home along with some other kids to her cottage, gave them a nice meal of stew and potatoes, and did her best to please Amy.

Nancy and Letty were taken off in a smart pony cart driven by the kind lady who had chosen them. 'I am Mrs Trelawny,' she said, 'but I would like you to call me Miriam.'

The girls were amazed at everything they saw as they drove up a long drive hedged by huge bushes with purple flowers and came within sight of a big house with tall chimneys. A large glistening pond broke up the soft, rolling carpet of lawn.

'This is my home,' announced Miriam with some pride. 'Do you like it?'

Nancy and Letty just stared, open-mouthed and speechless as a motherly, white-haired lady took their coats.

'This is my mother-in-law. My husband is away in the army,' Miriam introduced them. 'I am sure we will all get on so well together. While the men have gone away it will be nice to have you help me take care of this big house. I am sure you will love it here.'

Nancy looked all about her, taking in the lovely fireplace, the shining brass and the gorgeous flower arrangements. Always a lover of beauty, she gasped. 'It's lovely, just like in the films we seen.'

Miriam put an arm about her shoulder. 'You know, you are a lovely young girl,' she said gently. Then seeing Letty standing there looking so forlorn, she put out a hand to her too. 'You darlings will be safe here with me, away from all those nasty bombs.'

That night when the sisters snuggled down into separate soft downy beds, it felt like sheer heaven. They had never had a bed to themselves before, or such a lovely hot bath with all that perfumed water. 'Oh, ain't it grand to be rich?' said Letty.

Nancy agreed. But then her expression became grave. 'I am worried about Amy. God knows what Mother will say about me leaving her.'

'She'll be all right,' replied Letty sleepily. And Nancy nodded as she too drifted off to sleep. They were all safe and well. Everything would be all right.

But all was not well with Amy. In that small cottage in the village Amy was being very naughty and badly behaved. She grizzled, would not eat her food and wet the bed in the night.

Poor Lily got up and tried to rinse the sheet under the tap and dry it before the morning but it blew away in the night and was found in the morning hanging on an apple tree.

'Oh, what naughty children,' cried the fat lady. 'Does your sister always wet the bed?' she asked Lily.

'Only when she's upset,' said Lily.

'All right,' said the lady in a firm voice, 'then she must sleep on this camp bed in between the rest of you. I'll not have my mattress ruined.' She did not look so jolly now.

But Amy would not stay in the camp bed. She screamed and cried, climbing into bed on top of the other kids and punching and kicking them. Throughout the second night pandemonium reigned.

The fat lady smacked Amy's bottom and then took her right back to the billeting officer in the morning. By midday,

Amy had been sent on to stay with someone else in another village six miles away.

When Nancy and Letty found Lily wandering around the village weeping, they were horrified. Staging a protest, they sat on the steps of the village hall and refused to move until someone agreed to tell them where their little sister was.

They rang Miriam Trelawny up at the military hospital where she worked, and she came to them at once. When she arrived, she was hot and breathless, having driven the pony cart furiously all the way. After much argument and debating inside the hall, she eventually came out with a triumphant smile on her face. 'Come on, children, let's collect your sister,' she said. 'And Lily, go and get your belongings. You can come too. My first decision was a mistake. I can see that now there will be no peace down here until you Flanagans are all together. And we can remedy this present situation easily enough,' she exclaimed.

Nancy flung her arms around Miriam's neck. 'Oh, Miriam,' she cried, 'you are wonderful! I'll be grateful to you forever.'

Miriam smiled. She was already fond of her young charges. 'I was an only child. It must be nice to have a lot of sisters.'

They rode out to the next door village and collected Amy from a thin anxious woman who had tied Amy's hands up in her pinafore because she had picked her nose at the table, and was making quite an issue of it. The Flanagan sisters hugged each other tight, delighted to be reunited again.

That night they sat around the big log fire in the library; Miriam listened while they talked of their mum and older brothers and sisters and the little brothers who had gone astray, and above all, the street where they had lived.

Miriam took Amy on her lap and pushed back the straggly locks from her brow. 'Now that is a bad scar,' she said. 'Perhaps we can do something to hide it.' With gentle movements she began to brush Amy's hair into a fringe to cover up the red scar. Amy loved all this attention and snuggled up close. At last she had found a friend in this big wilderness so far away from home.

So the girls all settled down to a peaceful existence with Miriam Trelawny in the very big country house that had been in her husband's family for many generations. Soon it was only the five of them because Miriam's mother-in-law returned to her own home.

Nancy and Letty took care of the house so that Miriam could keep her wartime job at the hospital which she seemed to enjoy so much. It was a good arrangement. Letty took the younger girls to the village school, did the shopping and then returned to help Nancy, who loved to clean and polish the nice furniture, and helped get the meal prepared. It wasn't long before Miriam had begun to rely on Nancy, that slim chit of a girl who learned so quickly the ways of the rich folk and kept the house so nice and tidy.

Miriam would cook in the evening and Letty took care of Pedro the pony, Barney the cat, and Mick, the red setter. They would eat their supper together and then each evening they spent together playing games, listening to gramophone records and writing letters to home.

Life was really very pleasant and the months flew past. The war seemed far away. Even when the bombs began to fall on London, no hint of such horrors ever entered Miriam's home.

'Once I am off duty from the hospital I like to think only of nice things,' Miriam often said. Then she would play the piano to them – beautiful classical music that the girls did not understand but Miriam's soothing spirit gave off a happy aura as they lay around listening to the sounds produced by her fingers.

Amy soon became Miriam's pet, and every night she got special treatment. One of her legs was still thinner than the other one, a little wasted, having been in a plastercast for a long time after the accident. Miriam would take this leg up on to her lap as they sat around the fire and she would slowly

and affectionately massage the weakened muscles. She cut
Amy's hair and gradually trained it into shape so that it
covered the nasty red scar.

Amy loved all the attention and began to thrive. She was
still boisterous but not so naughty, sliding down the huge
banisters, and chasing the cat everywhere, but within weeks
there was a noticeable difference in her.

Nancy wrote to her mother: 'We are happy down here and
Miriam is a very nice lady. You are welcome to come down
and see us, if you like,' she added.

Sheila read this letter out to Annie as she sat enjoying a
much-needed cup of tea after having come up from a long
night of bombs. They had slept in the damp shelter beside the
canal. Annie's face was very red and her hair dishevelled, but
her hard eyes brightened with tears as Nancy's words were
read out to her. But she held back her feelings. 'Oh, well,' she
said casually, 'that's four less to worry over. They certainly
seem to like it down there.'

Sheila sighed. 'Oh, I miss them all so much,' she said. 'The
house is dead without them.'

'Better ger off to work, Sheila,' said Annie, refusing to
wallow in sentiment. 'You might miss that bus. They don't
run regular to the city now.'

Pale faced, Sheila put on her hat. 'Now mind you stay near
the shelter, Mum,' she said, as she kissed her goodbye.

Annie gave her a grudging peck on the cheek. 'Stop
worryin',' she said.

After Sheila had left, Annie stood at the small front door
and stared out into the street. Some men were on the corner
fiddling with a barrage balloon which had come down in the
night and all the houses had a gloomy air about them. Old
Gran and Grandfather had gone away. Mrs Appleby's shop
was closed. There was Emily's house all shuttered and empty
and those that still lived in the houses in the street nearly all
went out to work. Most of the old neighbours had gone but

those houses did not remain empty for long. Young men on leave got married and took them over and their wives got pregnant and now a new generation was growing up. All gone was the comfortable old street full of kids. The fish-and-chip shop and the cooked meat shop had been bombed, and Charlie was no longer knocker-up but instead was an air raid warden.

Annie stood gloomily in the doorway thinking on these things and not knowing how to pass the day away. She was forty-five years old and the family had always kept her going. Now the warmth and the comfort of them all was gone; only poor thin worried Sheila was left. Joe was in the army now as a sergeant, Billy was there too, and young Dan was in the Air Force. God knew where they were. And what about her little boys who had been sent to some God-forsaken farm in the Midlands? She hadn't heard a squeak from them for some time.

'It's just like hopping, Mum,' Wally had written, 'but we don't like it so much because we get cold at night. Please send some sweets because we are hungry.'

Annie had gone up to the town hall to show them that letter, but they had waved it aside. 'Children exaggerate,' she was told. 'They are all together at least. If you want them home, just give the correct notice and we will bring them back to you.'

But Annie had shaken her head. 'No, let 'em be,' she said. 'I don't want 'em back.' As she left the town hall she sighed to herself. 'No use grumbling, I suppose. We're all alive, so that's wot matters. I'll go in an' 'ave a kip. Don't s'pose we'll get much rest down that shelter tonight.' And Annie went indoors and slept the day away.

Sheila came home in the evening, and the two of them had a meal together and then waited for the warning siren. Once it sounded it was off to the shelter for the night, on that cold stone floor on that old mattress, with Sheila tossing and turning fearfully all night while Annie's hip started to throb with that bloody arthritis again.

Such was the picture of our street in 1941. All around them had been laid waste but still the old street survived, even though some doors were missing and most of the houses were windowless.

'It's the old Cut that protects us,' one wise old man said. 'The Germans follows the water and head in towards the docks and the City.'

'Well, it's the only good thing it's done for us,' retorted Annie caustically, 'and it stinks to 'igh 'eaven.'

The next day the air raids started early before Sheila was even home from work in the city. Annie began to get quite worried. The Spitfires and Messerschmitts were having a dog fight over the town and the drone of the incoming bombers throbbed menacingly through the air.

Sheila had got stuck in town when she was unable to get on a bus. The conductor had pushed all the passengers off shouting: 'Take cover! We ain't going through this!'

The docks were ablaze. Acrid smoke filled the air and people ran, white-faced with panic, towards the tube to take shelter.

Sheila was worried about her mum, so she started to run in the direction of home, her thin legs going nineteen to the dozen. She gasped for breath as she ran, sometimes glancing up at the sky where the dog fights were going on. Suddenly she saw a huge flash and heard a loud explosion as a plane came crashing down over the roof tops into the Thames. Sheila stopped in her tracks and watched in horror as the pilot's body whirled out all alight through the air to land entangled on the telegraph wires just in front of her. He was a fair young man – not unlike her brother Dan – and he screamed terrible screams as the flames consumed him.

Sheila fell to the pavement in panic and shock. A burly air raid warden came running to pick her up but by then she was

hysterical and fought him off with extreme strength, screaming and shouting at the top of her voice. Eventually poor
Sheila had to be tied up before anyone could get her into an
ambulance.

All this while, Annie sat in the shelter listening to the
screams of the bombs. Through them she knew she could
hear the screams of her Sheila.

'Lie down, Annie,' a neighbour said.

'No,' said Annie, 'somefink's happened to Sheila, I knows
it. Oh, the only little gel I got left,' she wailed, 'what shall I
do?'

Hot tears poured down her cheeks. The neighbours were
silent; it was not often that they saw Annie Flanagan cry.

In the morning a policeman came to see her. Annie stared
at him like a zombie. What else could happen to her now?

But his news was not what she expected. 'Your daughter
Sheila is safe. She just collapsed with hysteria yesterday. They
are sending her home in the morning.'

'Oh, fank gawd,' said Annie, in great relief. But the shock
had done its damage. From that day Annie's hair began to go
grey and she no longer was the lively woman she had been
before, leading the community singing down in the shelter
carrying her bottle of stout. She became withdrawn and quiet
and clung to Sheila who was in an even worse state. Sheila
was not fit to go back to work because she was still suffering
from that terrible shock. She just sat with her head down
shivering and sobbing every night and no one could persuade
her to pull herself together.

Danny got compassionate leave and Emily came back from
evacuation with her two babies. She had hated being billeted
with a middle-class family down in Sussex.

'Oh, blimey, Muvver,' she said, 'it was terrible dahn there.
Yer life's not yer own, and those toffee-nosed cows just don't
like yer.'

With Emily back in her house and Danny home on leave,

Annie's life was brighter, but Sheila still did not improve. She would not stay a moment on her own and followed Annie everywhere like some nervous little puppy dog. The folk down the shelter shook their heads in sorrow. 'Poor Sheila Flanagan,' they would whisper. 'Not quite there, she ain't.'

But between them Emily and Annie took care of Sheila and Emily's babies.

Dan was not happy about them staying in London. 'Go back to the country and take the kids with you,' he said. 'It's not safe here.'

But Annie was as obstinate as ever and clung on to her little house which by now had been badly blasted. They spent the days in their shattered home and went into the shelter at night, Annie keeping Sheila close to her and her grandchildren around her.

Those Londoners who survived the blitz would always remember the bombing of 1942. How short those dark days were! No sooner had everyone finished work than it was off to the deep shelter for an unsettled night of sleep, and then out again in the morning traipsing through the burnt-out streets to work, past the acrid smell of burning flesh, and the tired faces of the firemen and the air raid wardens, who had fought a long night of bombing with no respite. But many still managed to laugh. 'It's a wonder that we are alive to tell the tale,' they would say. And usually, no matter how terrible the circumstances, someone always managed to raise a laugh to cheer the others. Every day long funeral processions would go by, and the rationing caused hours of waiting in queues for the few luxury goods that occasionally came their way, such as an orange or a banana.

A well-known figure Annie was, toddling off down the market in her faded blue cardigan wearing her carpet slippers which had pieces cut out at the sides to allow her huge bunions to have more freedom. As she passed the still-smoking buildings, Annie never gave those tragic heaps a glance. Her mind was riveted on the lastest shop in the market to have been bombed, for it would be having a damaged-goods sale. Then she would come home later with little toys and sweets for Emily's children and damaged dry goods for the larder. She was always in search of little extras. Sometimes she managed to get under-the-counter butter, or a bit of offal that might be going. Such things would be great treats to add to an otherwise dreary diet.

Emily was pregnant again – after her husband's latest leave. She rarely left the house now, in case she had to dash over with the kids to the air-raid shelter next door. She had become quite nervous.

Annie would sit on the long wooden seat in the dirty old shelter, peeling a much cherished orange for her grandchildren. In many ways she still looked as if she never had a care in the world, as if she had a natural resistence to life's knocks. And strangely, not once did she mention her younger children who had been evacuated to the country. She never answered their letters and so eventually they stopped writing to her.

It seemed as if Annie had entered a world of her own and was determined to survive. But even her resilience gave way after that terrible night when a stick of bombs fell right across the poorest parts of London wiping out the small streets and generations of families.

Earlier that month, after a bomb had hit the big shelter in Shoreditch, not far away, there had been plenty of talk down the market of it not being safe even in the shelters any more. But Annie just thought it was panic.

Emily's husband came home one night because he was stationed nearby. Emily decided to stay in the Anderson shelter in their garden with him and the children. 'At least we will all be together,' she said to Annie.

Annie shiffed. 'It's up to you, but I'll take Sheila down the deep shelter. She can't stand the noise of the bombs, let alone the guns.'

That night was the roughest London had seen. At ten o'clock at night the air raid wardens began to watch the incendiary bombs raining down. 'It's going to be a rough night,' they muttered to each other.

Annie and Sheila were tucked up together near the door of the shelter, so they were just missed when a huge bomb came whistling down and hit the top end of the shelter. That section disintegrated, and disappeared, with a mass of bodies, legs and arms, into the canal. The lights had gone out and the screams of the injured and dying were terrible. A huge cloud of dust rose up and large bits of timber fell on them. Annie and Sheila lay still, too terrified to move. The people who did rush into the street got caught by the next bomb which hit the end of our street and swept away all those little houses.

After the bombers had left, Annie and Sheila were helped out of the piles of debris. When they emerged coughing and spluttering into the street, what they saw before them was a wasteland. Sheila collapsed in a faint, while Annie stood, just bewildered, looking over the road to where Emily's house had been. Now there was only a pile of rubble.

The air raid wardens were everywhere, carefully picking their way through piles of rubble in their search for survivors. Annie stared, speechless with shock, hardly daring even to hope that her eldest daughter and family were still alive.

But by some miracle, they were. They were pulled from the mangled remains of their Anderson shelter bruised and dusty but otherwise unhurt. Annie ran towards them all and flung her arms around them, 'Tahnk God,' she murmured, 'Tahnk God'. Tears poured down her cheeks.

'It's a bloody miracle,' someone said.

Annie stood blubbering. 'Oh, Emily,' she sobbed, 'I can't stand no more. I'm ready to go to the country.'

Through the dawn came a mobile canteen giving out hot drinks. As the dust settled the extent of the damage became clear. It was appalling. Over a hundred people lost their lives that night in one little block of slum streets. Both Emily and Annie had lost their homes; nothing was left.

'Right!' said Emily's husband. 'You must go down to Dorset to join Nancy and the girls. They seem to be all right down there.' And Annie could not wait to be off.

Someone had put an old fur coat around Annie's shoulders and they went straight to Victoria Station in a Fire Service van. All along the way to the station they saw that the East End was not the only place to have been hit. The whole of London was laid waste. A bus had been overturned in the road and a sad silence hung over the great city.

CHAPTER FOUR

Village Life

It was a very different scene in the little village of Ashmullen, down on the Dorset moors within sight of the sea. In the spring the marshlands were full of flowers – gold masses of marsh marigolds, tall purple irises, and delicate blue and pink flowers mingling in the long grass bordering the dykes that ran down to the river.

On the higher ground the wild heather bordered the moorland and the tall pines swayed in the sea breeze. Before the war, Ashmullen had been a quiet, sleepy village but now there was a large army camp up on the moors, and huge tanks rattled constantly through the village. The village pub, the Tavern, was always full to bursting every evening with soldiers from every part of the world. For this was a training camp where the young men came to do a specialized course before going into battle. And the cottage hospital was now a military hospital and had doubled in size.

The village inhabitants were not at all pleased by this invasion of their tranquil existence but did at least appreciate the fact that they got a good living working for the army. And they had by now become quite used to the little evacuees from London. At first it had been difficult having them all milling around the place, but soon the shopkeepers had learned how to handle them, and the school teachers likewise. In two years, those children who remained had become quite accepted by the country folk. Certainly the girls up at the

Cedars, Miriam Trelawny's house, had settled down very nicely.

Nancy had grown tall and willowy. At almost seventeen years of age, she was quite a young lady. She now ran Miriam's house to perfection and received a weekly wage from Miriam, while Letty was a maid at the family hospital in the camp, coming back home every evening. Lily and Amy were still at school. Lily was a real tomboy and could play football and cricket for the village team better than any boy. But the one who had changed the most in this time was Amy. From that small cheeky guttersnipe with a chip on her shoulder, Amy had emerged from the chrysalis to become a charming little girl. She was tall and bonny with ash blonde hair she kept in pigtails, and she had developed a very posh way of speaking (having imitated Miriam, her heroine, mother and auntie all in one). 'I live up at the Cedars with Auntie Miriam,' she would boast to the kids at the village school.

Miriam found what materials she could and, because Letty was very handy with the sewing machine, the girls all had excellent wardrobes. At Christmas when they had a village party, Letty had taken an old evening dress belonging to Miriam and picked it apart. It was made of beautiful pink satin and was cut in a flowing style with loads of material. Letty made a straight low-necked dress for Nancy and a wide skirt for herself. The bits that were left over made a little dress for Lily, and Miriam bought a nice one for Amy.

All dressed up they went to the village Christmas party and stayed late to attend the dancing which followed the party. Nancy sang in a crooning voice into the microphone. 'Mares eat oats and does eat oats,' and she got everyone jiving. She was a lively girl and very popular with the boys of the services. What fun that Christmas party was! They all talked about it right through to the spring.

Life went on at an even pace. No one talked about the blitz, even though some nights they could hear the bombs dropping in the distance as Southampton and other coastal towns were bombed.

Miriam would hug the girls tight. 'It's all right, darlings, you are quite safe here,' she would comfort them. And so, in the warmth and security of this lovely home, the Flanagan girls grew up into lovely young women.

Miriam Trelawny had a lover. He was a captain named Jack, and he had been injured at Dunkirk and spent some time in the hospital. Now he was quite well, and fit enough to spend weekends with Miriam. Jack was fun and Miriam was very happy with him.

The girls quickly realized what was going on and were surprised.

'What about your husband?' Letty asked cautiously.

Miriam suddenly looked sad. She shrugged. 'We'll cross that bridge when we come to it,' she said, 'I truly love Jack and no doubt that will happen to you one day.'

'Not me,' said Letty firmly. 'When I get old enough I'm going in the WAAF's.'

Nancy looked very dreamy. 'Oh, it must be nice to have a lover.'

And Amy began to giggle. 'What about Dick?' she asked with a mischievous look in her eye.

'Be quiet and mind your own business!' Nancy snapped, looking very cross all of a sudden. 'Go off to bed at once!'

Any mention of Dick always made Nancy very angry. Dick was the son of the local fruit farmer whose land adjoined Miriam's. Each day Dick would arrive at the kitchen door bringing the produce for the day. He was a big husky lad with dark auburn hair but was very slow of speech, shy and awkward. The boy had spent his entire life on that fruit farm and now that his father was an invalid, he was responsible for the entire tract of land and those famous apple orchards which provided the special apple for the Devon Cider.

From the very first day Dick had gazed cow-eyed at Nancy

as she swept the kitchen floor, her slim hips swaying, the short cotton dress displaying the long slim legs and her bud-like breasts sticking out under the clinging bodice. Dick was devoted; he had never seen anyone so beautiful. In all his twenty years this kind and gentle lad had only ever loved his horses.

Nancy, however, was a little impatient with him and would snatch the basket of farm produce from him saying, 'Mind your muddy feet on my clean kitchen floor,' and would grumble and nag if he brought the wrong sort of vegetables.

Dick loved it and would sit there with a silly smile on his face, which just aggravated this pert Cockney miss all the more.

Dick was a sore subject with Nancy. He offered to take her riding and to the pictures. At this second offer, Nancy had bent a little. They went off one Saturday afternoon to the cinema but came back early. 'Oh, he's such an oaf,' Nancy complained. 'I can't stand him. He tried to put his arm around me in the pictures.'

Soon Dick had become quite a joke among the girls, but Miriam would say, 'Well, he's not such a bad boy and he's got a comfortable future. He's an only child and that's a big property. I nursed his mother and I visit his father pretty often.'

But Nancy was not going to be persuaded otherwise.

'Sorry, Miriam, but he is so slow, I can't stand him.'

One morning after Captain Jack had left his weekend bag behind, his batman came to the house to collect it. Nancy took one look at him and fell head over heels in love. The batman was small dark and half French, and was called Gene.

Nancy gave him cakes and coffee and smiled right into his face. His dark eyes flashed in admiration. 'You sure are a pretty gel, Nancy,' he said. 'You coming to the camp dance on Saturday night?'

Nancy smiled her lovely smile. 'I'll have to bring my sister Letty,' she said.

'That's all right,' said Gene with a grin. 'I'll soon get her hitched up.'

And so began the romantic times. On Saturday night Nancy and Letty put on Miriam's high-heeled shoes, made up their faces and curled their hair and kept that date at the village hop.

While Nancy danced with her dark admirer, Letty was fobbed off on to a sergeant who ended up very drunk.

Looking very pretty in her pink satin dress, Nancy danced very close to Gene. Their bodies were close, hot and sweaty, and every time the lights were dimmed, their lips met.

On the way home, they lingered down the lane. Letty yelled back 'Come on, Nancy! Don't hang about.' She had got rid of the fat sergeant.

A trifle hot and dishevelled Nancy ran towards her. 'Oh shut up, Letty, don't be such a spoilsport! Gene is so charming.'

'That's not what I would call him,' said Letty. 'Better watch him, if I were you. Don't go out with him any more.'

Letty's words of warning were wasted, for every evening Nancy was out on the heath with Gene, lying in the purple heather lost to the world of lovers with her dark French passionate Gene.

Miriam was not aware of this affair. Not one of her sisters would have betrayed Nancy by telling on her.

The autumn laid a glorious carpet of red-brown leaves in the woodlands when Nancy was in Gene's arms for a last farewell. He was returning to the front with his officer. 'I will write, darling,' he promised. 'We will be married the next time I get some leave.'

'Where are you going?' Nancy asked, her eyes wet with tears.

'I cannot say,' said Gene, 'but I promise I will let you know. I love you, I will never forget you, whatever happens to me.'

Nancy returned to the Cedars and dashed up the stairs crying, her heart felt broken.

Miriam sat beside the fire drinking a glass of wine. Her face was white and sad, for Jack too had just said goodbye. Realizing the situation she went to comfort Nancy. 'Oh, don't get so distressed,' she said gently. 'There will be plenty more boys in your young life. But for me it is truly over. Jack has a wife in Canada.'

The autumn breezes gave way to the frosts of winter. Soft white snow covered the land. They all stayed around the big log fire in the evenings, the huge tree logs sent out a warm glow. 'What would I have done without Dick this winter?' murmured Miriam. 'He got us all those logs, you know.'

Nancy said nothing. She kept her head bent and continued sewing.

'And hay for Pedro,' chimed in Letty, who sat on the rug with her old friend the red setter, who rested his head on her lap.

Lily and Amy were doing their homework. It was a cosy scene as the winds howled over the moors and the snow froze hard. Not many people came this far out of the village in this kind of weather, so it was surprising when they heard the noise of a car engine.

'What's that?' said Miriam when she heard the noise outside. Amy dashed to the window. 'It's the station taxi, and it's coming down the drive,' she cried excitedly.

When the loud sound of the door knocker echoed through the house, Miriam looked a little scared.

'I'll go,' said Lily.

'No, wait for me,' said Miriam, but young Lily had already reached the door and opened it wide.

To everyone's amazement, standing there was a little crowd of wet and decidedly unhappy people. There was Annie all wrapped up in an old fur coat, Emily, heavily pregnant holding on to her two young children, and thin pale Sheila in her old woolly hat.

Nancy ran out into the hall crying. 'Oh, my God, it's our Mum, Sheila and Emily! What are they all doing here?'

Annie let out a big howl of welcome. 'Oh, Nancy, we've got nowhere t'go so we all came to find you.'

Nancy hugged that faded old lady, for Annie's hair was now quite white and her shape sadly deteriorated.

'Come in out of the cold,' cried Miriam, ushering them all into the hall. 'Take your wet things off and come near to the fire. Go and put the kettle on, Nancy.' She gave no sign of any annoyance, she was just concerned for those cold shivering people.

Emily rubbed the little girls' hands and warmed their toes to the fire, while Nancy got hot drinks for them all. Suddenly that cosy sitting room was full of people. 'Sorry to inconvenience you,' said Emily, 'but it got too bad in London and our houses got blitzed and the shelter received a direct hit. Lots of our neighbours were killed, so we packed to go away and this is the only place I could think of.'

'Well, you did right,' said Miriam, patting her hand and looking around her at this motley throng with a look of confused pity on her face.

There was Sheila who just dropped in a chair by the fire and simply stared into space and the little girls lay on the rug with Amy who gave them some of her cherished store of toffees. Annie sat in the middle of the room looking like some mournful cow while Emily sat back with her long untidy hair in a pony tail, no make-up, a tear-stained face, and her stomach very high.

'How long have you got, Emily?' Miriam asked.

'Two weeks,' said Emily. 'I fink I'll 'ave ter go t'the 'orspital.'

'Well, we'll sort it all out,' said Miriam reassuringly. 'In the meantime, you can all stay with me till we find somewhere for you to live. Come with me, Nancy, we'll try to get that spare room into shape just for tonight.'

Nancy went with her upstairs but stopped at the top landing. 'Miriam,' she said, 'if there was ever an angel it must be you. How could they do it? All of them descending on you like that? I feel quite ashamed of them.'

'No, you must not say that, Nancy,' Miriam said, 'For these are desperate times and they need desperate measures.'

Within a couple of hours Annie and her elder daughters were installed in the spare room, and Emily's little girls were in with Amy and Lily in their cosy bedroom. A good time was had by all.

Of course, it did not take long for this big family of the Flanagans to disrupt the tranquillity of the Cedars. Emily's girls played snowballs, built snowmen, ran in and out of Nancy's clean kitchen, and made the floor filthy, and during the night poor Sheila had screaming nightmares waking up everybody.

Then Emily went into labour and they had to get an ambulance to take her to the hospital. Miriam was as calm and smooth as ever, her medical training seemed to carry her serenely through these adverse circumstances.

Annie would insist on sitting in the middle of the kitchen, a bowl in her lap as she slowly peeled the potatoes and dropped bits on the floor. If she had nothing to do then out would come her packet of Woodbines, and the dog ends would be thrown in the clean grate.

Nancy cleaned up after her with dustpan and brush and was getting more and more exasperated every day. Poor Sheila did nothing all day. She just crouched in the same spot on the wide window seat staring out at the snow-covered garden, while Letty was always busy with the pony or the dog and cat when she was off duty from the hospital.

Lily, who often used to help, now larked about all day with

the small girls, playing hide-and-seek and rummaging in the big attics; they all had a good time except Nancy, who was very depressed.

When Dick arrived with the vegetables the first time after the family had arrived, he stared in amazement at Annie sitting puffing at her fags. 'You got a big houseful, Nancy,' he said slowly.

'Mind your own business!' she snapped. Then to prevent him making any further comments, she began to go down to the gate to intercept him.

Dick, however, was rather pleased with this arrangement and took it as a compliment. He would hang on to the gate looking at her and prolonging his visits.

But one day Nancy stood with her head against a tree and really wept. Dick put down his basket and put his arms around her, Nancy did not resist. His were warm and comforting arms, and she was feeling so very down-hearted. She had not had one word from her love, Gene, and it was breaking her heart. In addition to having the burden of her family, it was all too much to bear. She was weeping tears for her lost lover, and Dick was concerned. 'Don't 'ee cry, lass,' he said gently. 'I'll find them a cottage and that will make you happy.' Nancy did not pull away. She let Dick wipe her eyes and cuddle her close. She was so hungry to be loved and the sensual sexy Gene had awakened such emotions in her so that she did not know whether she was here or there.

Dick was as good as his word. 'There's a tied cottage down the road to the village,' he announced a few days later. 'The old folk who lived there have died but I'll get it tidied up for your family, Nancy, and maybe they can get work on the farm in the spring.'

When Annie was told about the cottage, she was not at all sure about it. She even went so far as to say that perhaps she ought to go back to London. But, Emily, exhausted from the demands of her newborn baby was quite adamant. 'For Christ sake, grab that cottage for us, Nancy,' she said. 'Why, it's a Godsend; you'd never get me back to the blitz,' she added. 'Got me kids to fink abaht.'

Miriam was delighted and thanked Dick for his help. Dick smiled in his slow way and said, 'I thought it would be better for Nancy, not having so many folks to take care of.'

Nancy smiled at him gratefully and allowed Dick to put his arm around her. And Miriam's eyes gleamed with amusement and pleasure at the sight of them both.

So it was that Annie, Sheila, Emily and Emily's three children moved into that small cottage. It was very old and small and lit by candlelight. But it had charm and was quite comfortable. Miriam had collected bits and pieces of furniture for them and even gave things of her own which she said she did not need. The girls all helped to make the place look nice and everyone was pleased.

Occasionally Annie grumbled about the place, complaining about how quiet it was and how far from the shops, but Emily was quite firm. This was their home and it would stay that way. They were not going back to London, she had had enough.

Even Sheila seemed to improve in the country quiet. She left off her woolly hat as the spring came and spent many hours walking along the woodland paths picking snowdrops and primroses to take home to put in a jar for the windowsill.

Slowly and quietly, Nancy's attachment to Dick grew. It became a common sight to see her walking out with him hand in hand through the woods and now she often went over for tea at the farm where Dick's Aunt Edie kept house and looked after Dick's father who was now crippled with arthritis.

Nancy came home one day looking quite flushed. When she was alone with Miriam, she told her why. 'Dick wants to marry me,' she said. 'Very soon.'

Miriam smiled and hugged her tight. 'Congratulations,'

she said. 'I'm delighted for you both – but what's the big rush? Don't you want to enjoy your engagement for a while?'

Nancy shrugged and looked away, a sad look in her eyes.

'But why so sad, darling?' asked Miriam. 'You are in love with Dick, aren't you?'

Nancy pulled her to her and tears fell down her cheeks. 'Oh, no Miriam,' she wept, 'but he does love me. Gene never even bothered to write to me.'

Miriam stared keenly at her for a moment and then stroked her hair gently. 'It's all right, darling, I'll see you have a nice wedding. And I won't lose you, you'll be my neighbour when the war is over. And it must end some time.'

The wedding of the pretty young Londoner to the local farmer's son was the talk of Ashmullen for quite a while. Nancy made a lovely bride and Dick, the big husky farmer lad, was very proud of her.

Big brother Joe came all the way from London to give Nancy away and Annie was made to wear a hat, which she did under great protest. It was a big black straw hat which Letty had trimmed with a bunch of artificial cherries, Annie wore it lopsided, her face a beetroot red. She had never worn a hat before and it embarrassed her.

Nancy's four sisters were bridesmaids and Emily the matron of honour. Miriam bought their headdresses and Letty made all the dresses. It was a big community affair and even with rationing they did well with legs of pork and turkey delivered at the back door. Even the village baker managed to bake an enormous fruit cake which he iced for them in elaborate patterns. The excitement was great. It was Easter and sunny. The village church was full of spring flowers. It was such a lovely peaceful scene that no one would have believed that not many miles away the army was secretly preparing for that big invasion of France where much blood would flow and many lives would be lost.

Joe was now a strapping great sergeant and physical training instructor, having served his time at various battle fronts he was now in England with a commando regiment. The Flanagans were all very proud of him and showed him off to the rest of the village. Joe, a happy-go-lucky character, had married a young Irish girl at the very beginning of the war. She had recently returned home with her children for the duration of the war, and it seemed that Joe was looking out for a good time.

When Joe first arrived, he told them the news of the three little brothers who had disappeared in 1939 during the evacuation. While he had been stationed in the Midlands he had tried to find out what had happened to them. When Annie never replied to their letters, the little boys had given up writing. No one had heard from them for years.

Joe had found out quite a bit about them. 'Those buggers played up merry hell in that village, I can tell you,' he informed his mother. 'When I got there they were in an approved school, something like Borstal. I protested right away but it seems they got no reply from you, Muvver, when they wrote.'

Annie shrugged. 'Ain't I got enuff to put up wiff wiffout them buggers playin' up?'

'Well, they are all right now. The twins are at the Duke of York Army school, but I couldn't get Wally in there, he's too young. But he's working on a good farm now and loves the life there.'

'Always was one for bloody animals,' grunted Annie.

'So you don't have to worry about the twins,' continued Joe. 'They'll go straight into the army when they are the right age. But I hope the war's all over by then.'

Although he did not show it, Joe was impatient with his mother. He could not understand her nonchalant attitude to everything, for he was a conscientious man, a hard grafter, and a leader who had made a good career of the army. Joe's only one failing was that he was a womanizer. At Nancy's wedding he got very drunk and made it obvious that he had his eye on Miriam who looked extremely chic that day.

Joe insisted on escorting Miriam, Amy and Lily back to the Cedars, and he did not return to the cottage that night. In fact, he was seen sneaking out of the back door of the house early the next morning.

'He slept in Miriam's bed,' Lily told Amy.

'Don't let on,' replied her sister, 'stay stumm. It pays.'

After Easter, with the long summer days stretching ahead them, Annie, Emily and Sheila got work on the farm picking fruit and helping in the packing sheds. Annie felt in her element. It was just like the good old days down at the hopping, sitting out in the fresh air with Sheila and Emily eating a meal under the hedge and Emily's baby in a carrycot beside them. The weather was good and the extra money they earned helped them live a more comfortable life.

With her face covered with freckles, and her long hair tied up in a bright scarf, Emily looked the picture of health as they picked the sweet strawberries. 'I've 'ad a few ups and dahns in me married life,' she said, 'but this is the 'appiest time I can remember. Here in the fields, it's so peaceful. Yer gets the backache but wot's that ter wot we bin frew in London?'

Annie squatted on a stool deftly putting the ripe strawberries in the wicker baskets. 'Yus, Emily,' she agreed. 'And just look at Sheila, she works wiff a will. I've seen a big change in that girl, I 'ave, since we come dahn 'ere.'

'I can't fank Dick enuff for it, our Nancy's done well for 'erself when she 'ooked 'im,' said Emily.

'Oh, well, she's a lovely gel, an' now got a baby due for Christmas. All the time the family grows, an' some goes,' said Annie. 'Poor Danny,' she added, thinking about her second son who had been killed in the Air Force.

'Now don't start, Muvver,' said Emily. 'Let's all be cheerful while we can. Wot abaht a song, eh? Emily did a little dance and in her Cockney tone sang, 'Wiff the partin' of the ways, you took all me 'appy days and left me lonely nights.'

Annie and the other field workers joined in.

Amy was now in the fourth form at school. She always studied hard, put on airs and graces to the village kids and spent very little time with her own family, preferring to pretend that she belonged to the more refined air of the Cedars than anywhere else.

Lily, however, was quite different and romped with her small nieces, Emily's children, taking them on long hikes in the woods and rambles over the common. Letty had turned sixteen and announced that she was going to join the forces just as she had always planned. She was now just waiting for her papers to come through.

'It seems that I am going to lose my little family,' Miriam said rather sadly.

'No, you are not, Auntie Miriam,' insisted Amy. 'I'll never leave you, ever.'

Miriam stroked her head where that faint line of the scar still showed.

'Yes you will, darling,' she said. 'It's a big old world out there but I will always love you.'

As far as the Flanagans were concerned the war could go on forever. They took little notice of events or news from the Front, and just merged into life of the village. Whenever Joe got a weekend leave he would come down and take them all – including Miriam – to the village pub, and they would sing all the Cockney numbers. The bar would be quite taken over by the Londoners.

Nancy, now a respectable farmer's wife, kept her own counsel but she would come visiting bringing eggs and butter, precious commodities that were rationed. It was all great fun, but as usual life was not going to allow them too much happiness.

When Emily's husband was invalided out of the army, he came down to stay at the cottage. Fred was always a worker but he hated rural life. 'It's fairly quiet up London now, Emily,' he said. 'Why don't you come home?' he begged.

Emily was not impressed, 'I can't leave Mum,' she replied flatly.

So Fred went back to London on his own and went into lodgings. Emily was very fond of him and got depressed when he wrote to tell her he was going to the Midlands where he had been offered a job in a car firm. Now she gave in, 'Find us a house and I'll come to live there,' she promised him in a letter.

So by autumn Emily had gone, taking her children to live in the Midlands. She said goodbye to her happy days, and was never to return.

Letty was the next to say goodbye, all dressed up smart in her WAAF's uniform. Then Lily, who had been working at the hospital as a maid, got a chance to train as a proper nurse and went off to Plymouth to be a probationer nurse in the big hospital. That left only Sheila and Annie in the cottage, and Amy living with Miriam.

Amy loved it at the Cedars. Now she did Nancy's job of looking after the house. As far as she was concerned this was her own lovely home and Miriam her auntie, her much loved auntie.

Joe's outfit was moved on. Billy was still in London and wrote to say he had been allocated a house and that his wife and baby were now back home with him. He said it was a big house with three floors in Gospel Street not far from their old street, and that if they wanted to come home they could live upstairs.

Annie began to pack right away. It was too lonely down in

the country for her without Emily. 'You coming home wiff us, Amy?' she asked.

Amy looked aghast. 'No, I'm not – certainly not, I'm staying with Miriam.'

'Please yerself,' said Annie, 'she won't want yer 'anging on forever.'

CHAPTER FIVE

Back to the Old Surroundings

With Sheila in tow, Annie returned to her own grass roots. She did not get on with Emmy, Billy's wife, who wisely stayed clear of her. Annie and Sheila occupied the upstairs flat of Billy's house, one of the strong, well-built houses in that street which had survived most of the blitz. The War Damage Authorities had renovated these buildings during a respite in the bombing. The raids tended to be lighter now and mostly on the coastal towns, the Spitfires having deflated Hitler's bombers and 'given them wot for', as the Cockneys expressed it.

Annie wasn't the only one home. The Londoners came back in droves to new accommodation for themselves and their children. They were all a bit older, there were more weddings and more babies. And life went on for a while quite peacefully for the ex-evacuees.

Annie put on her old cardigan and her tatty carpet slippers and toddled off each day down to the market stopping to gossip to the stall holders who remained and the conversation always revolved around the blitz. Everybody knew Annie and most of them liked her as she stood around gathering up the threads of the life she had left behind.

'Nice ter see yer back, Annie,' they said.

'It's good to be 'ome,' replied Annie. 'So yer got frew it, all right. Wat abaht old Barnet?' She pointed to the bombed-out shop that had once been the shoe shop.

58

'No, mate, he copped it,' said the stall holder.

'Oh, well,' said Annie, 'it's a good job some of us is left. I lost my Danny, I did. First time 'e was in that aeroplane. And I never wanted him to join the Air Force.'

'Never mind, Annie, you still got Billy and Joe and I see Siddy doing all right for 'eself.'

'Don't talk to me abaht that bleedin' Siddy,' said Annie. 'Never went to war and now 'e's a crook, so they tells me.'

'Oh no! not as bad as that, Annie, just a spiv – has a little fiddle, that's all.'

'Well, he can stay out of my 'ouse,' said Annie flouncing off in a very determined manner.

Always not far away from home was Sheila, who had gone back into her shell since they had come home. She found herself another woolly hat and drooped along behind Annie without a word to say for herself.

'Pull yer bleedin' self togeffer, gel,' Annie would say. 'You was all right when we was 'vacuated, wot's wrong wiff yer now?'

But Sheila's lips would twitch and her eyes would roll.

'Oh, my gawd, she's goin' ter 'ave a fit.' Annie would yell for Billy and he would lie Sheila down and put a spoon in her mouth. For Sheila's delayed shock had developed into epilepsy.

'Take Sheila to the hospital,' Billy would say, 'I am sure that someffink can be done for 'er.'

'Leave 'er be,' said Annie gruffly. 'She's all right wiff me.'

So lovely gentle Sheila, so fair and so sweet, was condemned in her early twenties to a life of misery.

Emily wrote very often to say that Fred had a good job and they had a nice house in the Midlands town, Joe had been posted out in the Far East.

One day Siddy came visiting. He had grown very big and broad shouldered and wore a pin-striped suit and a wide hat. He was carrying a big parcel of food, and when he grinned he revealed a gold tooth in his front teeth. Billy welcomed him in. But Annie refused to allow him up the stairs. 'I don't want that crooked sod up 'ere,' she yelled from the landing. Billy knew his mother too well to press the issue further, but Siddy had brought whisky and chocolates with which he treated Billy, so he was quite happy. 'How yer doin', Sid boy?' he asked.

'Okay,' Siddy said. 'Got a bar dahn Befnal Green Road. It's called a Beer Club, but you know how it works, still plenty of booze to be got under the counter.'

'Good luck t'yer mate,' said Billy. 'Glad some made it. You married?'

'No fanks,' said Siddy, 'but I got a nice little gel who runs the bar for me. You remember Sadie Goldman? Her old man is Yiddish, he used to 'ave a stall dahn the market.'

'Oh, yes,' said Billy, 'clicked all right there, mate. Not to worry abaht 'er,' he indicated upstairs. 'Knowing Muvver, she'll come round in the end.'

'But what happened to Sheila?' asked Siddy. 'She didn't know me. She just ran away when I spoke to 'er.'

'The blitz, mate, sent 'er crackers,' said Billy very noncommittal. Sheila was not his problem; she was Annie's.

Placidly Annie settled down to her own old surroundings and to everyone she met she chatted about the good old days before the blitz. But within two months of their return, one of the worst periods of the war began. It came without warning when everyone was settled to sleeping at home, starting as a curious kind of drone from the sky, just one stray plane that looked too small to worry about. Then quite suddenly the drone of the engine ceased and the plane dived down to earth devastating all before it. This was Hitler's new weapon – the dreaded buzz bomb.

Billy had been on fire watch that night and could see these small flying bombs coming down just outside London. 'Looks like a dog fight out there, mate,' he told his companion as with huge flashes the buzz bombs exploded in the air, the rest went down on built-up areas of the town.

In the morning the results were devastating. Hundreds had been killed and wounded but luckily the big house in Gospel Street was still standing. Billy sandbagged the cellar and made it secure for everyone to take cover. 'When the engine stops, dive down into the cellar,' he instructed them.

This had a terrible effect on poor Sheila and Annie, whose arthritic hip made it very difficult to get down there in time. The buzz bombs came by day, hour after hour, but as with most things, the Londoners got used to them. They would listen to them coming down and say, 'Yer number's not on that one, chum,' and go on with the day's work.

After a few days, Annie had had enough of being cramped in that cellar, and she began to go out on her regular trots down the market. 'I can't go runnin' away no more,' she told them. 'If it's me lot, that's it. Can't keep on dodgin' 'em.'

Later on, the rockets came, a bigger version of the buzz bomb but without the noisy little motor. These bigger bombs came with no warning at all and did a lot more damage, but the fighter planes went up and intercepted this latest hazard as they came in across the coast. And the British and Allied Forces stood their ground against Hitler yet again.

The war had been on for four years and Annie's family was now spread all over the war areas. Joe was out in the Far East, Letty was in Scotland on a gun site. Lily was in a Plymouth hospital and Emily with her little family was in the Midlands. Annie's twins were now in an Army Training School and Wally was a farmer's boy, though no one ever heard from him. Annie would sit and think of her brood of children, spread all over the place. For in her awkward way she was fond of them all except poor Siddy. There was just no way she would entertain Siddy, even though he left little packages of food on her doorstep, good food which she found very acceptable. But for his kindness, she would not acknowledge him.

One day Billy received the terrible news that a rocket had hit Emily's house in Coventry, and that the whole family had gone under – Fred, Emily and the three children. Billy stood in the passage sobbing. 'Who's going to tell Annie?' his wife, Emmy, asked gently.

'Oh God!' cried Billy, 'I can't do it, not yet, I can't.'

Emmy said, 'Well, don't say anything then, give yourself time to get used to it.'

Siddy was told and they all decided to stay stumm, for no one could face telling Annie. She thought so much of Emily her eldest girl and those three little granddaughters.

But of course Emmy told her mum, who in turn told someone down the market who told someone else and, as Annie came toddling down the market street one morning with a cheery smile on her face, a woman came to her side saying, 'Oh, Annie, I'm sorry about Emily and her kids.'

Annie stared back at the woman in amazement. 'She's gorn up to the Midlands. Ain't 'eard a word since before Christmas.'

'D'you mean she never got bombed?' continued the woman without a thought. 'Well now, I 'eard they all went under, 'er 'usband as well.'

Annie opened her big mouth wide as if to speak but not a word came out. Her legs crumpled and Annie fell face forward in the middle of the market street she knew so well. Sheila, terrified witless, ran away screaming her head off to find Billy.

Annie was taken to hospital where she was examined. 'She'll be all right,' the doctor told Billy, 'but she has had a terrible shock.'

'Oh, Mum, I'm sorry, I should have told you before,' wept Billy.

Annie sat up in bed and stared at him with a stony eye.

'Well, I knows nah, don't I?' And from that time on she never mentioned Emily again, but she became feeble and would sit outside the house on a chair just staring into space. Losing Emily and her little ones had been the final blow.

Finally the dark clouds parted and the blue skies appeared; the Allies were at last winning the war. Then came Victory night when it seemed as if all of London had gone wild and they had a big street party. Annie still sat outside her house, but her limbs had stiffened so she made little attempt to go far. They all danced a knees-up, and even Sheila wore a coloured paper hat. The horror of the blitz and the buzz bombs was soon forgotten.

They had lit a big bonfire and weird shadowy figures careered around it but Annie sat dreaming of those who would never return. 'Well, fank God I've lived to see this day,' she said, albeit sadly.

Sheila, who still seldom spoke, said shyly, 'Maybe our Amy will come home now.'

Down in the village of Ashmullen, they also celebrated the Allied victory with a big party on the green. Nancy was there with her little girl, Heather, who was now a year old. She was as dark as Nancy and Dick were fair, and her parents worshipped her. The night that Heather had been born Dick had got drunker than he had ever been in his life. He and all the farm hands had poured gallons of Devon cider down their throats. Dick was a happy man. Nancy seemed to have settled down and loved her role as a farmer's wife.

But there were quite a few farewells that summer. Dick's Aunt Edie went off to live in Florida, taking Dick's father with her, for the benefit of his health. Nancy had all the rooms of the old farmhouse redecorated, and polished all the copper and brass until everything shone clean and bright.

Nancy always referred to her husband as 'my old Dick', much to the amusement of Amy.

'Why *old* Dick?' she laughed. 'He's only two years older than you.'

'Oh, you know what I mean,' smiled Nancy, 'he's so sweet and so slow.' And now there was genuine affection in her voice.

Amy was fourteen. She had grown tall and had a pretty freckled face. Her hair was cut in a page boy bob with a heavy fringe which hid the scar on her forehead. Amy was actually feeling a little disgruntled, for Captain Trelawny, Miriam's husband, had returned from the war, and Amy did not like him one bit. 'He barks like a blooming dog,' she told Nancy. 'And he's ancient! Much older then Miriam. "Gel!" he shouts at me, "bring up my tea, quickly!" I told him I'm not a servant and he don't like me one bit.'

'Perhaps you should go home to London, Amy,' said Nancy. 'Or, better still, come and live with Dick and me.'

Amy pulled a sullen face. 'I won't leave Miriam and she doesn't want me to go,' she protested.

Nancy sighed. For Miriam had recently confided in her about her own plans for the future.

'But you can't stay on, Amy,' she said gently. 'Just between you and me, Miriam is going to Jack in Canada. But for heaven's sake, don't say I told you so.'

Amy stared at Nancy aghast. 'She wouldn't do that,' she cried in a low, frightened voice.

Nancy raised her eyebrows. 'It's no good you getting upset, Amy. What I said is true.'

'Well, then, I'll go with her,' declared Amy truculently.

'Now, you have to be sensible,' the sensible Nancy said. 'Now that you've left school, you'll have to get a job and you can't expect strangers to support you.'

Amy screwed up her face in grief. 'I don't want to grow up, Nancy,' she said plaintively. 'I've been so happy here.'

'Well then, stay,' replied Nancy, 'and come and work for Dick on the farm. But you do know that Mother hasn't been well since Emily and her kids got bombed. And there's only poor Sheila left to look after her.'

Amy put her hand on her chin and gazed obstinately into space. 'If Miriam don't want me, then I'll go home,' she said, 'but I won't leave till she tells me.'

Nancy shrugged. 'You're going to have to learn that we can't have everything we want out of life. We've all spoiled you, I'm afraid, and that's a pity.'

Within two weeks Amy had made her decision. She would return home to London. Miriam seemed a little distracted and worried, and not concerned about Amy's future. And when she told Amy that she and the Captain were going to buy a smaller house as her husband was retiring from the army, Amy knew that whatever Miriam's plans were, she was not included in them. It was final. She put her arms around Miriam's neck and sobbed.

'I'll never forget you, Auntie Miriam,' she whispered through her tears.

'Now don't be silly, girl,' said Miriam. 'We're moving into a nice house in Devon near the sea and you'll come to me for your holidays and bring your young man. You are sure to find a nice one back in London.'

So Amy didn't know if Miriam was still planning to join Jack in Canada or not but she was pleased to have a standing invitation to visit her.

Amy kissed the pony, the cat, and the dog goodbye and Miriam put a tearful girl on the train for London, off to a new destiny. Our Amy had suddenly grown up.

Billy met her in London at the station and took her in his old van back to that old slum district where she had spent her early years. Amy had a very sullen expression on her face as she stared out at the busy streets and the big empty spaces where there had once been houses, but when she saw the bent, tired figure of Annie sitting on a chair outside the front door, she burst into tears. She dashed up to her white-haired mother and slung her arms around her.

As always Annie showed little emotion, she just patted Amy on the back gently. 'Now don't cry, gel,' she said. Her voice was tired. 'I must say, you've growed up a nice gel.'

CHAPTER SIX

Rehabilitation

Annie squinted up at Amy through the haze of cigarette smoke. 'Bit taller than the other gels, I should say,' and she took another puff on her Woodbine. Going inside the house Amy stared in dismay around the untidy rooms, the rubbish on the floor and the table littered with used crocks. After all these years living with Miriam, she was quite unused to poverty and she was shocked.

Then from a dim, gaslighted corner shuffled poor Sheila. She had a woolly hat clamped down over her ears, and a grubby overall draped untidily around her thin figure. Sheila's pallid blue eyes stared vaguely at Amy, unable to recognize her little sister after such a long time.

'Oh, it's Sheila!' cried Amy. 'Whatever's the matter with her?'

'Nerves got bad, that's all,' muttered Annie. Turning to Sheila, she said, 'Pull yer bleedin' self togevver, Sheila, it's our Amy come 'ome.'

Sheila's face twitched spasmodically but Amy ran to her and gathered her in her arms. 'Oh, poor Sheila,' she cried. 'What have they done to you?'

Sheila rested her head on Amy's broad shoulders and smiled a gentle smile as her sister cuddled her.

Annie sat down on a chair without saying a word. She had a glum expression fixed on her face as she sat puffing madly at her fag.

'I'll make tea,' said Sheila, delighted to be able to wait on Amy. 'We've got a nice cake from the milkman.'

Amy sat down and surveyed her future home in silence.

'It's no good turning up yer nose,' said Annie. 'This is all we got left of our 'ouse. It was bombed to the ground, yer know. I lost all me nice fings, I did, that night.'

'Never mind,' said Amy as tears filled her eyes. 'I'll get a job and buy you and Sheila lots of nice things.'

Annie gave a shrug. 'That'll help I suppose, but I never looks forward to noffink these days. Tonight you can sleep in wiff us. Billy's got yer a camp bed but 'ees goin' ter do up the attic and then yer can go up there wiff Sheila. I needs a bit more room, I do, now that I'm disabled.'

Amy looked down at her mother's useless withered leg and love and pity welled up inside. 'It was about bloody time I came home, I think,' she said abruptly, and a strong urge rushed through her to make things better for her poor mother and sister.

So at fourteen, Amy got a job at Woolworth's and became the wage earner of the family. The hours were long and Amy had to stand behind the counter most of the day and was not allowed to sit down. It was exhausting but the thought of that wage packet at the end of the week kept her going. Most of the customers liked Amy. She was tall with ash blonde hair cut in a neat page boy bob. She had clean fresh-looking skin and a wide pleasant smile. And she was no fool; she minded her own business, and she never saw anyone shoplifting, though in this poor district that sort of thing went on all the time. On Friday evenings, Amy would go straight home with her wages. She always gave three pounds to Annie and kept two pounds for herself. She tidied up poor Sheila and took her to the Britannia Cinema on Saturday nights. Sheila loved it. Back home the girls had pinned pictures of their favourite filmstars on the attic walls and Sheila would spend hours staring dreamily at these photographs of Clark Gable and Betty Grable with a beautiful smile on her face.

Sheila seemed to have improved since Amy had come home. She had filled out and now kept herself clean and tidy. Amy gave her some nice dresses and help to roll her hair into a neat style. She never allowed Amy to cut her hair. Amy learned this once when she had wanted to trim Sheila's ends, but Sheila had panicked at the sight of the scissors. Amy never tried again but now rolled up the blonde tresses for her, and put lipstick on her lips and powder on Sheila's shiny red nose. Sheila was thrilled. She loved Amy passionately. Every day, as soon as Amy got home from work, Sheila would be ready with a cup of tea for her, and took off her shoes and fussed around her. Annie actually felt a little jealous at times but her financial status had improved so much since Amy had come home and she was too wise to make any comment.

Sheila's housekeeping habits improved vastly. She swept, dusted and polished the two slum rooms until they shone with cleanliness, and she continued to care for Amy's treasures, peeping at herself in the nice hand mirror, pouting her lips like the film stars did.

Although Amy quarrelled frequently with Annie, she never did with Sheila. She was always so sweet, kind and gentle to Sheila that the older girl could do little else but improve. But Sheila was still very nervous and easily disturbed, and often had bad nightmares during which she huddled close to Amy in bed.

On such nights, as Sheila clung to her, Amy would lie awake and think of the fresh country air, and in her dreamy thoughts she could see the green fields and the farm she had come to love so much. And she would wonder if she would ever go back.

At Woolworth's she now had her own counter. She was bright and alert, and just the kind of girl the shop liked to train. She did not have that brash Cockney accent the other

girls of that area had, she never swore and she took little notice
of the lads. Amy enjoyed earning money. She liked to be
smart, and to have nice clothes to wear, for she had good
taste. But things were still a little hard to come by, but there
was her older brother Siddy who would often help her out in
that area, she discovered. Siddy had come down in the world
a bit since the war years. He no longer ran his bar and his
little Jewish bird had got married to Izzy Simons, who had a
drapers shop in Pimlico Walk, at the far end of the market.

Although Sadie was married, she and Siddy were still in
love and deep in the throes of an affair. Sadie was a nice, well-
brought-up Jewish girl who had been in a boarding school
during the war. Her father, Jack Goldman, decided it was
time to get his daughter a nice Jewish husband and told her to
stop working at the bar. Sadie obediently married Izzy
Simons, a very respectable local man, and with a very bored
expression served babywear and wool in Izzy's drapery shop.
But she always had one eye down the street watching for
Siddy to come visiting. Jack Goldman was a big shot down
the market. He did not run off in the war, but had been an
air-raid warden and kept his business going. His wife had
been killed when their shelter was hit during that bad blitz
when they had a stall that sold surplus wear, old army
equipment and articles that had been damaged in the blitz.
Now, after the war, Jack was doing well. He had two shops,
one in the city and one in the market, and he was well liked
and respected by the Cockneys. He gave plenty of money to
charity and had helped to build up the market after the war.
That year he had become head of the traders' association
which met weekly in the Coster's Hall, and ran raffles and
had collections for the poor folk in the district. Jack liked
Siddy, even though he wasn't Jewish, and he shut one eye if
Siddy went up to see Sadie when her husband was travelling,
trying to sell ladies' underwear. Jack employed Siddy in his
shop and relied on him quite considerably. The two men

respected each other and knew each other's secrets. Jack had a secret business which he had started when the Yanks were here – selling dirty pictures of lovely nude ladies. Recently he had progressed to hard porn, which he sold outside the Windmill Theatre in Piccadilly, and business was doing very nicely.

'Everyone to his own peculiar perversions,' Siddy would say. 'Meself, I wouldn't touch that stuff with a barge pole.'

Still, Jack and Siddy were good friends. With his short square shape and a big trilby hat propped up by extraordinarily large ears, Jack was a well-known figure down the market. Siddy with his long lank brown hair and sallow face was always joking and skipping in and out of the shop chatting up the girls.

Amy would often meet him on Saturday afternoons as she rummaged through the bargain rails to try to find an expensive suit, perhaps only smoke damaged, which could be cleaned and be an excellent buy. Siddy was sure to find anything she wanted.

'Ten bob to you, love,' he would say, and then give her five bob back saying, 'Buy Muvver a bottle of stout with that.'

But still Annie would not acknowledge her son.

Amy would often try to encourage her to make an effort. 'Take a little walk down the market, Mum,' she would say. 'You might meet someone you know.'

'No bloody fear!' Annie would retort. 'Might bash into that bloody Siddy. Crooked little sod.'

'Oh, Mum,' Amy would sigh. 'Siddy is all right. He works in a shop now and everyone likes him.'

'They don't bloody know him,' Annie would grouse.

Commodities were still a little short. Butter was still rationed, as was sugar. But every weekend a box of food was put on Annie's doorstep. Sheila would go down to get them, and there was Siddy with a wide grin on his face as he put his finger to the side of his nose. 'Stumm,' he'd say.

Sheila understood, 'Just been down to get the things from the milkman,' she would tell Annie.

'Don't run up no big bills,' Annie would sniff. 'Can't afford them.'

The secret was safely kept from Annie. In no way would she welcome Siddy in to her home; it was as if she blamed him for the loss of the rest of her family.

Amy became very fond of Siddy and they confided in each other. She felt quite sorry for him when he told her that he and Sadie really loved each other, but because of her religion they could not get married.

'Oh, it's all so silly,' said Amy. 'But suppose you give her a baby?'

'It's a wise child that knows its own father,' grinned Siddy, enigmatically. At that time Sadie was three months pregnant.

And so Amy grew wiser and not a little wary of the ways of the world. At sixteen, she had matured into a wordly young woman, who knew how to dress and behave. She now had a new job working in a big West End department store where she was to be on a training programme until she was eighteen. Amy loved her new job. Carefully dressed each morning, she would get on the bus, walk down the street wearing neat little gloves and carrying a rolled umbrella.

Shelia would wave goodbye to her. She would have got up early to make Amy's breakfast which she had then served to her as well.

Annie changed very little in those last two years, though her arthritis slowed her down increasingly as it crept up to her hip. She would sit on a chair outside the door most of the day, for it was so painful to move, and she quarrelled incessantly with Emmy, Billy's wife, who lived downstairs with Billy and her two children.

It was mostly the little boy they quarrelled over. Emmy was terrified of Sheila because she was so peculiar, and she did not like her children to go near her. Whenever Sheila sat on the stairs and talked sweet nothings to the little boy, Emmy would dash out and snatch him up and run inside with him.

This behaviour infuriated Annie who would hurl insults at her daughter-in-law. 'All right,' she would yell, 'we ain't goin' ter bleedin' eat 'im.'

Then Emmy would complain to Billy, who worked hard on the transport and came home very tired, and did not want to get involved in any arguments. He usually tried to dodge Annie and seldom went upstairs to visit.

Amy was rarely affected by such scenes. 'Been playing happy families again?' she would comment after some noisy fracas.

But all this came to an end when Billy changed jobs and went to work for a frozen food firm in Chelmsford. He and his family moved out of the downstairs flat and a West Indian family moved in. Sheila was absolutely petrified of them, even though they were perfectly nice and friendly. There was only one toilet in the house which was downstairs next to the kitchen occupied by the West Indians, so to go down those dark smelly stairs to the toilet became too frightening for her. Someone always had to go with her. If Amy was not around, she would sit doubled up in pain and terribly constipated waiting until her sister came in from work to accompany her.

One evening, when Annie was dosing poor Sheila with liquorice powder, Amy suddenly became very annoyed. 'Why I put up with this place, I really don't know. They're building new council flats down in Shoreditch. I'm going to write and put our name down for one.'

'Won't get one,' moaned Annie. 'Got a long waiting list, they have.'

'Well, I am not staying here,' declared Amy. 'You'll just have to go with Sheila to live at Nancy's and I'll get some lodgings up west near my work.'

Sheila blubbered and Annie nagged. There was no way she was moving out to live in the country again. And poor Amy trying hard to keep the home going was at her wit's end.

When Siddy saw her looking so harassed, he was worried. 'What's up, sis?'

She confided in him. 'It's the conditions we live in,' she said. 'There are just too many of us in that house and Sheila is terrified of the West Indians who have moved in. We deserve a better place to live, and I have to find something.'

Siddy looked at her thoughtfully. 'I've only got a little dump meself,' he said. 'You know, sometimes I'd like to live in a house with the family, but I know it's no good crying for the moon.'

'There's not many of us left now,' said Amy. 'What with everyone all over the place. And to think we were a great crowd, us Flanagans, when we were kids. We ruled the street, we did.'

And that was how they eventually got a nice council flat down at the other end of our market. It was not a sky-high block – it was just three storeys high and they were given a ground floor flat because of Annie's disability. It was spanking new and there was even a small patch of grass outside where Sheila could walk about safely.

Amy threw caution to the wind and immediately treated themselves to a three-piece suite and a carpet, all on hire purchase, to be paid back weekly from her wages. But they were at last happy and comfortable and very close to each other.

Nancy and Dick came on a visit with their little girl, as did Lily, and Letty came to see them before she left with her new husband for Canada. Amy organized a little celebration to show off their new home. Siddy sent beer and wine, though he did not come in, but his sisters went out and talked to him outside. They kissed and cuddled him there, for there was still a lot of affection left in this sadly depleted family.

CHAPTER SEVEN

Courting

At seventeen Amy was a handsome young woman, who dressed and carried herself well. She had kept the smart clipped accent she had copied from Miriam who had always moved in posh circles. During the week she worked hard but every Sunday was spent at home with Annie and Sheila. Sheila always cooked a roast with baked spuds and a pastry for afters. She had become quite a good cook but Amy and Annie always had to watch out for her because the slightest disturbance could cause her to drop dishes and upset saucepans.

Later in the afternoon Annie would sit out on the green chatting to the old folk who lingered there too. Mostly they nattered about the blitz and harked back to the good old days when all the small streets had criss-crossed the market and had been a big community in which everyone knew each other. But those days had flown by. All around high-rise flats had been built and in those post-war years many of the East Enders did return to the areas they knew so well, even if the war had changed it all so much. And certainly the East End's criminal element was still there; but now tucked away in those modern little boxes. At one time the criminals had openly ruled the area.

'There used to be old Janey Richard,' Annie recalled. 'She wore a man's cap and a big sacking apron rolled up over her arm. She'd go straight into old Scheiderman's shop, nick a joint of meat and hide it in her apron. Old Scheiderman used to jump up and down with exasperation but he never dared do or say anything in protest.'

Annie's eyes gleamed with delight at the memories. 'Then off Janey would go to unhook a nice pair of kid's pants hanging outside Long and Doughty's,' she continued, 'and that's the way Janey did her shopping all the way down the market. Not one penny would she spend.' Annie would tell this story with glee.

The old lady listening to Annie would cackle with glee. 'Yes, those big boys, the heavy mob, were always just behind her. Nobody had a chance with the heavy mob guarding her.'

'Disgusting old woman. Don't tell me about her,' Amy would mutter if she overheard these reminiscences.

'Ah,' replied Annie, 'but there's many a poor sod arahand 'ere remembers 'ow kind she were. And she put many a meal on their table an' boots on their nippers' feet. When she died it was a real splendid funeral, with a great big wreaff from the neighbours inscribed to "the Angel of Hoxton, our Janey".'

And thus Annie would spend her time talking about the old days in the East End, and clearly revelling in them. But she would never dwell on stories closer to her heart or talk about her beloved kids, like Emily, lost with her own children in the war. The hurt was too deep for her to recall. No, her memories dwelt on the Cockney characters of the past. 'And they're still there, Amy,' Annie announced jubilantly. 'Saw two of them brothers only yesterday, going to the pub. They must 'ave been inside, 'corse they was mixed up wiff that Yank's murder wot happened just up the road, it did.'

'Oh, stop it, mother!' exclaimed Amy in her poshest voice. 'I don't want to know about those low-class people.'

'Oh, hoity-toity,' called Annie. 'Yer might be glad of 'em yet, yer never knows.'

Sometimes on Sunday evenings Amy would feel rather low and depressed. She would remember how she used to cuddle

up to Miriam on the big Chesterfield and hold her hand. She
felt as if she was crying inside, but she did not understand the
feelings she had deep down. She would stare at Annie's moon
face surrounded by the haze of cigarette smoke and look at
Sheila slumped in the armchair with her mouth open and her
face devoid of all expression. This was a hard life, Amy
thought, for the hundredth time. She didn't mind it so much
now, and their situation had certainly improved. They had a
nice bathroom and she had her own bedroom and the flat was
filled with pretty things that she had bought for it. But was
this all there was to life? It would be nice to have someone to
cuddle her, and wine and dine her, just as they did in the
films. But the reality of it was that she kept her nose to the
grindstone at her job. She now travelled each day on the tube,
being squashed twice daily in that train with hundreds of
other people on their way to work and no time to talk to each
other. Their only thought was to fight for a place to strap-
hang. The tube train went back and forth from East End to
West End taking Amy to the posh department store where she
still worked. Nowadays Amy worked on the cosmetic counter
which, along with the expensive perfumes and soaps, sold
bright fripperies to please the rich, bored young ladies who
spent their time idly shopping each afternoon. Bright silk
scarves were hung artfully on stands, while earrings and
perfume bottles were placed in tasteful displays on the glass
counters. Customers were encouraged to take a nice squirt of
perfume to test its fragrance, and Amy in a friendly but
precise voice would persuade them to buy. She had become
an attraction to that counter, with her carefully cut blonde
hair and just the right amount of costume jewellery to go
with her black dress.

One afternoon, as she was rearranging the silk scarves, an
unusual type of customer hovered at her counter. He was a
tall slim young man, casually dressed, and with dark auburn
hair which stood up on end as if it had never been brushed

properly. He had a wide grin which revealed a set of perfectly white teeth and he smiled as Amy looked on in astonishment as he picked up one of the test bottles and squirted a spray of perfume into the air.

'Do you mind?' Amy snapped. 'That is very expensive perfume.'

'No, darling,' he said still with a grin. 'I just wanted to see if they worked. Don't use it meself.' He put the bottle down and continued to hover while Amy tried to ignore him and went back to arranging the scarves.

With hands in his pockets the young man looked her up and down, then finally said in broad Cockney. ' 'Ow much is them, then?' He pointed to the bottle he had squirted.

'Seven pounds each,' replied Amy very coldly, knowing that he wasn't interested in buying.

' 'Ere, I didn't wanna buy the bleedin' store,' he said, and slouched away.

Amy flushed scarlet and felt quite uncomfortable. She comforted herself by deciding that the man was just a nasty character to be ignored.

Wednesday afternoons, Amy got off work because she worked late on Saturdays. As she sat on the tube the following Wednesday wondering how she would pass the afternoon, she was suddenly aware of this same rude young man sitting opposite her. He had stretched out his long legs in front of him and was gazing mischievously at her.

' 'Ullo, doll. Got an' 'alf day, 'ave yer?' he asked.

'It's none of your business,' returned Amy very annoyed, and feeling a blush creep up her neck.

The man lurched over and sat next to her. Amy stiffened, absolutely petrified.

'It's okay,' he said. 'I ain't goin' to interfere wiff yer. I'd just like to get to know yer, that's all.'

Amy stared at him. There was some cheeky look in those

greeny grey eyes that suddenly made her giggle nervously. She tried to stop herself but couldn't.

The man grinned even more. 'That's it, doll, cheer up, 'ow far yer going'?' he asked.

'To Mile End,' Amy replied, looking down at her hands coyly.

'Funny, I could a' swore you was an East Ender in spite o' that posh voice.'

Amy smiled. She was feeling a little more relaxed. 'How come you are hanging around the West End all day?' she asked boldly.

'Noffink else to do,' he said. 'I'm waiting for a ship. I'm just goin' dahn to the pool office to see if I can get back to sea. I'm just pretty fed-up hangin' abaht 'ere,' he said. He hesitated for a moment and then looked at her eagerly. 'Why not ger off at Tower Bridge wiff me and we'll walk over the bridge and 'ave a cuppa by the gardens? It's just the day for it.'

Amy paused. It was indeed a lovely day and this young man seemed very friendly. 'Oh, all right,' she said. 'Why not?'

Why or how she made that decision she would never know but suddenly finally she found herself walking over Tower Bridge with a handsome young man who took her hand gently in his and squeezed it. A shiver of excitement ran through her veins. Amy had never felt anything like it. They stopped for a while on the bridge and looked down the great river.

'The Pool Office ain't open yet. It'll be open after lunch. Let's sit dahn and wait.'

They walked on and sat on a bench in the Tower Gardens and talked about themselves and their experiences during the war. It turned out that Jimmy Spinks, as he introduced himself, was one year older than Amy.

'I was in a bad boys' school and I kept running away. Finally I got on a boat in Liverpool – I lied abaht me age – and was on the convoys. It was a good life if a bit dangerous one. They calls me Sparky, 'cos I got on the radio deck.'

Amy found herself very interested in him. 'Where did you grow up?'

'Befnal Green,' said Sparky. 'Me family got blitzed. Me muvver and me sister was killed, so there's only me left. Never 'ad a farver that I remembers.'

Amy squeezed his hand in sympathy. After all, her own father had died when she was very young.

Sparky suddenly got to his feet, he bent down and gave her a swift kiss. 'Okay, darlin',' he said, 'I'll just pop over and register for another voyage and then we'll go out an' 'ave a good time.'

While Sparky went off to the Pool Office, Amy sat demurely on the park bench. She could not think what had got into her. What on earth was wrong with her? Why did she not get up and trot off home, when surely by now Mum and Sheila would be worrying about her?

Sparky came back. His long shadow fell on the path as he stood smiling and looking down at her. 'Well, I done it. I got four days now 'fore it takes orf,' he said. He held out his hand to her. 'Come on, let's 'ave a cuppa.'

They sat by the river in the summer sunshine eating sticky buns, drinking tea from paper cups and watching the kids playing on the pleasure boats. They walked hand in hand around the Tower looking at the ravens and the red-coated, stern-faced, Beefeaters, and the hordes of tourists.

'I've been all over the world,' Sparky said. 'I've been to New York, Ottowa and San Francisco, and they ain't got nuffink like this out there. Our London was somefink really worff 'angin' on to. It often amazed me,' he continued, 'how they knocked out all our slum 'ouses and killed the poor people. Why didn't they get this big place like the Tower and St Paul's or Buckingham Palace? I think 'cos they was bloody scared. They just chucked dahn their bombs and ran, the bastards.'

'Oh, Sparky, don't swear,' said Amy.

Sparky roared with laughter. Catching her in his arms, he swung her in the air. 'Oh, I finks yew are the cutest little bird I've ever met, an' I'm goin' ter spend ev'ry minute of the next three days with yer.'

'. . . ,' gasped Amy. But the force of his kiss silenced her. She had never been kissed on the lips before but this was the most exciting thing she'd ever experienced. She let herself relax in his arms and between kisses, she murmured, 'I can't stay out late because of Mum and Sheila.'

'I'll take yer 'ome early tonight,' he said, 'but tomorrer and the next days I tells the time yer go 'cos yer goin' aht wiff me.'

Amy smiled. She liked his authoritative tone. And so in the cool of the evening, they walked all the way back to Shoreditch, chatting nonstop. He kissed her again before they parted, and he said, 'Don't let me dahn, will yer, darlin'?'

Annie and Sheila were in a terrible state when Amy finally tripped in at nine o'clock. There were dog ends everywhere, because Annie, in her anxiety, had just smoked cigarette after cigarette and dropped all the ends on the floor. In the corner Sheila was sobbing hysterically.

'Oh, what's all this about?' asked Amy. She was rosy cheeked and her eyes were shining. 'I've never stopped out before. It was my half day.'

'You should 'ave told us,' grumbled Annie, 'Fair upset poor Sheila, it has.'

'Oh, some girl had a birthday party,' said Amy. 'Now shut up and let's have some supper. Tell you what, I'll treat you to fish and chips – coming with me, Sheila?'

Sheila had stopped sobbing but she stared sadly at Amy and shook her head.

'Well,' said Amy impatiently. 'You make the tea and lay the

table. And stop snivelling,' she snapped. 'I'll go round the chippy.'

Later that night as she lay in bed, Amy thought of those delicious deep kisses and the strength of Sparky's arms as he had held her. Oh, she felt so happy. She could hardly wait for the next day when she would see him again.

Next morning she dressed with extra care. 'I'll be late,' she told Annie and Sheila. 'Don't wait up. I'm going to the pictures in the West End with a girl from work.' The lie came easily.

Sheila pouted her lip. 'Can I come?' she asked.

'No, love, it's too busy up there. I'll take you to the Britannia Cinema on Saturday.'

Amy sighed as she travelled to work. It was clearly not going to be easy having a boyfriend with Annie and Sheila being so possessive and dependent on her. But then a little voice nagged at her and suggested that Sparky might not turn up anyway and all her newly stoked emotions would be frustrated.

She did not have to worry. At the end of the day, as the shop was closing, he arrived, dressed in a very smart suit and holding a box of chocolates under his arm. 'I booked us in for an early show so we can get out in time for a meal and a drink,' he said.

They went to Leicester Square cinema, but they didn't see much of the film. Their kissing became so very passionate and intense that even the chocolates got hot and sticky.

'Let's get out of 'ere,' said Sparky. 'I need a drink.'

They stood in a dark doorway holding each other tight. Amy felt the heat of his body through her thin summer dress, but she felt no fear.

'Look what you've done to me,' he joked.

When Sparky had cooled down, they went to a pub. At first Amy was reluctant to go in.

'I've never ever been in a pub,' she said.

'Oh, Amy,' he cried. 'There're so many things you ain't never done. Well, this one I can handle,' he laughed as he guided her into the pub. 'You needn't drink anyfink 'eavy. Wat abaht a shandy?' he asked. She nodded, so Sparky ordered a shandy for her and a pint for himself.

Amy felt strange and far away but drank the cool drink.

Sparky said, 'If I wasn't goin' away, I'd ask yer to marry me.'

'But you just met me,' said Amy, amazed.

'Well, I know I want yer and I ain't never felt like this abaht a bird, 'specially one like you, Amy. I can't believe you ain't never done it.'

'Oh, Sparky, don't talk about it,' Amy's face flushed scarlet with embarrassment.

He cuddled her tight. 'Yer haven't done anyfink really bad yet, Amy, but darlin', I will teach yer to luv' me but yer gotta belong to only me and it don't seem fair me goin' orf and leavin' yer. So I promise to behave meself, until I comes back and, oh darlin', yer must be there waitin' for me.'

Amy got home at midnight. Before she left Sparky again they kissed passionately near her home. And this time Amy knew she wanted him as much as he wanted her, but she pulled away before they went too far. 'I must go in, Sparky,' she whispered. 'I'll see you tomorrow, darling.'

So almost weeping with joy, young Amy crept into bed that night. As she settled into the cool bed, she heard Annie's gruff voice call out. 'Is that you, Amy? Hope you bolted the bloody front door.'

CHAPTER EIGHT

Her Man

That last night before he sailed, Sparky took Amy to a party. 'We're goin' to me mate's house,' he said. They went down the back streets of the East End to a small house where the seamen were saying goodbye until next trip.

It was a good party with plenty of drinks and 'knees up'. Amy had relaxed a little and drank gin and orange. At the end of the evening, the other guests were slowly leaving to go home, and Amy was feeling a little drunk. She lay on the settee in a happy, dreamlike state with her Sparky. The hostess said a hasty goodnight, turned out the lights and left them alone in the room.

Amy pressed close to Sparky, feeling his strong muscular body. 'You can do it, darling,' she whispered, 'if you want to.'

'Do you?' asked Sparky, surprised by her boldness, but he did not give her a chance to change her mind. And so Amy surrendered her virginity to Jimmy Spinks. He was her man, the first and last one, as far as she was concerned.

Very early in the morning as Sparky walked her home, Amy had cried a little.

'I'll be gone six weeks, Amy,' Sparky said, 'but you can write to me at this address.' He handed her a piece of paper. 'We will get married when I come back. I feel sorry about last night,' he said. 'I never wanted to do that to a lovely gel like you, but I promise I'll come back for you.'

'It was the most wonderful happening in my life,' answered Amy enthusiastically, 'and I'll wait for you because I love you.' So they had parted.

When Amy got home, Sheila had to come creeping down the hall to let her in quietly so that Annie would not know she had been out all night.

Amy had hugged her sister. 'Oh, Sheila, I'm so happy. I've fallen in love.'

It didn't take long for Annie to learn about Sparky. She was not impressed. 'Soppy cow,' she muttered, 'mooning over a bloody sailor. Got a girl in every port, they have.'

Amy frowned. 'Not Sparky,' she insisted. 'He's mine.'

Siddy was pleased to hear that Amy was courting. 'But you take care, ducky, and if anyone tries to take liberties with you, refer them to me. I'll get the boys to beat them up.'

'What boys?' asked Amy impatiently. Sometimes Siddy's secret life puzzled her. 'I'm going to get married when Sparky comes back,' she told him.

Siddy looked at her affectionately. 'Don't be in such a hurry, sweetheart. Marriage is not all it's cracked up to be.'

Siddy had had troubles of his own recently. Izzy had quarrelled with Sadie and she had fled to Siddy asking him to run away with her. But Siddy was too afraid of her father Jack who told him in no uncertain terms that it was a bad idea. 'Now pack it up, Siddy, my boy,' he said. 'Sadie is a Jewish gel and she's got her own family so don't spoil it for her.'

Siddy knew that Jack was right. He told Sadie to go back home and then spent his time at the dog track or down Petticoat Lane on Sunday mornings where he would sell balloons or any sort of cheap stuff from Jack Goldman out of the suitcase. The coppers continually moved him on but he made a lot of odd friends. The end had come to the surplus stores, so Jack Goldman concentrated more on his porno book shop in the West End. But here he met trouble, for the coppers up West were a little more nosey than the good old friendly well-bunged East End ones and often came to turn over the shop. When they did this Jack would toddle off with his suitcase full of porn to a new hiding place till the coast was clear.

So far Jack and Siddy had kept out of trouble but Siddy knew it was risky — mainly for Jack. 'It's like sitting on the edge of a bloody volcano,' he would remark to his mates. 'Something's gonna blow soon and if they get that dirty old sod he'll go down, that's for sure.' He did not confide in Amy over such matters. She was just his little sister who would never understand the ups and downs of a market trader's life. She would never understand him and his ways.

Meanwhile, Amy went happily to work and began to buy herself pretty underwear from the store, where she was allowed a discount. She whispered to the other girls that she was going to get married soon.

'Why, Amy?' said the staff manageress when she heard. 'You have only just met him. Why don't you wait till you know each other a little better?'

'Oh, I don't think he will wait, and I couldn't bear to lose him.'

The manageress was a worldly woman but was not going to interfere. She shrugged. 'Well, I wish you luck anyway, Amy.'

Those six weeks for which Sparky said he would be away turned to eight. The time dragged by and for Amy the period he was away was very long indeed. She put his photograph beside her bed and wrote long letters to him. A picture postcard arrived from Canada. Sparky had written in a very untidy scrawl and did not have a lot to say, but Amy's heart beat excitedly every time she looked at it.

Sheila watched Amy these days with a very worried expression on her face.

At last one evening, as the store closed, Amy suddenly

gasped and rushed towards a tall, tanned, red-headed figure crying, 'Oh, Sparky! You came home!' Her work mates looked at each other and smiled. They were all a little surprised.

Amy was over the moon. She felt as if she was walking on air. They sat on the tube holding hands and Amy thought her heart would leap from her breast as Sparky talked about Canada, and all the places he'd visited, the wonderful cities with lots of space and how nice it was in the autumn, with the sun still shining even in October.

'That's what I would like to do,' Sparky said, fired with enthusiasm. 'Marry you, darlin', and get us a nice place out there.'

'My sister, Letty, is in Ottawa,' Amy said timidly. 'She went there with the WAAF's.'

'All the better. We'll save up and go stay with her. I'll get a job out there.'

It all sounded very nice but Amy was afraid even to think about it. She was already feeling nervous about introducing Sparky to Annie and Sheila. How would they react, especially when he talked about taking her away from them?

Now she began to enjoy a regular sex life with Sparky. They made love whenever they could – at parties, in doorways, in the park and even in the sitting room when Annie was in bed and Sheila sound asleep. Sparky had no home. His home was a sailor's club since he had had no regular residence since the war and depended on the generosity of his many mates. He was a popular fellow for he was generous himself and a very good entertainer. He played the piano and sang rude sea ditties in the pub, and sometimes he would dress up and do a fat woman act at parties. Everyone loved having him around.

As it turned out, Amy need not have worried about bringing Sparky home and introducing him to her mother and sister. Like everyone else, they adored him. There had never been so much laughter in that little flat. He charmed everyone and teased Annie, calling her 'Fanny Annie', and tickling her big bunion which stuck out of her carpet slippers.

'Me name's Annie Flanagan,' Annie would protest, unable to suppress her giggles or her delight at having so much life around her once more. She took to Sparky in a flash. 'He's a real cough drop,' she told Amy approvingly one day.

To Sheila Sparky was also very kind, stuffing her with the crisps, sweets and lemonade which he brought home from the pub. 'Who's goin' to be a good girl, then?' he would say, holding up the goodies in the air just for a frustrating moment before handing them over. Once she had the booty, Sheila knew what to do. 'I am going to bed now, Sparky,' she would say.

Then Annie with a great grunt, and perhaps burping from the two bottles of stout inside her, would go. 'All right, give us a hand up,' she would say. 'I'll have an early night.'

Grinning broadly, Sparky would escort Annie to her bedroom door always keeping up his banter. 'Let me come with you, love,' he'd whisper. 'I'll keep you nice and warm.'

'You cheeky bugger!' Annie scolded him, but always with a nice warm smile. Seldom in her whole life had Annie had so much attention.

When the others were safely in bed, Sparky would hold Amy in his arms and waltz her around the room. 'That's it, darlin', now the night is ours,' he would laugh.

Sparky was often still sleeping on the settee early in the morning when a weary Amy got ready for work, but he would walk as far as the tube station with her.

Amy would kiss him goodbye with passion. 'Don't sit in the pub all day, will you, Sparky?'

Never the less he always did just that, what with all these mates of his who were still ashore and spending their shillings, backing horses and playing cards. This lazy side of Sparky's character did bother Amy at times, but every time she saw him outside the department store waiting for her at night her reservations would disappear and her heart always skipped a beat. Sparky was such a fine fellow — clean and neat with a healthy glow to his skin, a tall, lithe figure with those fine white teeth. She could never reject him; he was her man.

The marriage was often discussed but the details were still not entirely settled.

'We would have to find somewhere to live first,' said Amy one day when they were talking it over once more.

Sparky frowned. 'That's not going to be easy. Couldn't we pack in with old Annie? We could get spliced at the registry office and then I'll do another couple of voyages to get some money in the kitty. After that we can try to buy our own little house.'

The discussions rarely got further than that but Amy felt that she was already having a hectic honeymoon and so there did not seem much point in worrying too much about it. Although Sparky had a room at the sailor's hostel he spent most of his time at Annie's place anyway.

'I expect the family would like me to have a nice wedding,' said Amy, on another occasion, 'and my sister could come and I'd have my nieces for bridesmaids.'

'You'll 'ave wot yer want, darlin',' said Sparky generously as they lay on the settee. He nibbled her ear and brushed his tongue along her neck. Amy's skin tingled with delight and she shivered gleefully as she snuggled up tight.

Sparky stroked her hair. 'We really tick over, you and I,' he said approvingly.

'I'm afraid sometimes that I'll get a baby,' she said in a low, anxious way.

'If you do then we'll get spliced,' Sparky said lightly, 'but meantime, darlin', it's time for me to make another voyage as I have run out of dough. I'll sign on for the Middle East. They're lousy ships but the pay is good and the voyage not too long.'

Amy was silent. He was going away again with nothing settled and clear cut.

So early in November, Sparky sailed away and a silence descended on the flat. All three women were affected by Sparky's absence. Annie sat puffing mournfully at her fags and Sheila snivelled and became quite despondent. And, of course, Amy felt utterly alone. But she decided to work with a will and earn all the commission she could on her sales to save up for the wedding. She wrote to her sisters Nancy, Letty and Lily and told them that she was getting married in the spring. She even ordered a white dress from the store.

Sparky had been gone about three weeks when Amy began to get worried that she might actually be pregnant. When she thought about it, her feelings swung up and down. On the one hand it would be so nice to have a baby but where on earth would they all live? Also – and this was very important – she would not be able to get married in her white dress. Would Sparky come home in time? Oh, suppose something happened to him! Poor Amy found herself full of these woes and worries, though she always kept them to herself. Sometimes she noticed Annie staring at her suspiciously but she did not dare say anything to her mother.

A few weeks before Christmas Sparky arrived on the doorstep. He was a little thinner but still full of beans and, of course, loaded with presents for them all. That first night, when the rest of the house was asleep, Amy confided her worries to him expecting him to be angry. But Sparky's reaction was quite unexpected. With a muffled whoop of delight, he undid her dressing gown and pulled up her nightdress.

'Stop it, Sparky!' Amy protested, wriggling around angrily.

But Sparky knelt on the floor and placed his ear on her bare stomach. 'Hullo, son!' he whispered, 'your daddy is home.'

They both burst into fits of laughter.

'Hush,' said Amy, 'you'll wake Mum.'

'Not with all that rum inside her, we won't,' said Sparky. 'Now, darlin', let's make more love and give 'im good nourishment.'

'Oh,' sighed Amy, 'you are terrible, and not a bit romantic.'

'Me? I finks I'm very romantic,' said Sparky, pressing hot lips on to hers.

It was soon obvious that she was indeed pregnant. She cancelled the white wedding dress and told everyone that the big wedding was off. She never said why but most of them guessed.

Just one day before the wedding Siddy got arrested. Sparky heard the news on the grapevine.

'What for?' demanded Amy when he informed her.

'Well, you won't like it, but they say he was trading in porn.'

'No, not Siddy! I'll never believe it. But for gawd's sake, don't tell Annie.' Amy was appalled because she was very fond of Siddy.

But it said in the papers the next day that the police had entered a shop in Soho that dealt with dirty books.

A very determined Amy went marching down to Sadie's shop to find out what was going on. Sadie was sitting there looking very haggard and her eyes were red. 'I'm truly sorry,' she said. 'Siddy carried the can for my father, you know. That was Siddy's way. We knew the police were on to us and Siddy said, "He's an old man, Sadie. I can take a spell in the nick, and he can't".'

'Oh, the silly bloody fool,' declared Amy, 'and I wanted him to give me away at my wedding.'

'Not a lot we can do now, love,' Sadie said sadly. 'I suggest you get on with your own wedding and good luck. I'm going to see Siddy, he's on remand in the Scrubbs. I'll tell him you sent your love,' she wiped her eyes and kissed Amy on the cheek. 'It's a lousy thing to have happen at this time,' she said woefully.

'Well, I suppose things happen the way we make them happen,' returned Amy unsympathetically, 'but thanks all the same.'

Siddy's plight was put to one side as the wedding festivities took over.

Amy and Sparky got married on New Year's Day at the local registry office. Amy wore a nice blue suit that Siddy had come by and even though it was not a white wedding, it was certainly a noisy one. Annie's flat was full to bursting two days before the great event and for two days after it with the succession of Sparky's mates and their wives, who brought presents and congratulations with them. The night they got married they cleared the pub for the Flanagan's wedding festivities. Nancy and Dick came with their young daughter, Billy and Emmy with their two boys. Then late that night two tall six foot soldiers appeared in the form of the twins, who flew in from Germany. There was a telegram from Letty in Canada, and one from Lily who was out in Malaya nursing the troops.

Annie was in her element. Dressed up in a new silk dress and real shop hair-do, she sat at the head of the table in the place of honour as her family began to gather about her for the first time in years.

Even Joe appeared just as Annie began to wonder if he would. He strode into the pub, a tall, upright man with white hair and a tanned face. Marching across the room, he swept his little sister up in his arms. 'Congratulations, little Amy,' he said. 'I left Maureen and the kids with her mother in Cork. Must celebrate our Amy's wedding, I told myself.'

And, celebrate he did, along with everyone else. Those celebrations went on for days, back and forth to the pub with all guests kipping on the floor of the flat.

Amy and Sparky spent their first night of marriage in the spare room of one of his many mates' houses but then they went back with Nancy and Dick to Ashmullen the next day, leaving the family still celebrating.

Down in Ashmullen, Sparky charmed the local villagers who all remembered Amy as a little girl and were delighted to see her again now. Nancy had made a fine comfortable home of the old derelict farm house. Her husband Dick was still very sweet and very slow. He had become quite fat and jolly. He worshipped his daughter Heather. She was a small and dark child with long black curls. Amy thought she was very spoilt and watched how she twisted her father around her small finger.

'She's a little monkey,' Amy remarked to her elder sister.

Nancy smiled indulgently. 'She's very sweet really. In fact, she's rather like you when you were young,' Nancy added. 'I don't suppose I'll have any more children so we give her a good life to make up for my own childhood.'

Amy glanced at her wondering why Nancy should be so sure there would be no more children, but did not pursue the matter. She changed the subject. 'It's so lovely down here,' she exclaimed. 'Almost just as it always was. I've been up to the Cedars and looked over the gate. I can't believe that Miriam isn't there any more.'

Nancy smiled sadly. 'There aren't many people in this world like Miriam Trelawny.'

'Have you heard from her?' asked Amy, suddenly feeling bad not to have kept in touch. 'How is she?'

'Well enough,' replied Nancy. 'She and her husband have a cottage in South Devon. We write and phone each other occasionally. Captain Trelawny is not in very good health and seems to be a bloody devil to live with. Miriam doesn't deserve that.'

Amy nodded. 'I'm sorry if she's not happy.' Then she paused. 'Do you think that I am going to be happy, Nancy?' she asked, looking up with a look of such innocence that Nancy had to smile.

'Well, you've got the man you wanted, so now it's up to you to see that it works,' she said, looking at her shrewdly.

For those few days in Ashmullen Amy was so happy she could not believe it was happening to her. In spite of the freezing weather, she and Sparky walked across the heather-covered moors for hours. The air was fresh and invigorating and her heart could never have felt more lifted.

Wrapped up in his thick coat Sparky put his arm around Amy's shoulder as they stopped to stare at the bleak but magnificent view. 'Great, isn't it? It reminds me of Canada, you know. You'll love it out there.'

Sparky hadn't mentioned Canada for some time, and Amy was surprised. She frowned. 'But, Sparky, what about the baby?' she asked. 'I can't go out there till it's born.'

'Why not?' asked Sparky. ' 'Avin' a baby is nothin'. They do it all the time. Just look at yer Mum, she 'ad you on a bus comin' back from the 'oppin', or so she tells me.'

Amy blushed. She hated to be reminded of Annie's bawdy tales. 'I won't go till I've had her.'

'Whatcher mean, her? It's a boy!' exclaimed Sparky. 'A big bouncing son.' He picked her up and ran along with her bouncing in his arms.

'Oh, Sparky, be sensible,' she begged. His boisterous irresponsible ways worried her sometimes.

Their honeymoon over, they returned back to a cold dismal winter in London, where they packed in with Annie and Sheila who had to sleep with Annie so that Amy and Sparky could occupy the other bedroom. Not that Sparky took up much space. All he had brought with him from the sailor's home was a sea bag full of underwear, a few shirts and toilet accessories and his best suit on a hanger. 'That's all I got to worry abaht,' he said. 'Lived out of a bag for years,' he boasted. 'I'm used to it. Noffink will worry me as long as yer wiff me.'

Amy was determined to get their own place. Since Annie's

was a council flat and technically they were not allowed to have lodgers, Sparky should not have been living there. Not that anyone would have squealed. But Amy had to go by the book and she told Sparky that she had put her name down for a council flat, now that she was a married woman.

'What for?' asked Sparky. 'Just another couple of good voyages and we'll be able to get out of this dump as soon as we get the fare to Canada.'

'I don't want you to go back to sea,' protested Amy. 'Stay with me till the baby is born and get a job. There must be some other things you can do.'

'I can't do me own job,' said Sparky a bit huffily. 'I'm one of the best radio operators there are, but it's a specialized job at sea, and not easy to break into in civvy street.'

'What about the telephones?' declared Amy, determined to hold him in England.

Seeing the desperate look in his wife's eye, Sparky relented. He pecked her on the cheek and squeezed her. 'For you, dear, I'll try anyfink, but whether I can stick an eight-hour job in an office, I'm not sure.'

Delighted to have been able to influence him, Amy hurriedly got application forms for jobs in the Post Office and various other big companies, carefully filled them in for her man.

Sparky hung around and tried for the jobs that came up but nothing came of any of them. Each time he never got through the first interview, there was always some silly reason why he missed out.

Things were difficult. Each day after work Amy would come home a little tired to Sheila's weak tea and Annie's grousing, and find Sparky out in the pub. She was beginning to show quite a lot and already had given her month's notice.

Sparky was now completely broke except for his dole money. Still he did not get a job. The only bright event during that period was that suddenly they were offered a council flat in the same block as Annie's. It came just at the right time. Amy was feeling very unfit and could hardly wait to retire from her job and get off her feet as her legs had swelled badly.

Sparky also suddenly had some good news, too. 'Got a chance to get on the Hamburg run,' he said. 'I'll only be gorn three weeks at a time. We'll take the flat and go and get a nice lot of gear on the 'ire purchase and set up a swell 'ome. I'll get good pay and you can stay at 'ome.'

Heartened by the fact that some money was coming Sparky's way, Amy set about getting their flat ready, buying a cot and making a nice nursery. The next few weeks were hectic but by the time Sparky set off, they were moved in and settled in to their new home.

Sparky came home from the ship for one week out of every four. He earned good money and was very happy. But at home he always attracted a string of mates who aggravated Amy now. When Sparky was at home, he and these men sat having boozy gatherings in her flat every Saturday night with Sparky always popping off somewhere else at a moment's notice. He would return home very merry and generous to her, loading her with goodies. Amy liked the presents, but the excessive boozing between trips annoyed her, particularly since Sparky seemed to spend all their money on drink and would borrow back whatever he had given her to save, just before going back to sea. Still, she loved him, and in no way would she complain about him. Occasionally she would nag at him a little but he just covered her face with kisses to keep her from complaining. 'Oh, little Amy, how I love you,' he would croon.

So Amy would tell herself, 'I have nothing to grumble about – he's my man.'

CHAPTER NINE

Visiting

Amy was expecting her baby any day now and every morning she popped in to see her mother. Amy was a little bit afraid of the pregnancy, a new thing happening to her, and did not like being alone during these last days. It suited Annie who liked having an audience and in her usual tone was chatting about something she had recently heard out on the green.

'This woman I met was so posh, "Anyone heard about what happened to Mother Rain?" she asked us. "Wot?" says I.'

"I am doing research for a magazine" she says, "it's on freaks. I heard Mother Rain was quite an unusual person."

"Oh, yes," says I, "pigs' trotters she 'ad for 'ands – seen 'em meself in the chip shop. Used ter put 'er change in a kind of little pocket in 'er paw."

"How interesting," says she.

"Well," says I, "that ain't all – 'orses 'ooves she 'ad, and all the kids would chase 'er to lift 'er skirt 'cos it was rumoured she 'ad a long tail. And as gawd's my judge, she was ever so old. Why, me muvver said she was around in 'er days but she disappeared in the blitz, she did." She wrote it all down, this posh woman did, so I says, "It used to be said that it was 'cos 'er muvver 'ad a lot of men." And d'yer know wot? She larfed and said, "It don't sound like men with the pigs' trotters and a donkey's tail." Now, wot d'yer fink of that? "Well," says I, "we know abaht 'er – us folks in 'oxton – she lived 'ere wiff us." '

Amy's child was kicking lustily in her belly and suddenly it seemed to turn in the womb. 'Oh, for God's sake, Mother,' she snapped, 'be quiet, keep your horror stories to yourself.'

'Miserable cow,' grumbled Annie, lighting another Woodbine.

Then Sheila dashed to the door as Sparky came rolling over the green. To see Sparky was the heyday of poor Sheila's life. Amy's husband staggered in with a small dog tucked in his pullover. Holding it up by the scruff of its neck, he laughed, 'Look at this scruffy old mop I got for yer, Sheila, darlin', it's called Bridget.'

Sheila squealed with delight and took the terrified little dog into her arms.

Amy stared at Sparky in astonishment. There was lipstick on his face and on the collar of his shirt. The stench of whisky hit her as he collapsed heavily into the armchair.

'What you doin' 'ere, Amy?' he asked. 'Thought you'd gone to bed.'

Sheila was fondling the dog and pouring it a saucer of milk.

'Why do you call it Bridget?' Amy asked dryly. 'That can't really be its name because it's a male.' Her tone was acid for she knew that the barmaid who worked in the pub Sparky frequented in Bethnal Green was called Bridget.

'Yer all right, darlin'?' Sparky asked, looking at the worried expression on her face.

'Of course I am all right,' Amy snapped. 'And if you are fit enough to walk, I'd like to go home, if you don't mind.'

Sparky was concerned even in his drunkenness. He wanted to cuddle her as they walked to their flat but when he tried she pushed him away. Never before had she disliked her Sparky, but tonight she hated him.

Early the next morning she was in labour in the maternity wing of the local hospital. At midday she gave birth to a big bonny girl. She knew that Sparky would be disappointed but she didn't care. Still angry with him, she actually felt glad, that in some way she had got her own back on him.

But when Sparky arrived at the hospital that afternoon all neat, clean and perfectly sober, he looked delighted. He kissed the baby gently and affectionately and said, 'We got a lovely gel, Amy, isn't she pretty? Wot we gonna call 'er?'

Amy's anger disappeared at the sight of Sparky as the proud father. 'You choose,' she said, feeling supreme happiness once more inside her.

'How would you like Rachel?' he asked. 'It was me muvver's name.'

'It's all right,' said Amy, 'but I thought it was a Yiddish name.'

'Not on yer nelly,' he laughed. 'Me muvver were Welsh and real chapel,' he added defensively.

That was the first time she had ever heard him talk of his own family, and they sat holding hands till visiting time was over.

'You're not disappointed because it's a girl?' she asked timidly.

'Nah!' scoffed Sparky in his Cockney manner, 'we still got plenty of time to make a bleedin' football team.'

Amy smiled. There was no one like her man. Sparky was so happy-go-lucky and full of generosity and warmth. So what if he went off the rails occasionally? What man did not?

Now Amy was a young mother and settled down into a regular pattern of life. Every day she would take the baby for a walk in her pram and wheel it around to Annie's. Annie still sat on the seat outside on the little square of grass each day, always on the look-out for someone she used to know and with whom she could gossip.

Sparky had gone back to sea and, left alone, life, Amy though, was pretty dull. The baby had to be fed on time, and the nappies washed. It was all very monotonous.

One day when Rachel was three months old, Amy had a

long letter from her brother Siddy and a visitor's card to go down to see him in the open prison on the Isle of Wight where he now was.

Sparky happened to be at home when this letter came, and he was very insistent that she go and see Siddy before he had gone back to sea. 'Go and visit the poor sod,' he said. 'I know how lonely yer can get for the sight of yer own folk. Go and visit the poor sod.'

Amy liked the idea but didn't know if she could go. 'But what about Rachel?'

'She will be all right for one day with Annie and Sheila,' Sparky reassured her.

Rather nervous about the whole project, Amy went to visit Siddy after Sparky had gone back to sea. It was the first time she had left her baby but prayed that Rachel would be all right. She had given strict instructions to Sheila about bottles and nappies.

'Can't tell me anyfink abaht babies,' jeered Annie, 'had firteen, I did.'

Any knew that her mother would nurse Rachel on her lap most of the day and that by the time she came back the baby would be throughly spoiled and crying for attention all the time. But there was nothing else to be done, so Amy accepted it. So, wearing the nice blue suit she had worn for her wedding (and which Siddy had got her), Amy went on the tube to Waterloo Station. She already had a ticket and a special concession, which put her right away with several other young women standing at the barrier waiting for it to open. Some had small children with them and tense expressions on their faces. Amy noticed that they naturally split up into little groups; some were smartly dressed while others were ragged and poor. But they all got in the same end of the train.

'Going to the Island?' asked one shabby woman with two small children.

'Yes,' replied Amy.

'Get used to it. I've gone it for two years now. He gets parole soon, and I'm not sorry it's over.'

Amy was amazed at the woman's ability to talk about her husband's situation so freely. To her it was a quite disgraceful thing to happen to one.

'Who you got in there? Your husband?' the woman asked her.

'No, my brother,' replied Amy. 'And this is the first time I ever did this.'

'I've never missed a visit and all my husband does is give me the third degree when I get there. He even pumps the kids to find out if I've been going out and leaving them.'

'Oh dear,' sighed Amy but not too sympathetically. She would never put up with that sort of life, she thought to herself, feeling rather superior.

Just as the train started to pull out of the station, along the corridor came a lively old lady who was obviously well known. Small and sturdy with nicely set iron-grey hair, she wore a black coat and dress and was adorned with several long gold chains from which a locket and a Star of David hung. She looks rather prosperous, Amy thought, watching her with interest.

'Hullo, Dolly,' everyone smiled and greeted the old lady as she went along the compartment.

'Hullo, ducks,' she replied in a lively tone. 'Another month gone round, then.' She moved on down the train stopping to gossip here and there until she reached the very smartly dressed bunch who sat together. 'Just going down to get a drink at the bar,' she told them. 'Coming, gels?'

The women all got up laughing and went with Dolly on down the corridor to the bar. That was the last Amy saw of them on the train.

Once on the ferry from Southampton, Amy avoided the shabby woman because her kids were playing up and their noise gave her a headache, so once the ferry docked on the Isle of Wight, she was not sure where to go to next. She stood amongst a crowd of other travellers, some with suitcases, buckets and spades and a line of kids all going on their holidays. But in what direction did one go for the big prison way out on the island? Just as she stood there, a taxi went past with those four smart women in it. Another taxi followed and it slowed down as a voice called out: 'Waiting for a cab, love? Ger in here. We're going in the same way.' It was the old lady who had been so popular on the train.

'Which one you going to?' she asked as Amy got in the taxi.

When Amy told her, she grinned a crooked grin. 'Oh that's the open nick, I'm going to Parkhurst, so you'll be getting out before me.'

'Oh, there's more than one, is there?' Amy commented, trying to be sociable.

'Yes, love, three all told. Some worse than others. This must be the first time you came.'

Amy nodded.

'Me, I been doing this a long time now,' Dolly chatted cheerfully. 'Got three boys and there's always one of them in bloody trouble. Still, never mind, good boys to me, they are, and while I'm able I won't neglect them. Two of 'em are twins and they usually get nicked together, but this time only Morry is inside. He was always a bit highly strung – got a bad temper, and that's what gets him in trouble.'

Amy listened with interest, thinking that there was a lot of Annie in this old gel. They were similar in many ways except that Dolly was so lively and active and did not seem to mind that her boys got in trouble. That certainly wasn't the case with Annie and Siddy.

'Who you going to see? Don't I know you?' Dolly peered at Amy.

'Don't think so,' said Amy. 'I was evacuated all the war,

but now I live in Shoreditch. It's my brother Siddy I'm
visiting.'

'Not Siddy Flanagan?' Dolly cried. 'Side-kick of old Jack
Goldman? Well, fancy that.'

Amy blushed. She was not sure she wanted to be associated
with all this criminal activity. 'Yes,' she said quietly.

But the old lady jawed away, 'Used to be a mate of my
eldest son, Reggie.'

'Did he,' said Amy, rather haughtily.

But the old lady did not bat an eyelid. Out of her coat
pocket she pulled a packet of peppermints. 'Have one,' she
said holding them out to her. 'I like to have a peppermint
before I go in. I don't let them know I've had a drink with the
gels. You get used to it you see, love. I've been up and down
the country visiting all the nicks, I have. I like to make it me
day out. You see them nice smart women I had a drink with
on the train, did yer? Well, they'll be old ladies by the time
their men get out. Come from around your way, they do.
Twenty years some of them got. What do you think about
that?' She sat back in her seat, sucking a mint and rolling it
around her tongue.

Amy did not reply; she felt a little sick.

'Here you are, that's your stop, good luck, cock,' called
Dolly as Amy climbed out. 'See you again.'

Amy found herself outside a pair of massive iron gates. A
uniformed policeman stared coldly at her as she produced her
pass. After checking it, he allowed her to go in through the
gates into a large courtyard. Along the path, young lads idled
about with brooms in their hands and others sat outside huts
in the sunshine. It seemed to Amy that there were whole
armies of them, just sitting their lives away. What a depressing
sight.

Siddy was in the visiting room. With an exclamation of
delight, Amy went towards him, her arms outstretched, to
greet him, but he waved her off. 'Hullo, darlin',' he smiled.

'Yer mustn't touch me in case old Bill sees yer. Sit down and let's have a good long chat.'

Amy looked him over. He seemed very well and healthy. He was clean and had a short haircut which suited his long lean jaw, and he wore washed-out blue overalls.

'If you brought me anything don't give it to me yet,' he whispered. 'I'll tell you when.'

'I got some fags,' she said.

'Good,' said Siddy with that devil-may-care grin. 'Seen Sadie?'

'Occasionally,' replied Amy. 'And someone said her father had gone away somewhere.'

'Done a runner, eh? Got the wind up,' said Siddy. 'Never mind, time's passing fairly quickly and I got a few pals in here. How's Sparky and the baby?'

So they talked about the family and agreed that it was better not to let Annie know too much about anything. Or big brother Joe, who could be hard on a loser.

The journey back to London was uneventful. From the prison Amy found herself a cab easily enough and at Southampton got into another part of the train, away from the smart gels who meandered back and forth to the bar chatting in loud voices as if they never had a care in the world.

Amy was very glad to get home. It had been a long day and a tiring journey. She was just glad to have had the chance to talk to poor Siddy even for only an hour, and the lively fast talk of old Dolly stayed in her mind.

The baby was sound asleep, well tucked up in her pram by Sheila. As usual, Annie was dozing, but she woke up soon enough. 'You look done in,' she said as Amy sat in the chair. 'Fancy going all that way and spending money to see that crooked sod. I wouldn't cross the road to see him, I wouldn't.'

'Oh,' sighed Amy, 'you don't change much, do you, Mother?' Collecting her baby, she wheeled her home across the dark green. She tucked Rachel into her cot and climbed into her own bed clutching Sparky's photograph. 'Oh, I do wish you would stay at home with me all the time,' she whispered as she kissed it.

On Sparky's next leave, he was full of beans and ready to make love as usual. But Amy pushed him away. 'No,' she said, 'it's too soon, the baby is only twelve weeks old.'

But Sparky said, 'Amy, my love, me mates tell me it don't matter. Some women starts another one at three months.'

'Well, not me!' said Amy. 'I'm certainly not going to lumber myself up with a lot of kids like my mother did.'

'Well, you please yerself,' said Sparky slightly annoyed. Without another word, he got dressed and went out visiting his mates.

Amy sat down on the bed and cried her eyes out. What was she going to do? It obviously wasn't a good idea to hold out on him like that. He was too popular with the birds and she could lose him if she was not careful. Thinking carefully, she decided to change her tactics.

'Let's prevent me having another baby for a while,' she said to him later. 'If you want to save up to go to Canada, it will be better. And I might get a job later on and let Annie and Sheila mind Rachel for a few hours a day.'

Sparky was quite happy with this suggestion, so they made up and spent a happy week together. They left the baby with Annie and even went out to the theatre up west. The play bored Sparky stiff but Amy was thrilled at the star performances.

'We ought to do that more often, Sparky,' she said afterwards.

'Not if I knows it,' retorted Sparky grumpily. 'I was so dry, couldn't 'ave spit a tanner.'

'Well, they had a bar, didn't they?'

'I had to fight my way through all them toffee-nosed sods to get a rotten warm 'alf of bitter,' he grumbled.

It was just not his scene, and Amy had to face that. But

apart from such incidents they were a fairly happy couple. He loved small Rachel and whenever he was home he would wheel her out in the pram and would stand talking to the neighbours for hours. He still had many friends who were always pleased to see him. Amy never sought after that kind of social hospitality, and had few friends. Her closest confidantes were Sheila and Annie, and she seldom stood gossiping. She always carried herself proudly and walked very sedately, when she walked, nicely dressed, down the market.

'That's Siddy Flanagan's sister,' the Cockney traders would comment. 'Fancies 'erself, don't she?' 'Married to that young Sparky and he's a bit often away, they tells me.'

Had Amy come down to earth it might not have been such a big shock to her when Sparky fell in through the front door at two o'clock one morning beaten to a pulp, with a big gash in his head and his arm broken.

Worried sick, Amy put a towel around his head and gave him water.

'I'll be all right, love,' he said. 'I was just in a bit of a car crash.'

Amy ran to the doctor's surgery and dragged the reluctant doctor out of bed to attend to Sparky, whom he sent off to the hospital immediately to get his head stitched and his arm set.

And so began six weeks of nursing Sparky back to health. The accident made him miss his ship and he was not likely to be able to sign on for quite a while, so they had to live on his sick pay. Amy was struck by how very vague Sparky was about his accident.

'Who was driving the car?' she asked.

'One of me mates,' replied Sparky evasively.

'Did he get hurt too?' she asked. 'Whose car was it?'

Each time she asked questions he told her a different version of the affair until, very frustrated, Amy finally said to Annie one day: 'Here we are practically broke and Sparky has been injured. I'm sure he could get some compensation because of the accident.'

'Don't be such a silly cow,' scoffed Annie. 'The boys done him up.'

Amy stared at her in amazement. 'What boys?' she demanded.

'Don't ask me,' returned Annie, looking away. 'We don't mention names dahn 'ere but I was told by someone on the green that 'e got a bit cocky in one of their low-down clubs, so they set abaht 'im.'

Slowly but surely her mother's words sank in and a harsh light revealed a sordid aspect of her life that she had always ignored. With her head in the clouds always looking upwards, she had had illusions about her life. She would constantly think about Miriam's home with the antiques and beautiful furniture, the big brick fireplace, and the lines of books. At times she had dreamed that they would live in a place like that too, and that Rachel would even have a little pony when she got older. But now all those illusions were shattered. Her dreams came crashing down like a house made of cards. The problem, she decided, was the area. Sparky wouldn't hang out with the wrong types if they lived somewhere else. They had to get out of this gutter, that was the next thing to do. But how?

First she decided to tackle Sparky's drinking, and she started by refusing to give him money to go out with his mates. Sparky grumbled about this a lot but Amy was not going to listen.

'Listen,' she said, 'if it wasn't for your drinking habits, you wouldn't have got into a bother with those villains in the first place. It's time to stop.'

'Well, you know what it's like when a fella's away from home,' whined Sparky. 'It's the life at sea – all booze. And so when yer get ashore yer can't help yerself.'

'Right then,' said Amy with determination, 'don't go back

to sea. You must try to get a job. I've decided that I'm definitely going back to work to save up money, too, and I definitely don't want no more kids for a few years yet. I'll not let you pull me down into the gutter, there's too much of that going on around here anyway.'

Sparky knew there was no point in putting up any resistance when she was in such a mood. 'Okay,' he said, 'don't argue. We'll do what's best. I'm nearly finished with the therapy at the hospital, so I'll find something to do. In the meantime I'll help Annie and Sheila mind Rachel, if that will please you.'

So Amy went back to work in a big store in the city. It was an old-fashioned sort of shop which dealt a lot on credit, but the wages were good and Amy did not have far to travel.

Sparky was still having trouble moving his arm so he had to go to the hospital for physiotherapy every day. He would wheel Rachel round to Annie's before he went for his hospital treatment and Sheila took over watching and playing with the baby while Annie sat outside in the afternoon amusing herself and her cronies with that neverending 'good old days' gossip. Then in the early evening Sparky would go to the pub to have a drink, but only one half. 'It's all I can afford,' he would say, 'but I like to see me mates.'

Amy worked eight hours a day. She had always been a little solemn but now, as she entered her twenties, her face had assumed a rather hard expression. She seldom relaxed and had little time for anyone but Rachel. She even became quite impatient with Sparky and often cross-questioned him on how he had spent his day. She loved him but the pressures on them were so great and he still had done nothing about getting a job himself.

Sparky was usually quite tolerant of her questioning, but one day he completely lost his temper. 'Wot the 'ell is this, the effin Gestapo?' he yelled at her.

'No need for that kind of language,' Amy replied haughtily.

Even though they had very little of it, Amy was very careful with her money and would not waste a penny of it. That way they managed to get through the bad winter. And at last Sparky got a job. It was only a weekend job in car sales near where he used to live. 'One of me mates,' he told her, 'is gonna give me cash in 'and, no questions asked, it will be a help.'

Amy agreed and accepted the idea of spending Saturdays and Sundays alone if it meant bringing in money and adding to their savings. Gradually her dreams came back again and the motivating force in her mind was a picture of that nice house in the country. One day they would have it. . . .

Sparky was earning a bit now and seemed to bring home quite a lot of presents for Amy and Rachel. There'd be a short fur coat or some nice glassware, which someone, he'd say, was selling cheap. Amy, remained blissfully naive of the details and divorced herself from East End life. She did not visit Siddy again but she did know that on his release from prison Sadie had been outside to meet him and that together they had fled to somewhere up north.

Late one evening, as Amy and Sparky ate their tea, they heard the tramp of heavy feet on the steps outside the front door. Suddenly there was a heavy thump and some policemen rushed in and grabbed hold of Sparky.

Amy was stunned. It was like a nightmare. Through a blur, she watched Sparky struggle and protest, but the police stood firm and announced, 'You are under arrest.' The words were still ringing in her ears as they carted Sparky off to the police station.

Amy took her baby and ran over to Annie who, for once, was kind and sympathetic. 'The bastards,' she said, 'he ain't done nuffink. Someone's set 'im up, they 'ave. That's 'ow it is around 'ere, they can't bear to see yer gettin' on, they can't,' and she wept with Amy who was too scared to go home.

In the morning one of Sparky's dodgy mates came looking for Amy. 'Got a message from Sparky,' he said, 'you're not to worry, and that he never did anything. Old Bill are holding him for a few days, 'cos they are after the real villains, that's what.'

'But what's it all about?' asked an agonized Amy.

'Well, it's a big showdown at the garage, there's been some dodgy insurances, and buying of hot cars. It's nothing to do with Sparky, it's the guys who run it.'

'Well, then, why doesn't he tell them?' demanded Amy in bewilderment.

'It don't work like that, missus,' Sparky's mate tried to explain. 'It's just that it's a big deal and the old Bill will hold him to get the big guys. He's coming up in court in the morning. He said you're not to go 'cos he don't want you involved.'

'Oh dear,' she wailed. 'What can I do?'

'Nothing. They will acquit him. Old Bill knows Sparky's just a mug; they don't miss a trick.'

'But who are those criminals?' cried Amy. This conversation was above her head.

'Well, missus, don't ask me, and if I was you, I'd stay out of it. Sparky will be home, you can count on it. It's his first time in trouble so they can't hold him long.' With that, he put on his checked cap and went on his way.

Alone in her flat Amy sat weeping, and was just too miserable to even think about going to work. She sat there feeling as if she had not a friend in the world. Where were all her brothers, Siddy, Billy and Joe? No one wanted to know.

Annie, however, came up trumps. She was so kind and thoughtful. Somehow she understood Amy's heartbreak. Amy who had always thought of her mother as a very cold unsympathetic woman, could hardly believe how kind she was being, making Sheila go and get the meals, helping to cook and being very maternal. 'Don't go home, Amy,' she said, 'stay 'ere wiff us.'

Amy leaned on her and wallowed in the comfort she

offered. They spent many happy hours chatting out on the green. 'You're better off staying wiff me,' Annie said. 'Yer never knows how them bleedin' crooks will turn, yer can never trust 'em. Mind you, they won't get past me,' she added with belligerent pride.

'Depends if Sparky grasses,' said the gossipers.

'No, he won't do that, he's a very fine, principled boy, my son-in-law,' said Annie with pride.

In fact, Sparky was held for three months. The police knocked him about a bit in an effort to make him talk but there was no evidence of him being in any way a party to this insurance fraud, so they eventually acquitted him. Sadly, Sparky came home a very bitter disillusioned lad with a seething hatred of coppers that would never leave him.

During those three months that Sparky was on remand, Amy's savings had dwindled to almost nothing. On his return, Sparky got a loan from a mate of his and bought an old lorry. He began to do some freelance transport and started making a fair living. Amy stopped work and stayed at home. She and Sparky grew very close again and she began her second baby. Sparky was delighted. 'Maybe I'll get a son this time, I can't keep on being so unlucky.'

But the stars were not in his favour. Amy had another girl. Sparky welcomed the baby but Amy knew that his heart had been set on having a son. Life settled down again; they were all together and getting by. For the time being Amy knew that she had to accept that this was to be her existence and so she might as well get used to it. Besides, the council flat and the two babies took up most of her energy and she had little time for dreaming nowadays.

Poor Annie was getting old. Her health was deteriorating and her legs getting worse. One day Sparky brought home a wheelchair for her and after that Sheila was often to be seen pushing Annie along with Sheila's little dog sitting in Annie's lap yapping at everyone who passed.

Amy was most pleased about the change in Sparky. He was no longer irresponsible. He seldom went out drinking but was a good family man and worked hard to build up a good business.

'I'll own a fleet of lorries before I am finished, love,' he would tell his delighted wife. And Amy was very proud of him.

CHAPTER TEN

No Escape

By 1956 the East End of London had changed radically. Big rebuilding programmes had injected new life to this run-down, badly blitzed area bringing shops, supermarkets and high-rise flats for a new generation, instead of the slums that had been there before.

Amy's life went on just the same, though they lived more comfortably with a better flat and nicer furniture. It was still not too far from Annie and Sheila so that Amy could pop over each day to help Sheila get Annie out of bed and onto her seat on the green. Annie's limbs continued to stiffen and it was difficult for her to move about, but mentally she was fine. She was always ready to chat about this and that, and once she started on the good old days it was a job to stop her. With snow-white hair and a blue woollen cardigan, she was a well-known sight on that green in Shoreditch. Every day it seemed that more and more people she knew returned home to their grass roots after the war and its aftermath, like migrating birds, to the old haunts of their youth. Annie was always delighted about this and would say excitedly, 'Guess who I 'ave just met, Mrs So and So, you know, 'er daughter married that fella', you know who, 'er 'usband got killed in the war . . .'

Amy would pretend to listen but her mother's chatter would go in one ear and out the other. While Sheila pranced around and played ball with her dog Ben, Amy would sit back and let herself be flooded with her old dreams of living in a great big house in the country with a log fire.

Sparky's transport business had done well. From a small company it had gone slowly from strength to strength, expanding until it was a large international concern. It was quite an achievement, particularly in such a short time, and he was proud of it.

He gave Amy good money and took her and the children to the seaside once a year, but otherwise he had little time for them, always staying at the office late in the evenings to catch up with the growing paperwork. He now had a lot of lorries and other drivers working for him. He worked very hard but some of his old habits remained. He still liked, for example, a Sunday morning drink with his pals and would go to the pub off Brick Lane to meet them, leaving Amy, as always, alone to cope with the kids.

Amy's feelings about Sparky were confused. She did love him and she was delighted by the way in which he had struggled out of the gutter and become a man of substance, but there was always a remoteness about him, a barrier, she could never break through. But he was so good to Annie and Sheila, and was an excellent father to his daughters, and materially a good husband. She felt that she should count her blessings; she could do no better. Certainly from the outside they were doing well, and Sparky was always keen to show Amy off as his wife. Whenever they went to one of the many flash parties given in the neighbourhood, he insisted that she be the best dressed woman there and wear all the jewellery he had bought her.

But whenever Amy mentioned the idea of a little house in the country, Sparky would say: 'One day, Amy, I'll quit and we'll go off to Canada, I promise. Just be patient, darlin'.'

'I don't care if I never go to Canada but I'd like to bring the girls up in a nice area,' Amy would say timidly.

'What the bleedin' 'ell is wrong wiff the East End?' Sparky

shouted one day when she said this. 'Why all the brains and the money is down 'ere and I'll get my share of it if it kills me.'

And Amy would retire back into the shell she had built up around herself, knowing that it was hopeless to argue.

That year a pale, washed-out and very dejected looking Siddy returned home. Amy bumped into him on a Sunday morning in Petticoat Lane, where he was selling very unreal-looking gold watches from a suitcase.

'Oh, Siddy,' she cried, 'why didn't you let us know you were back?'

'Wasn't sure you would be interested,' shrugged Siddy despondently. 'Not now that Sparky's Jack the lad.'

'What do you mean by that?' Amy demanded defensively. 'Sparky's worked hard and got a good business going. Don't begrudge him that.'

'Sorry, sis,' replied Siddy, looking sorry and humble.

'Well, from now on you come to Sunday dinner with us,' decided Amy. 'I suppose you're in lodgings.'

'Yes,' said Siddy, closing the suitcase with a bang. 'Now I gotta move – old Bill's coming along. See you Sunday next week.'

'Three o'clock is dinner,' said Amy, giving his hand a little squeeze as he dodged off.

'Poor Siddy,' she said later to Sparky, when she told him she had seen her brother. 'He looked right down on his luck.'

Sparky glanced at her, and she was disturbed to see that his eyes had a hard, unfeeling look about them. 'Okay, so what did he want?' he asked.

'Oh, Sparky!' cried Amy. 'You're getting real mean and very hard. Poor Siddy. Well, he's coming to Sunday dinner next week and he don't want anything from you. He's just coming to see his own family, that's all.'

Sparky noticeably relaxed and then smiled charmingly. 'All right, darling,' he said with a sigh. 'Do as you wish.'

The following Sunday, Amy cooked roast beef, baked spuds and batter pudding, and Sparky brought in bottles of beer. Siddy arrived looking very thin. He huddled pathetically by the big fire.

'Oh, Amy, there is no place like home,' he said. 'And you sure got it set up nice here.' He looked around the flat appreciatively.

Sparky quietly poured out the beer but made no comment. To his mind, Siddy was a lame duck. Amy loved lame ducks but Sparky had no time for them.

'Sadie ditched me,' said Siddy as he scoffed his dinner. 'Wasn't her fault – her old father put the arm on her.'

'If she had really loved you, she would have stayed with you,' said Amy.

'I don't blame her,' replied Siddy defensively, 'after all, Jack's got an inn out in the country, so they tells me, and now Sadie and her old man run it. Jack lives with them now that he's retired. He got me duffed up and dumped in an alley down the Lane, he did,' he added bitterly.

'Rotten old devil,' said Amy.

Later, when Siddy had left, she confronted her husband. 'Now, Sparky, you got to help Siddy. You give him a job or I'll know the reason why,' she said.

Sparky's lip set with grim humour. 'Thought you said he was to stop out of trouble, not to buy it,' he said.

Amy stared at him. 'Oh, don't be funny,' she said. 'You see to him or I'll be very annoyed.'

So Siddy got a day job in Sparky's yard. Sparky had not been at all keen to employ him, but he knew that it would make Amy very happy, so he was prepared to take him on.

Thus, in that typical Flanagan way Amy looked after her brother Siddy. He found himself new lodgings but spent most mealtimes in Amy's flat.

Annie was most incensed to learn about this. 'Bloody mad, you must be, takin' that Siddy in. Sparky don't really want 'im in the yard, he's bloody trouble, that Siddy, like some bleedin' Jonah, he is.'

'Oh, what are you talking about, Mother?' snapped Amy impatiently. 'Siddy has had a bad deal and you certainly haven't helped him by your attitude.'

'Don't say I didn't warn yer,' cried Annie, as aggressive as ever.

Sparky's business continued to grow. Siddy turned out to be very useful about the place and he certainly knew how to keep a still tongue in his head. So, after that difficult start, he and Sparky got on quite well together.

A big racket was going on in dockside London at that time and the lorry owners were all involved. The Big Boys, as the crooked element were known, still ran the vice and crime of East London and all had their little men working for them in their small clubs and pubs where many of the rackets went on. This latest racket was that of hijacking lorry loads so that the owners could put in false claims to the insurance company, and get compensation. The gangsters would then call for their slice of the cake, having dispersed the booty via the well-concealed channels run by the old war-time black marketeers.

This sort of thing went on all the time but as far as the rest of the residents of the East End were concerned, what went on in gansterland was not their business. The art of living down there was keeping your nose clean.

That Christmas Annie's twins arrived home from the army. It was their last leave before they were to be demobbed. They had volunteered to join the Hong Kong police, so it was hallo and goodbye. Annie welcomed them warmly. They stayed at her flat and slept on the floor in sleeping bags. Amy cooked for them and gave them a big party on Saturday night. The twins regaled them all with juicy indecencies about their lives in the army. They told one story about how they had both courted the same girl and when she got pregnant she did not know whom to blame when she came up to identify the man. 'Thought she was seeing double,' they guffawed.

Amy did not think this very funny, at all, nor the other stories of their escapades out East, 'keeping the wogs in order' as they put it. She thought it all a bit distasteful but did, nevertheless, put on a good party for them. Halfway through the evening, the twins went down to the pub to get extra beer, and in no time at all, a big fight had started which went on until after midnight when the police finally arrived and arrested the twins, who had actually started it.

Amy had to take her rent book down to the police station at Old Street to bail her brothers out. Sparky had missed the whole event, having had to go out, supposedly to pick up a lorry which had broken down. 'Who was they fightin' with?' he asked Amy when she told what had happened.

'It was those terrible Palmer twins that everyone is so afraid of.'

Sparky's jaw dropped. 'Oh no!' he exclaimed. 'A lot of bloody good the twins 'ave done me.'

'I don't know what you are talking about,' snapped Amy, 'and anyway, they are on their way back to camp now.'

'And, I hope they bloody stay there,' snarled Sparky.

'Oh, Sparky,' wailed Amy, 'why are you like that with my family? I sometimes think that you are jealous because you haven't got a nice big family of your own.'

She had touched a nerve. Sadly, Sparky picked up his little daughter Annie, and kissed her. She was known to him as Tosh. She had bright red hair and was very sturdy and very much a favourite with her dad.

'Who said I ain't got a family?' he said. 'Let's have another baby, Amy. Might get a boy this time.'

'No, thanks,' replied Amy. 'Not till we move out of this rotten slummy street.'

Later that year Sparky suddenly said to her. 'Written to Letty lately?'

'Well, I do owe her a letter but now with Rachel going to nursery school and me helping out at Mum's every day I don't seem to get a lot of time.'

Those hard bright eyes stared at her across the table. 'I didn't ask for a long comment about the family,' he said harshly. 'Write to Letty and tell her we are coming out for a holiday. Ask if she can put us up.'

'Oh, Sparky, oh, that's great!' cried Amy excitedly.

'Well, I am not too sure yet, but keep it under yer 'at. I don't want anyone else to know about it – not Siddy nor Annie, no one. You understand that, don't yer, Amy?'

'Oh yes!' she said, but she didn't. Why all this secrecy about a holiday abroad? But she kept her promise to him. All that spring he was often bad tempered and quite often drunk at the weekends. Amy felt sure that he had more on his mind than he was prepared to share. She wrote to Letty, who replied immediately to say that she was delighted and that they could stay with her whenever they wanted.

Now they did have a date. 'July, but stay stumm,' Sparky told Amy. 'I'll see to the tickets and everything. You just collect up your and the kids' gear.'

Of late Sparky had been very close with one of his drivers, a big, loud-mouthed fellow called Tom Evans. Amy could not abide him. They had been at a party one weekend and Tom Evans was there with an extremely young blonde. She could not have been more than sixteen. Amy remembered this girl being born to a family who lived down their street. Her parents had moved the family out of London soon after the blitz started. So to see this lovely child, who everyone called Bubbles because of her blonde curls and her sweet dolly face, was quite a shock to Amy. 'What's he doing with her?' she muttered to Sparky in a low voice. 'Why, his daughters are older than her.'

Sparky said, 'That's Tom's business, he's left his wife, packed in with her, so I've been told, so keep yer mouth shut, and don't let him hear you talking like that. Bubbles is no angel. She ain't nothing like she looks, I can assure yer.'

Amy was quite disgusted by the sight of this little blonde girl, who still lisped like a child, cavorting about the room swinging her hips and wobbling her breasts while the tough-looking Tom Evans drooled over her. At one point, when Bubbles lay back in her chair with her legs spread wide showing her thighs, Amy felt she had seen enough. 'Pull your clothes down, love, all the men are getting a good view,' she said tartly.

Bubbles sat up and stared insolently at her, 'You mind your own bloody business. People like you ain't got much to show.'

As Amy retired to the kitchen in a fury she could hear Bubbles' silly immature voice ringing across the room, 'Who's she then? Old bent nose – some sort of prize-fighter?'

Amy instantly demanded to be taken home. If there was one thing that upset her it was any reference to the bend in her nose. 'I'll give her prize-fighter,' she raged at Sparky. 'She can have a bunch of fives from me any day, saucy little cow,' she said when they got home.

'Don't go on so, Amy,' said Sparky. 'The kids that are coming up now are different in more ways than one to us.'

'You're not kidding,' declared Amy, 'and that old Tom Evans ought to be shot for carrying on with her.'

Sparky grinned. 'Someone might do that yet.'

'Oh,' said Amy impatiently. 'I'm not coming to any more of your bloody flash parties.'

'You won't have to,' said Sparky. 'Get them glad rags in a case. We're off to Canada next week.'

Amy packed excitedly and sent a wire to Letty. At the weekend, Sparky brought home a big pile of account books from work and burned them one by one on the kitchen fire.

'What are you doing?' asked Amy in bewilderment.

'I'm getting out,' said Sparky. 'In fact, I've already sold out. Don't ask me too much, but Tommy Evans is taking the business over. Siddy still has a job, so don't worry,' he added hastily.

'Mean to say that after all those years of hard work you sold out to that rotten Tommy Evans?' Amy could hardly believe what she had heard.

But Sparky came and cuddled her close. Tears came to her fine eyes. 'Don't bother your pretty head, darlin',' he cajoled. 'Come, let's get the kids together. We're off tomorrow – I've got the plane tickets.'

'But what about Annie and Sheila?' cried Amy. 'And how long are we going for?'

Sparky sighed. 'For once in your life, Amy, think of me. I've been saddled with your bloody family too long. Now I'm getting out.'

'But, it's only a holiday, isn't it, Sparky?' she asked anxiously.

'Yes, if you like,' he mumbled and started to empty the whisky decanter into a glass.

Annie was very annoyed to discover that Amy was planning to disappear for a while, and even more annoyed that she couldn't say how long she was going for.

But Amy herself was not at all sure what was happening to her. She gave Sheila some of her dresses and make-up and told her to take care of Annie.

It was all a big rush. The next minute Sparky arrived in the car outside and tooted his horn for Amy. 'Ain't he coming in to say goodbye?' cried Annie in despair.

'Mum, the kids are asleep in the back and Sparky's asked you not to talk and not to say where he's gone.'

'Oh,' Annie's big mouth drooped down at the corners. 'Trouble, eh!'

'Oh, no, Mum,' said Amy impatiently, but she leaned

down and gave her a sudden big hug before running out to join Sparky.

They drove to Heathrow Airport and boarded the plane for Canada. Still Amy was not sure if she was doing the right thing. It was very unpleasant, that journey, a long flight on the crowded plane. The kids were very restless and, Amy, who had never flown, was extremely nervous. Sparky drank steadily all the way over and said very little. He just kept checking his watch all the time. It was very long and tedious.

Fortunately, Letty was at the airport to meet them. Amy had not seen her sister since she had left Ashmullen for the WAAF's but Letty had grown into a very lovely mature woman. Her husband, Frank, was a tall, healthy looking man who was a schoolmaster. Right away, he got along with the little girls. Tears of happiness were shed as they drove out to Letty's suburban home outside the town. It was a very smartly furnished house high up on a hill surrounded by tall pines. In the distance they could see a big lake.

'It's just like Ashmullen,' said Amy.

'Yes, that's why I'm so happy here,' said Letty. 'But, how fortunate you are, Amy, to have such lovely children. I don't take after mother – so far there's no sign of a child.'

After a few days with Letty and Frank, the family all settled down. Sparky cheered up and was more of his old charming self. They went out on picnics and life was one round of exciting things happening.

The months flew by, and Amy began to get a little concerned. 'I wonder if Sparky has booked our return flight,' she said to Letty one day. 'We can't abuse your hospitality for ever.'

But Letty's eyes darkened with sadness. 'Oh, Amy, don't you know? He's staying on. He's asked Frank to help him find an apartment and he is going to apply for a work permit. I thought this was all agreed between you.'

'Oh, my God, what a dirty trick to play on me!' Amy cried.

'Well, it seems he has his reasons,' said Letty very quietly.

'Well, he had better bloody tell me them,' said Amy in a fury.

Sparky made no excuses and did not deny that he had intended to stay from the beginning. 'I shall see if it's possible,' he told her.

'But, my God! Why didn't you say so? Poor Mum and Sheila, and what about Siddy?'

'Here we go,' declared Sparky rolling his eyes. 'But just you take a look at this.' He pulled from his pocket an evening paper and there, spread across the front page, was a big story from London of how the police had smashed a racket in the East End and arrested two Palmer brothers for a whole catalogue of crimes, including murder. The big racket concerning the hijacking of lorries had been exposed. There were pictures of Sparky's old yard and poor Siddy, looking very depressed, standing in the entrance. 'Quite a few arrests have been made,' Amy read in disbelief, 'and the police were still looking for important witnesses.'

'What is it all about?' she stared at Sparky in bewilderment.

'You wouldn't understand,' he said, 'but they had the arm on me for years.' He smirked. 'Now I've left them all holding the baby.' With a grim smile, he folded the paper and put it back in his pocket. 'So, Amy, you understand that we stay here, like it or lump it, my love.'

Amy sank down into a chair. 'Oh, Sparky, what on earth will they do to you?'

'I don't know but I've certainly made a few bloody rotten enemies,' he said. 'But don't you worry, love, I've got enough money to set us up over here. Forget about home for a while, will you?'

There was no choice now. With the money Sparky had managed to get away with, he bought Amy a nice house not very far from Letty. It was the house she had always dreamed of owning, with a big brick fireplace, a modern kitchen, and a grand view of that big lake. There was a convent school nearby so the two girls, neatly dressed in school uniform, went off to school there each day, while Amy spent her time polishing and painting her nice house. When the deep snow of the Canadian winter came down it wrapped them around warm and cosy in this new nest. And Amy found that she was happy. Although there was often a deep tug of remorse in her heart when she thought of Annie and Sheila back home, these were the most contented days of her married life.

Sparky was no longer called Sparky. Now he was known as Mr Tony Spinks, or just plain Tony. He had had several jobs, but now worked in a car-hire firm in the town which also supplied a car for them to use. So at the weekend Sparky would take his family on long trips into the deep Canadian forests.

The little girls readily took to their new life. They would play football out in the park and when there was deep snow, they went tobogganing down the hill. From the kitchen, Amy could hear the sound of their happy laughter.

Tosh was becoming quite a tomboy, while Rachel was a little more solemn, more like Amy. Since she had been going to the Catholic school, she had become very interested in religion.

Amy would watch Rachel, her long blonde hair hanging over her face as she wrote in her exercise book, and think it was the best thing she ever did for her family, to agree to leave the slum where she had been born.

Sparky, or Tony, as she now tried to call him, was very good to her and often wooed her to get pregnant again. 'Let's have another baby. This time I'm bound to get a son.'

'You have Tosh, she's more like a boy than a girl,' Amy joked.

'But I want a son,' insisted Sparky. 'I always have done.'

'Well, it's all in the hands of fate,' she said, 'for I don't seem to fall for children so easily as I did.'

Letty came to visit every weekend, and they all spent the holidays together. Letty worked in the local library and Frank taught at the nearby school. They were a hardy pair who loved the outdoor life. They frequently played tennis and took long hikes into the country, which Amy found very tiring. So she usually kept herself occupied at home with Rachel while Sparky joined the others on their hikes, taking young Tosh with him.

All in all they became a happy and devoted family, but Sparky was still restless. When the spring came, Amy and Sparky went down to walk beside the broad swift-flowing river. Huge lumps of ice still floated on the black water as they watched the long, low-built ships sail up to the arctic wastelands.

'There's a big world up there, Amy,' murmured Sparky. 'I'm only standing still here because you want it, but I can't do this forever.'

'Oh, whatever is wrong with you?' snapped Amy. 'I settled here because you wanted it. Don't uproot us again. I'll tell you, if I go anywhere, I'll go back home.'

'Over there is Detroit.' Sparky pointed towards the bridge, ignoring her remark about home. 'Once over that bridge you are in the United States, and that is a thriving place; there's money there.'

Amy gazed dismally over the bleak river to the skyscrapers of Detroit and longed to be back beside her big log fire. She had been aware for a long time that Sparky was restless and it worried her. A wave of homesickness suddenly washed over her. She was learning to like Canada but it was occasionally hard. Sometimes when she went shopping in the town, the flow of the traffic bothered her. And everything was so big – the shops and the streets all so widely spaced. It was nothing like those small slum streets of London.

It was during their second cold winter that Amy caught a virus which affected her chest. She felt pretty poorly and had to stay inside, unable to go out in the arctic conditions.

Sparky was very good to her during this time. He took the children back and forth to school and got books from Letty's library for her to read. He fed her with hot spiced drinks and cooked her hearty meals. But it did not seem to help. Slowly, Amy grew very thin and very depressed.

Sparky joined a sports club and went out in the evenings often leaving poor Amy sitting gloomily by the fire thinking of her mum and Sheila and poor Siddy. They all seemed so far away and she often wondered if she would ever see them again.

Then one day she got a long letter from Nancy which shocked her. Nancy wrote to say that Mum had gone into hospital and that they had taken Sheila away to be taken care of. On reading about this, Amy wept solidly for an hour.

When Sparky came home that evening, he comforted her gently. 'When the spring comes, you go on holiday back home,' he said. 'I'll try to save for it because you know we are only just getting by. All the money I had out here went into this fine house because you wanted it so much.'

'Don't worry,' snivelled Amy, annoyed by the sudden bitter edge to his voice. 'I'll be all right, I'll forget it.'

Yet the worry of Mum and Sheila was like a yoke on her shoulders. She could not get rid of it, and it weighed down on her constantly night and day. This concern added to her general feeling of homesickness and contributed greatly to her depression as she sat there so far away from home and the members of her family she loved.

CHAPTER ELEVEN

East End Troubles

At first Annie had been devastated when Amy wrote to tell her that she and her family were going to settle in Canada. Illiterate, she had not been able to read the letter herself, and had had to wait several weeks before her son Billy popped in to see her. He read it to her slowly.

'Don't surprise me none,' she said gloomily when he had finished, but inside she felt quite shocked. It *was* a surprise.

'Sparky was in a lot of trouble, I heard,' said Billy. 'Those rotten sods, them crooked brothers, was after him. Some says he grassed on them, and I'd not give tuppence for his life if he did,' said Billy.

'Oh well,' sighed Annie. 'Well, now they're all in Canada, so there's not much I can do. And I got Sheila to fink of.'

One day a fellow in a cap and muffler came and sat next to Annie as she sat out on the green. 'Hello, Annie,' he said.

'I don't bleedin' knows yer,' she replied grumpily.

'Yes, you do. I'm Siddy's mate.'

That was like a red rag to a bull to Annie. 'Sling yer bleedin' 'ook!' she yelled at him. 'Sheila, come and give us an 'and, I'm going in.' She pulled up her enormous bulk and waddled inside.

Poor Sheila flapped around every day after that peering outside to see if that bloke was there, because Annie said she would not go out if he was.

'E's a copper, I can smell 'em a mile orf,' she said. 'Ain't gettin' me ter talk. Not on yer nelly.'

Siddy had been arrested and tried. He got a suspended sentence and was now out and living in Amy's flat. Tommy Evans had gone down for two years, but the Palmer brothers brought in a clever crooked lawyer to fight their case. He got them acquitted but they had to pay heavy fines for their part in the lorry insurance racket.

'There is no such fing as bleedin' justice in this bloody country,' snorted Annie when she heard the verdict.

'It's just as well Amy and Sparky gor aht. The East End ain't safe while those Palmers is still around, I assure you.'

Indeed, fear and violence continued to skulk in London's back streets. A new generation of tough kids had grown up since the war as the gambling clubs and the strip clubs came to the fore and now a new kind of evil reared its ugly head. Once drink had been the worst problem but now it was drugs. There was a lot of money to be made so the racketeers did not care how many lives their activities might destroy. The drug trafficking began in those low-down clip clubs in the West and East End, run and organized by the big time crooks as they peddled their wares and made a fortune.

One of the victims of this racket was the young Bubbles, who Tommy Evans had set up in a nice flat in South London, with strict instructions to stay out of the East End until he had done his time. He warned her that he would do for her should he hear that she had got involved with another guy.

Bubbles was only eighteen, immature, hot natured and psychologically hooked on cannabis. She drove a big red car which Tommy had left behind and which could be seen every night parked outside Amy's old flat while Bubbles spent the night with Siddy.

'Sheila!' Annie would say. 'Put yer 'ead rahnd the corner and see if that car is still there.'

And Sheila, like a scared rabbit, would come running back a few minutes later to tell her it was.

'There!' Annie would declare. 'Told yer about that Siddy, didn't I? Never was no good, he wasn't. I don't know why Amy let 'im live in 'er flat.'

But Sparky had paid six months' rent in advance to give himself time to get away, so Siddy had no immediate worries about that.

Annie would sit out on the green her mouth working angrily at the thought of what Siddy was getting up to with this blonde young woman. 'I knows 'er, I do,' she would mutter, 'and 'er muvver. Never was no good, she weren't. Used ter go dahn Aldgate after the men. Well, what's bred in the blood comes out in the flesh, so they sez, and that Bubbles will come to a sticky end, she will,' predicted Annie.

At the end of the six months, when the rent had run out, the council commandeered Amy's flat and all her furniture was placed in storage. Despite this, Siddy's romance with Bubbles continued, much to the surprise of the local inhabitants.

Siddy moved away into sleazy lodgings, and Bubbles worked in the strip clubs. Siddy always looked after her; he got her home when she was high on drugs and put her to bed. Once she was settled, he would then go around to his low down haunts to get a supply of this cannabis she was so fond of. And Bubbles spent. Bubbles spent all of Tommy Evan's money which he had stashed away.

For once in his life Siddy had someone of his own in this lovely wayward young girl. She played up to him and would lisp like a child, 'I love 'oo, Thiddy,' she would simper. 'Don't go and leave me will 'oo, Thiddy?'

Siddy stayed with her and she became the be all and end all in his life. This romance was much talked about among the criminal element, and it was always treated as a joke, for in spite of Siddy's love for her, it was well known that Bubbles was promiscuous and that she liked old sugar daddies and just took them for their money.

When he got the news of their love affair, Tommy Evans, still in the nick, uttered threats to Siddy's life. But poor Siddy was infatuated and was just like a dog on a string; when Bubbles needed him, he was always there for her.

The affair ended abruptly when Tommy got a week's parole. He arrived to catch Bubbles at home and began to beat her up. She managed to run out into the street to get into the car to warn Siddy. But as she unlocked the car in that dark street, Tommy secretly got into the boot, and Bubbles in her upset state drove on without even realizing that she carried trouble to poor Siddy. As she ran up the steps of Siddy's lodgings, he came out to greet her and Tommy Evans dashed up the steps waving a big gun. As he came near, he fired straight at Siddy's lower parts and Siddy collapsed on the floor screaming. Evans dragged Bubbles down the steps, bundled her into the car and drove off.

Poor Siddy rolled around on the ground. The bullet had wedged in his private parts. An ambulance was called and in the hospital they had to remove poor Siddy's balls and part of his penis, so he really was in a bad way.

The next day, news of this incident spread like a bush fire around the neighbourhood.

'But who did it?' No one would say. Those harassed detectives got no information out of anyone – it was all stumm, finger to the nose – and Tommy Evans was safely back in the nick having reported back in good time from his parole. No one seemed to know where Bubbles had gone, for she had disappeared into the endless web of vice that operated in the East and West End.

Not long after all this, Annie was sitting outside on the green, still gossiping about the old times, when Dolly Palmer came to visit her. The old lady dropped a box of chocolates in Annie's lap and said, ' 'Ullo, Annie, and 'ow are yer?'

'I'm fine,' said Annie. 'Wot d'yer want?' She was not very friendly.

'Oh, only to say I'm sorry about your Siddy. My boys send their respects to you.'

'Well, they can keep 'em to their bleedin' self,' said Annie, 'and I ain't got no son called Siddy.'

'What a funny woman,' muttered Dolly, as she went on her way.

'Don't know abaht that,' Annie said to another close neighbour later on, 'if anybody's funny, she is. Them bloody boys is a nuisance arahn 'ere, and she encourages 'em.'

'Fings ain't wot they used ter be, Annie,' said the wizened old woman sitting next to her.

'No, they ain't, and that's a fact,' said Annie. 'They tells me that our old street's now a block of bleedin' sky-high flats and all them old shops is gorn up that end of the market.'

'No,' said the old woman. 'Anderson the baker's still there and old Paget's son, he got a shop up there.'

'Oh, I 'members 'im, old Paget,' said Annie. 'Dead and gorn now, used ter go rahnd wiff a donkey and cart.'

'Nice man he were,' related the old lady, and so they went on and on, these memories of the good old days. The present day was getting too much for Annie, she had to hark back to the past. When Billy next came to see her he said: 'Mother, I think you should move out of this district. Come up our way, and you'll get a nice council house in the country.'

'What?' roared Annie. 'It took bloody Hitler and his bombs to move me aht of London and was I bloody glad to get back, so no crooks is goin' ter drive me aht.'

Billy retired from the fray, leaving his Nancy to try. All fresh complexioned and clean in her summer dress she arrived with a basket of farm goodies for them. 'Mummy, dear, be sensible. You don't know what you are bringing on the family by your defiant attitude,' she pleaded. 'Look how they ran Amy out and what they have done to poor Siddy.'

'No, gel, go back to yer nice 'ome and little kid and leave me an' Sheila be,' replied Annie aggressively.

'You know you can come back to Ashmullen,' begged Nancy. 'Dick will get you a place of your own if you won't live with me.'

Annie lit a Woodbine and puffed at it angrily. 'Now will yer go? And, mind yer own business, me and Sheila are all right 'ere.'

'Oh,' said Nancy exasperated. 'You are a selfish old woman. What about poor Sheila? Why, she is not much older than I am but she looks like a middle-aged woman. All this tension is making her more nervous.'

'Leave me and Sheila be!' yelled Annie. 'And sod off! I don't care if I see any of yer, I'll get by.'

Nancy wrote to Amy about all this. 'It's quite hopeless,' she wrote. 'We can't budge her. She is more stubborn now than she was in the blitz, but I have done my best.'

Sometimes Joe, who was working in the oil fields, sent her a money order, along with a letter. Annie was unable to read the letter and just took out the money order and treated Sheila to the sweets, lemonade and crisps that she loved, and got herself plenty of stout and Woodbines.

There was not one line on Annie's brow even though she was often in pain from her arthritis. The smooth skin and halo of white hair remained with her, and still full of jaw herself, she would sit listening to the chat from old neighbours which kept her in touch with the old times.

One highlight of her life, every two weeks, was a visit to the hairdresser's, which she had done since Amy's wedding. There they trimmed and set her hair keeping it a lovely white with silver rinses. Sheila would push her along to the end of the market where Esther had a shop that had been there many years. Esther's parents had been the old-fashioned men's barber's shop with the long candy-striped pole outside the shop. This was when men did not use electric razors and liked close shaves. Old Manny Webb had cut hair in his shop which had been a hive of gossip all about the First World War. In the latest war, the bombs had disposed of his little shop and Manny and his wife had died in the Jewish Old Folks' home. After the war, their eldest daughter, Esther, came back from evacuation and started up in a brand new premises and added a ladies' department.

Esther Webb was now in her sixties and had known Annie all her life. She was a nice and homely woman whose dumpy little shape bustled here and there across the shop. And as she worked she talked incessantly. A visit to Esther was a tonic to anyone bored and lonely and there were many that way in those high council flats. So Esther's shop was always busy, packed with long lines of old ladies sitting under driers or waiting to be attended to. Whatever they were doing, they chatted, relaying the news of the day and harking back to the old times before and during the war.

Annie was in her element there. Nothing would make her miss this trip to the hairdresser once a fortnight. Sheila pushed her mother along in the wheelchair and helped her inside. Then she would sit very quietly, her little dog, Ben, on her lap. Sometimes she would comb his coat and tie a blue bow on it. Everyone knew Ben, who snapped and snarled at strangers, but was friendly to anyone he knew and he liked. Sheila was never anywhere without him.

Esther would say: 'Come on, Sheila, let's make you look nice too. I'll cut your hair and perm it.'

But Sheila would shrink back into her seat shaking her head and staring in confusion all around her.

'Let 'er be,' Annie would say. 'She won't let anyone touch 'er. Only our Amy was allowed to do that.'

'It's a bloody shame,' said Esther. 'Your other gels are so smart, and poor Sheila looks about forty.'

Sheila would cuddle Ben, kiss the top of his head and make no comment.

During Annie's visits to her shop, Esther was wise enough never to mention Siddy. She would ask after Amy, Joe, Billy – anyone but Siddy.

So Siddy's accident was talked about in whispers and everyone shut up as soon as Annie arrived. But without the bright gossipy Esther and that nice hair-do, Annie would have found life a little tedious.

Then one bright summer day Annie was sitting outside in her wheelchair having just returned from the hairdresser's. 'Go and make a pot of tea, Sheila,' she said. 'Let Ben stay on me lap for a while, he's having a kip.'

Willingly as always, Sheila went inside to put the kettle on while Annie and Ben quietly dozed in the sun. Annie's hair was white and silvery shining brightly in the sun, her face still quite red from the heat of the drier. She did not notice the two lads lurking about on the other side of the green watching, as they often did – kids playing truant from school, out to nick from the cars or anything left on park benches. Suddenly they swooped, running past Annie, and scooping up the dozing Ben from her lap. They ran off down the road with the dog which yapped like mad in their grip.

'Oh, you sods!' screamed Annie.

At the sound of the commotion, Sheila came dashing out and ran after them. 'Ben! Ben! Don't take my doggie! Let him go,' she called.

The lads disappeared like the wind, laughing gleefully as they leaped over the high railings and disappeared with Sheila's beloved dog in their arms.

Poor Sheila stood screaming in frustration by the railings which she could not get over. Annie struggled to rise in panic and fell out of her wheelchair. There was no one around on the green. Most of the flat dwellers were out at work and the kids were all at school. Still screaming, Sheila ran back towards Annie who was now lying helplessly on the ground, but suddenly fell down in a fit in the middle of the green.

Annie yelled frantically for help. At last a little old man came out from next door. Realizing what had happened, he helped Annie back in her chair, but she fell forward again, her mouth all twisted. She was unable to speak. He ran to the phone box and called the ambulance and the police. Both Annie and Sheila were taken to the hospital, but no more was ever heard of little Ben.

The whole district got roused up over this incident. Down at Esther's the customers all shed tears. 'Oh, she had 'er hair done only that day,' said Esther. 'It gave 'er a stroke, it has. They sez she can't utter a word.'

'Oh, gor blimey!' said one customer. 'Poor Annie, that's gonner upset 'er.'

As always, Billy was sent for. Nancy came, as did Lily, who was now a big busty woman and the matron of a home for deprived children.

Annie just sat up in bed and stared apathetically at them. Sheila had first been sent to a psychiatric hospital because of her screaming nightmares but now had been returned to the general hospital. But they could not really cope with her there so she was sent back to the psychiatric hospital. In the end Annie was sent home and Lily stayed a while to clean up the flat and organize the home-help, such as meals-on-wheels. But she could not stay for too long. 'I have my own group of children to think of,' she said.

No one bothered about Sheila. No one even visited Sheila. Poor Annie would sit mouthing silent words which seemed to say, 'Where's Sheila?' But no one could cope with her, it was all too much for them all.

In the end Nancy wrote to tell Amy the bad news.

Back in Canada, Amy's depression had not lifted. Sparky could not put up with it any more. 'Right,' he said one day. 'Go home, if you like, but leave Tosh with me.'

There was no question in Amy's mind of splitting up her family. 'Come home too, Sparky, it's all blown over now. Let's get back to where we belong.'

'Look, Amy, I'd have to sell this house. I can't just walk out on it, and I will need money to start again in England.'

So the arguments and debates continued until one day when Sparky placed a wad of notes on the table. 'I quit my job,' he announced 'and got a bonus. Go take a plane home now if you want to.'

'What about you, Sparky?' sobbed Amy.

'Look, I've decided to stay and sell this 'ouse, and then I'll work my passage home on the boats. I'll get across that bridge to the States and go home that way. It will be easy to get a job on one of the Atlantic Liners. It may take longer but like that I'll not bring too much attention to myself, just in case they have a contract out on me.'

Amy held her head in distress. 'How can I leave you? How do I know you will come home?'

'Well, doll, you will have to trust me, won't you?' said Sparky with a smile.

The following week Amy said goodbye to Letty and Frank, and Sparky, who was putting the house up for sale and selling all the furniture. He was to stay with Letty until he had completed the deal. He stood there at the airport with the wind blowing across the tarmac, ruffling his red hair which he now wore much longer so it had begun to curl. Amy glanced over his long lean healthy body in the casual shirt and tight jeans which had become his normal mode of dress, and she smiled sadly at him. 'I'll be waiting for you, Sparky,' she said quietly.

The plane took off and Amy was on her way home at last.

It was a more comfortable flight this time as the plane was not crowded, and Amy managed to get a good rest. She sat staring out into that wide air space. The fluffy clouds down below looked like a snowfield and way up there in the blue empty void it was all so peaceful. Suddenly she was a little girl again and Miriam Trelawny was sitting next to her, her soft hand holding hers. Her soft voice was saying: 'Now, Amy, be a good girl, Auntie Miriam is here.'

Amy woke from her reverie with a start. It was now night time and the air hostess was pulling down the blinds. 'Have a good sleep,' she said. 'I'll wake you all for breakfast.'

Amy's little girls were facing her, cuddled up close together. Amy looked tenderly at them; there was a sweet smile on Rachel's face.

Suddenly a pang of fear ran through Amy's body. All at once she felt afraid that something might go wrong and they would never meet up as a family again. It ruined her night. She could not sleep but instead tossed uncomfortably in her seat, sweating and biting her fingernails.

In the early morning, when the dawn shed a pink light on all the other sleeping passengers, the stewardess brought Amy a cup of tea. 'It won't be long now,' she said. 'We will be landing in twenty minutes.'

Amy had never felt so grateful in all her life.

CHAPTER TWELVE

Coming Home

It was raining in London when Amy came home. The shiny wet pavements and the stiff breeze blowing off the Thames seemed to bid her welcome. The children were tired, but uncomplainingly helped to carry the bags. They travelled by bus into the West End, then by tube to the East End. By the time they neared home they were all very weary, trudging along dragging two heavy suitcases. It was very comforting for Amy to spot Annie's flat just before it began to get dark. There were no lights on but the front door was on the latch. Amy pushed it open, and switched on the light, then went inside.

Annie sat slumped in her wheelchair in the middle of the sitting room. Her head had dropped against her chest. She was dozing and the whole place looked as if it had been hit by a tornado. There were empty bottles everywhere, cigarette ends overflowed the tin stuck in front of Annie's wheelchair and an overpowering stench of urine and bad food permeated the air. It was all a dreadfully squalid scene of neglect. Amy stood still, gasping for breath. Her two little girls who had crept in behind her looked around and started to giggle.

Annie slowly raised her big head. Her hair, no longer a silvery white, was just a kind of dirty grey.

'It's Amy, Mother,' Amy cried. 'I've come home.'

As Annie stared at Amy, her mouth worked but no sound came, and tears poured down her faded cheeks.

'Oh, Mother,' exclaimed Amy. 'What have they done to you?' Tears fell down her own cheeks as she put her arms around her mother and cuddled her. Pointing to the bedroom, she said to her wondering children: 'Go in there and unpack. It's Auntie Sheila's room. You can tidy it up for her.'

Amy made Annie a cup of tea, washed her face, helped her to the toilet and found clean knickers for her. Poor Annie had just sat and wet herself, it being too difficult to propel herself to the bathroom. She was indeed very feeble. Amy nagged all the time. 'How could they leave you alone all day? Wait till I see that Billy.'

Annie just wagged her big head pathetically, her mouth moving wordlessly. But Amy could tell what she was trying to say. 'Sheila, where's Sheila? Bring her home, Amy.'

'Yes, Mother,' replied Amy reassuringly. 'Tomorrow I will do just that. Now you relax. I am staying with you,' she consoled her. Annie's wrinkled hand grasped hers so gratefully.

The little girls were having fun in Sheila's room and put on the old portable gramophone, which Amy had brought back from evacuation and which Sheila had taken such good care of. The strains of that old record came drifting out, 'Amy, wonderful Amy,' and filled the whole flat. Annie gave a twist of a smile and touched her ear as if to say, 'I don't speak but I can hear good.'

The next day Amy went to the welfare and complained bitterly in an effort to get Sheila out of the hospital, and about the conditions in which her mother was left to live.

The welfare people were apologetic but explained that Annie was awkward and would not allow the flat to be cleaned up or let anyone in to wash her.

Amy would not listen. 'It's a bloody disgrace, is all I can say, it might be your mother to be treated like that some day. You get your bloody wages, so do your job. And I want my sister Sheila sent home.'

They told her that they weren't sure if this request would be possible to meet as Sheila had deteriorated in the hospital.

'I'll go and see for myself then,' stated Amy, marching out smartly.

Back at the flat she told the girls to stay and look after Granny, and then she set off by train to Essex to see Sheila.

It was a soul-destroying sight that met Amy's eyes at the hospital. There was Sheila crouched beside her bed, her hands over her face. The ward was very overcrowded, the windows were barred and the floor was bare. The beds were packed close together and it was impossible to escape the weird antics of the disturbed patients.

Amy and the authorities argued at length about Sheila. They said she had to be examined but in the end Amy had her way.

At first Sheila did not know Amy and would not look at her. The young nurse roughly pulled Sheila's hands away from her face. 'She is very different you know.'

But Amy's sturdy shape almost pushed the nurse over as she shoved her out of the way. She pulled Sheila to her feet and cradled her in her arms. Sheila started to sob heart-brokenly. 'Don't cry darling,' said Amy. 'Amy's here, you remember.' And Sheila put her arms about Amy's neck and repeatedly kissed her.

'Take me home, please take me home to Mother,' Sheila whispered.

'I will, darling, where are your outdoor clothes? Come on, we'll see the matron. No one's keeping you in this terrible place any longer.'

After a big battle with the staff Sheila was eventually allowed to go home with Amy. They travelled back by train. Amy got a taxi to the station and Sheila was supremely happy. She did not say a word; she just sat staring at her beloved sister Amy.

Amy wanted to scream she was so angry at the injustice of

it all. Poor sweet Sheila who wouldn't hurt anyone, shut up in that grim asylum. 'Some one is gonner pay for this,' she vowed.

When they finally got home, Annie was over the moon with joy to see Sheila at last. Her wide grin appeared on her face once more as she held her daughter to her bosom and her mouth worked as if she had so much to say but could not tell them.

And so part of the family was reunited under one roof.

Amy called the council in to clean up the flat, and arranged for a nurse to come each day to help wash and dress Annie. She got sheets and an allowance to feed them, and all the commodities and welfare facilities needed to take care of Annie. She did not leave a stone unturned in her battle to get what they were entitled to.

During the day the girls went to a local school and Sheila and Annie sat out on the balcony, while Amy cooked them all good nourishing meals. She was now so busy there was no time to think of Sparky or what he was up to.

Sheila and Annie developed a kind of sign language between them, so that Sheila was able to transmit to Amy all Annie's needs. It worked very nicely. Slowly Sheila got some of her confidence back. Amy would tuck her up each night with one of the girl's toy dogs which looked a little like Ben and leave the light on for her. Sheila had told Amy that in the hospital they had always turned the lights out, something that terrified her ever since that shelter disaster.

Bravely Amy coped with Annie and Sheila in addition to her two little girls. Her sister Nancy came visiting, bringing with her a big basket of farm produce and home-knitted woollies for the girls. Emmy, Billy's wife, sent sweets and toys. Even Lily turned up, leaving a gift of money for them all. Each one in turn Amy lashed with her tongue, blaming them for the neglect of Sheila and their mother.

'But Amy,' pleaded Nancy tearfully, 'she is so obstinate and won't do anything for us.'

'Well, you seldom came by to see her,' declared Amy.

Nancy burst into tears. 'Oh, don't pick on me now, Amy,' she sobbed. 'I'm so upset about poor Miriam – she was like a big sister to me.'

'Why? What is wrong with her?' asked Amy, a little surprised.

'Oh, I was going to tell you,' wept Nancy. 'She got killed in an air crash. The same day as you came back, she was flying to Canada. She had lost her husband and was at last flying out to join Jack. He had a ranch out there and had waited all those years for her.

Amy's big brown eyes widened in horror. 'Oh, no!' she cried. 'Not our Miriam!'

'It's true!' said Nancy. 'Dick rang up the airline. They told him that the plane crashed off the Newfoundland coast. There were no survivors.'

Through Amy's mind flashed that strange dream in which Miriam had seemed to be so near to her in the plane when she was coming home. She covered her face with her hands. 'Oh Nancy,' she wept, 'and she came to say goodbye to me.'

Sadly the sisters comforted each other, and even the unemotional Lily was distressed when she heard the news of Miriam. 'Miriam was like a mother to us all,' she said. 'We had little love from Annie, so that's why we are a little careless now.'

Annie was in bed in the next room and she banged violently on the bedside table with the stick.

'Oh, there she goes,' said Lily. 'I don't envy you your life, Amy.'

Amy smiled. 'She hears everything. She can't utter a word but has earholes on sticks.'

Rachel and Tosh giggled. 'She is always so funny, our granny,' they said in unison.

When the sisters returned to their own homes, Amy felt very down-hearted, but she coped with her family to the best of her abilities and as far as the money she got from the welfare would go.

At night she went her rounds. She covered up the little girls who slept in the single bed next to Sheila. Sheila would lie cuddling her toy dog in her arms, her mouth open as she snored noisily but peacefully. Then she would go in to see Annie who would still be sitting up in bed puffing her fag. 'Put that out, it's bedtime,' Amy would say firmly. 'I am going to put out the light.'

Annie always grimaced in a kind of grateful smile, and she held Amy's hand as she kissed her goodnight.

Amy knew she was needed but once she was alone, her mind began to be tormented with questions. As she made up her own bed on that old put-u-up in the sitting room, tears would pour down her cheeks. 'Oh, Sparky,' she wept, 'where are you? This waiting is driving me mad.'

All night long she tossed restlessly. She missed his strong body beside her at night and his noisy antics as he played with the kids or sung and whistled all the time. Would their lives ever be the same?

One day, when morning dawned, she heard the latch on the door rattle. Thinking it was the milkman, she got up, pulled on her dressing-gown and opened the door. There stood a tall young man in a dark blue sailor's outfit. He had a seabag slung over his shoulders and wore horn-rimmed specs. He dropped the seabag, put out his arms and grabbed her. 'Oh, Amy, darling, you sure are a sight for my weary eyes.' Any sighed as she sank into his arms. Sparky was home once more.

Great was the excitement when the rest of the household rose. Sheila was very excited and kept grinning. Rachel kept jumping up and down and little Tosh never left her father's lap. Annie was got up and wheeled into the sitting room very early, while Amy cooked eggs and bacon for them all, leaving her no time to talk to her returned husband. Sparky looked so different. He had lost weight, he wore his hair long and it curled up at the nape of his neck, and he had grown a moustache to match his long ginger sideburns.

That evening, the atmosphere was a little quieter. Annie was in bed. Sheila was in her bedroom playing Ludo with the little girls, and Sparky and Amy were alone at last. He pulled Amy down on to the settee beside him. 'Oh, Amy,' he said, 'how I've missed you all.'

Amy gently stroked his untidy hair. 'Take off those specs, Sparky, it don't look like you.'

He removed his glasses and kissed her passionately. 'I wear them as part of my new image – like it?' he asked cockily.

'No,' she said, cuddling close to him. How she was enjoying his lovely male smell of fresh skin laced with tobacco. This was her man: how had she managed without him?

As his hands roamed urgently over her body, he whispered, 'Where do we kip?'

'Oh here,' she said. 'There's nowhere else, but wait until they are all in bed.'

So Sparky and Amy became true lovers once more on that same old settee where they had done their courting. Annie could be heard snuffling and twisting about in her bed and Sheila let out frightening little cries throughout the night. But the world was theirs; they were lost in the land of lovers.

By morning, Sparky, in his shirt sleeves, served everyone tea in bed and was his bright breezy self. Before the girls went to school, he stood them together and said, 'Line up.' Then with a serious expression on his face, he said, 'Now it's stumm.' He put his finger to the side of his nose.

'Yes, Dad, stumm,' the little girls replied.

'You don't go telling the kids at school that your dad is

home, right? Because I'm on a special secret mission for the government, savvy?'

'Oh yes, Dad,' they cried, and went off to school giggling at the excitement of it all.

'But why does your return have to be a secret?' asked Amy later that morning.

He cuddled her. 'Look darling, these bastards might have a contract out on me. I don't trust them. I've got enough to start again – but this time it's on the level, I ain't getting mixed up with the big boys again – no siree! I have learned my lesson.'

Amy looking a little afraid and put her arms about his neck. 'Oh, don't scare me, Sparky, don't spoil it all.'

'Well, doll, it must be faced. Why do you think I took so long coming back to you? I was trying to fox them. Didn't want no reception committee waiting for me.'

Tears poured down Amy's cheeks. 'Oh Sparky, don't tell me it's as bad as all that?'

'No, not really, but you can never be sure, Amy. They are a bloody evil lot, you know, and it don't take a lot to get on the wrong side of them. After all, I did clear out and leave them holding the baby. But don't worry, love, the best place is home and we will get by.'

For a while Sparky only went out when it was dark. Even then he wore a black trilby hat and a long black overcoat, avoided the trouble spots and most of his old mates.

Every time he went out, Amy would wait anxiously for him to come home, when she would throw herself into his arms. They were so loving and so sweet to each other that it seemed that they had begun another honeymoon in that warm nest with Annie, Sheila, and the two girls. The flat was very overcrowded but there was plenty of love and warmth and happiness within.

But after about three months of this fugitive existence, Sparky came back one night to tell Amy that he had got a little business started. He had rented an arch near Liverpool Street Station where he was going to repair electric faults on cars, and buy old cars to do them up and sell for profit.

Amy looked anxious.

'It's quite clean, and no one knows me. I'm Tony Binks from now on. We'll stick it out here until we get enough money to buy a house in one of those new towns and take Annie and Sheila with us.'

He was generous and so considerate to her family, how could Amy not agree and trust him as she would do all her life?

Then began a peaceful year. The little business thrived but never did too well. Amy took a part-time job in the baker's shop in the market. Sparky bought and sold his cars and became quite famous at doing repairs. His training at sea had given him useful skills. Tony Binks, as he was now known, was a real wizard with old cars, repairing and refurbishing them and then selling them at a profit. But unfortunately because of his generous ways he often got knocked and rarely paid, but all the same, he made a fair living and they all seemed quite content, though there was never enough money in the kitty to put a deposit down on the nice new house that Amy longed for. Eventually they settled for another council flat in the same block as Annie's but four floors up. It was a bigger and more spacious home. Sparky bought some new things and got Amy's old furniture out of storage. Life was not all sunshine and roses but fairly content. Amy would pop in each day to see Annie who never got her voice back but was fairly fit otherwise, though still unable to fend completely for herself. Sheila was able to cope quite well because Annie did not sit out on the green any more but instead sat on the balcony when the weather was good, looking out towards the old places she used to know, and pointing frequently to the old square tower of the parish church.

It was while working in the baker's shop that Amy made

contact once more with her brother Siddy. She was at first very disturbed to realize that the lean gaunt man who came in to buy a couple of rolls, a shabby, down-at-heel creature, was her beloved brother. He limped badly and wore very old shabby clothes. He was indeed, very down and out.

'Oh, Siddy!' Amy cried. 'What has happened to you?'

That old devilish grin appeared as he replied, 'I'm okay, sis.'

'But where have you been? Are you working? Why do you look so ill?' Questions poured from her.

'Can't stop, sis,' he said briskly. 'I'm helping out on the tater stall. See you later,' and Siddy limped off.

At three o'clock Amy finished work and went up to wait outside the school to meet the girls as they came out. She was feeling most upset about Siddy but when she mentioned him later to Sparky, all he said was: 'Can't carry the world on your shoulders, Amy. You do too much for your family already.'

'Oh, Sparky, he looked a proper down-and-out and limped along so badly,' she said sadly.

'Well, seems that they really nobbled poor old Sid. That's why he lost his privates. He has to wear a kind of plate down there, I gather. It's finished him with the women, it has.'

Amy felt sick. 'Oh Sparky, we must help him,' she begged.

'There's nothing you can do, and Siddy wouldn't thank you. Let him alone. He's got plenty of friends and I don't want him to know that I am home.'

'Oh, why not? You can trust Siddy.'

'Amy,' said Sparky, his voice suddenly hardening. 'After all I've been through I don't trust no sod.'

So Amy went back and forth to work, she often stopped to say hello to Siddy who hopped around the big vegetable stalls fetching and carrying for their owners. Sometimes Amy would slip him a packet of fags but that was all she could do. Much as she wanted to, she did not ask Siddy to come home any more, she was too afraid of Sparky. For if Sparky said no, it must be no.

Siddy was not bothered. 'I'm all right,' he told her. 'Got good lodgings, and all me pals are around here.'

There was no mention of that dangerous love affair with Bubbles or of Sadie, his lost love. To Amy it was as if Siddy was only a shadow of his old self.

One day a big story splashed across the newspapers when the beautiful blonde Bubbles had been found dumped in an East End alley, her fair body ripped open and her lovely face battered and bruised.

Siddy was grabbed by the police, and everyone was quite agog at this terrible murder. Bubbles had only been twenty years old and had grown up in the district; it was indeed a dreadful thing to happen.

But Sparky was a little alarmed. 'Blimey, I hope it don't bring old Bill nosing about down here. Siddy would not hurt a fly, so they'll let him out in no time. They just got to get some information from him.'

Amy was very worried for a while, but Sparky proved to be right. The police let Siddy out again once he showed that he had a good alibi.

'She was just a whore, that Bubbles,' said Sparky, 'and they finished with her, chucked her out into the dustbin. I've been told she was full of dope.'

'Oh, don't talk about it,' wept Amy. 'I never liked her, but I feel so wicked at what has happened to her.'

'Amy,' said Sparky, 'you know very little of what goes on out there, so let's keep ourselves to ourselves, shall we?'

Three weeks after Bubbles was buried they found Siddy's body on the railway line just outside Broad Street Station.

Amy and Billy had to go and identify him, but Sparky stayed out of the way. When Siddy was buried it was the grandest funeral that had ever been seen down the market, for the trades people had a whip round to see poor Siddy off great style. Huge wreaths and long lines of cars followed his cortège to Manor Park. The verdict was that Siddy had fallen over while trying to get across the railway line, as some often did, in a short cut from East to West. Therefore his was declared an accidental death rather than suicide. But Amy knew, Billy and Sparky knew, and all of Siddy's friends knew otherwise. Poor Siddy, who had never amounted to much and had been rejected by his own mother, went off in grand style nonetheless.

'Poor Siddy who had loved and lost,' Sparky said. 'Poor sod, he was a born loser, but at least no one can kick him in the arse now.'

Amy went with Billy in the principal mourners' coach, as they drove past the hundreds of people lining the roadside, she realized how few of them she knew. Some came in big limousines. She recognized the Palmer boys with their big heavily padded shoulders and smart suits, and their small black-clad mum between them. It was Dolly, the old woman she had met when she had visited Siddy on the Isle of Wight. The sight of them worried her. How deep had Siddy been with them? Then to her surprise, sitting in a big Rolls Royce, Amy spotted Sadie and her father. Sadie had grown very stout and was weeping copiously, while Jack Goldman, now a white-haired old man with his fur hat on top of his head, looked very serious. Then there were the various car loads of Siddy's market friends. The stalls had all closed for the day, as had the pub.

After the funeral, a noisy party was held in the pub, but Billy and Amy went back to Annie's house. Annie did not know where they had been and stared suspiciously at them. Amy wanted so much to tell her of the son she had rejected and of how well he had been loved in spite of all his troubles, but knowing Annie, she thought it was all better left unsaid.

'Let sleeping dogs lie,' as Sparky had advised.

CHAPTER THIRTEEN

I'll Wait For Ever

The building continued throughout the East End. The council were making huge improvements everywhere, and were now demolishing what was left of the old shops and houses, and building a new market in a covered arcade. Lots of the older costers objected but the council compensated them and moved them on to the new towns.

Esther the hairdresser was one of the first to go. She came to Annie one day bringing her a present, and the two women sat gossiping in a kind of sign language all afternoon. Annie had cheered up immensely since Amy's return but was still unable to speak clearly, so when Annie and Esther came to a point when they couldn't understand each other, Sheila would step in and translate what Annie wanted to say. Otherwise Sheila sat peacefully crocheting lots of round woolly hats, some of which she wore. She had a different one for each day. Sheila's hats were the joke of the family. She presented them to her nieces and nephews, who never ever wore them, and all the hats eventually ended up on some stall at a charity fair or a jumble sale down in Dorset or up in Chelmsford. Nevertheless, this hobby kept Sheila quiet and content and everyone bought her skeins of wool or gave her old jumpers to unpick to make more woolly hats. Sheila, in some ways, found herself in her element looking after her mother. She liked to be needed, but could not be expected to go far from home; sometimes just a walk to the chip shop would terrify her.

But Amy thought this was a blessing. 'It's just as well Sheila doesn't go out much,' she said. 'The area is fast becoming fairly dangerous. The old folk we knew are not there any more.'

Sparky remarked, 'Be patient, doll, one day we'll make it rich and move to the country, but at the moment it is all graft and I have to stay near my work.'

Amy plodded on with her own work, spending the mornings in the baker's shop, and the afternoons with Annie. Her little girls had grown quite independent of her. Tosh had her sports and Rachel her studies. Both girls had chosen their own kind of friends. Tosh's friends consisted of all nationalities and all colours – black, white or brown. As long as they could skip and jump or play netball, they were her pals. Rachel was inclined to stick to one nice girl whose folk owned the baker's shop.

As the years went by, life for Amy did not change. She had reached a point when it did not matter any more. Sparky was still very good to her and whenever he made a lot of money, he bought her gold bracelets and diamond rings. 'Keep them safe,' he would say. 'They can always be pawned if we are ever broke.'

Recently Sparky had begun to make some more friends – 'smart-alec guys', as Amy called them, who liked fast cars and night clubs. Often Sparky would get taken out on stag nights or when some young fellow was getting married.

Amy did not mind, but she would say: 'Don't get mixed up in anything dodgy, will you, Sparky?'

'No, love, I've learned my lesson,' Sparky would assure her. 'I am Tony Binks now, superman with cars and much appreciated. The old Sparky died a sudden death.'

For some reason a cold shiver went down Amy's spine. 'If it wasn't for Mum and Sheila I'd put my name down for a council house out in Essex. I get afraid of this place sometimes.'

'Amy!' he cried, forgetting what he had said about moving to the country. 'My little Cockney gel, this is where you and I belong. We proved it, didn't we, by coming back? So let's dig in our roots and make ourselves a fortune until the bloody taxman chases us out.'

Amy smiled. Sparky was always so full of humour nowadays, she could not be angry with him for long. But, in fact, slowly and surely Sparky was being lured back to his old haunts; he even took to going for a Sunday lunchtime drink at his old pub in Brick Lane.

Amy would warn him. 'Mind what you are up to. Don't get thick with those crooks again, will you?'

'The brothers have all gone for the big time up west now,' Sparky told her. 'Trans-Atlantic deals are what they are after, not little tiddlers like me. It's the big fish they hook these days.'

Even though Amy found herself worrying inwardly, it was nice to see Sparky happy and his confidence restored. He started to wear smart clothes and aftershave, and went off for his nights out whenever he fancied them.

On Sparky's nights out, Amy would go with the girls to the cinema and on her return would sit with Annie and Sheila. That she was sometimes very lonely she would not admit, but she took good care of herself, dressing carefully and very smartly, and having her hair done every week. She was only in her thirties but she was slowly becoming 'her indoors', as they called a woman who was very respected but played no part in the deals that were set up in pubs and clubs by the sharp male East Enders. Occasionally there was a social occasion, a wedding or an engagement party, to which Amy had to go and be the best dressed one there. She would wear all her fine jewellery, and Sparky would be very proud of her, twisting her around and saying, 'Gee! you'll knock all those lads for six when they see you, my lovely Amy.'

Despite Sparky's flattery, Amy was conscious of her defects

and did her best to disguise them. She kept her figure and had a rather haughty bearing. Her smooth ash blonde hair was cut in a dainty little fringe across her forehead in order to hide her scar. And at these occasions she was very proud to be admired as the wife of Tony Binks, that astute, much-sought-after business-man.

It was on one night after one of these parties that Sparky had said: 'Oh, life is just great for us now. I'm not sorry I came back, but one thing that is still missing in my life, is that son I never had.'

'I don't think I want any more children, Sparky,' Amy said quietly. 'It will mean losing that nice little job if I have a baby to look after.

But Sparky frowned. 'Fuck the job, Amy! It's me you will look after.' With that, he unzipped her fifty-quid party dress and carried her to bed. 'From now on, you are my lovely woman and we will make love while we are young and healthy. We're going to have as many kids as I can get.'

'Oh, no Sparky,' protested Amy, but her voice was lost as his lips pressed down on hers, and that lovely thrill of being close to her man, who so badly wanted her, overcame everything else. From then on, Amy's life was a constant honeymoon. Sparky showered her with gifts. Every night he brought home bottles of brandy and boxes of chocolate. They would sit around their big coloured television and get sloshed, and once the little girls were in bed, they too would go to bed for a night of love.

Amy bloomed. She was happier than she had ever been, though she kept telling herself that such contentment could not last. Always inside, she felt a feeling of apprehension. Often Sparky came to meet her at lunchtime, wearing his greasy old overalls and driving an old banger. He would pick her up from the shop after work saying: 'Come on, darling, let's have a little session before the kids get home from school.'

'Oh, Sparky, you are getting so sexy,' Amy would say but

her heart was beating with excitement at the thought of his strong arms around her. And he was so good with the children. Whenever Rachel got sulky, demanding to have some expensive thing such as some fancy shoes to be like her friend, Sparky always gave in and bought them for her. He played football on the green with Tosh on summer evenings and arm-wrestled with her on the rug in the winter. Amy would say, 'You are encouraging her to be a tomboy, Sparky.'

'Well, it's a tough old world she is going into, and she might need those muscles,' he would reply with a laugh.

Every day it seemed Sparky was happy whistling and singing and bustling with energy. One day, on a Sunday morning, he came home looking quite excited. 'Guess who I met down the pub?' he said.

Amy, serving lunch, paused to listen.

'Tommy Evans,' he said.

Amy nearly dropped the plates.

'Oh no!' she cried, 'Not Tommy Evans! I heard he moved to Harlow.'

'Well, he has, but he comes up now and again to have a prowl around the old places. He's back with his wife and kids and been going straight. Now he does long-distance lorry driving – goes right out to Germany and France.'

Amy put Sparky's dinner in front of him with an unsmiling face. 'All I can say, Sparky, is that I don't know how you can even speak with him after what he did to poor Siddy.'

Sparky's eyes gleamed in temper. 'Now Amy,' he said, 'your Siddy asked for that, knocking off Tommy's bird and doing in the money he had stashed away while Tommy was in the nick.'

'I don't believe that,' Amy said obstinately. 'And what about that poor girl who got murdered? For all we know, Tommy Evans did that.'

'Oh, for Christ's sake, shut up!' Sparky pushed his dinner

away impatiently. 'Don't go on about something you know nothing about. I'm going to bed.'

So for the first time in many months Amy did not join him but sat watching the film of the week on the telly and having a little snivel whenever she thought of poor Siddy.

After that exchange, Sparky continued to be a little cool towards her, and on Sunday mornings she would now often spot the portly shape of Tommy Evans hanging about waiting for Sparky, and watch wistfully as they went off down to the old pub together. Sparky would always return in the evening much the worse for drink.

Amy did nothing. It was no good arguing with Sparky once he was set on something. Every Sunday she looked over the balcony to watch Sparky greet Tommy Evans, she felt very afraid, but she did not know why.

A month later she had some wonderful news to tell him which brought them close once more, pushing Tommy Evans to second place. Amy discovered she was pregnant.

Sheila giggled and hugged herself when told about the expected baby. She was so happy it might have been her baby.

Annie shook her head at the news. 'Boy this time,' she said in her own kind of language which they had all begun to understand. It was so difficult for Annie to pronounce the words, but the speech therapist called once a week and Annie was improving vastly. She had begun to say simple words and enjoyed the attention she was getting.

Rachel was not sure about the new baby at all. 'It will be a bit embarrassing when my friends find out,' she muttered.

But Tosh was very pleased. 'Won't it be great to have a brother?' she exclaimed.

Sparky laughed and whirled her around. 'That's it, Tosh,' he roared, 'you really cracked it.'

Amy gave up her job without complaint and lived peacefully through her period of waiting. Sparky was as good as gold but was eaten up with his own shady kind of business. 'Got to get a bit of money in the kitty,' he would say. 'We're going to have a big family.'

The shady figure of Tommy Evans still lurked around but nothing would induce Amy to acknowledge him. She heard in the baker's shop that he had moved back into the district and had a council flat in Hackney Road.

'I don't know what you got against him, Amy?' Sparky would say.

'He's a real villain,' she would reply. 'It makes me feel cold every time I see him.'

'Well,' grinned Sparky, 'ain't we all? But he's me mate and that's it.'

In spite of this, Amy was fairly content. She would sit out on the balcony with Annie in the afternoons during that summer knitting little woollies while Sheila crocheted no end of little white bonnets.

Annie would sit sucking a sweet in quiet contentment until the little girls came out of school. Then Amy would go home to get Sparky's dinner ready. It was a calm and placid existence and Amy wanted for very little.

At Christmas the family got together as everyone came visiting. Annie sat like a queen surrounded by presents from her children – from Joe in Dublin where he now ran a hotel, the twins in Hong Kong in the military police, and Nancy and Lily and Letty – in Canada – and all her grandchildren.

Amy was happy for her because Annie had had a hard life and now it seemed that it was all good things happening to her at last.

As New Year approached, Sparky said, 'There's going to be a big party on New Year's Eve around at me mate's house in Stepney. Get yer glad rags on, Amy, we'll go together.'

Amy was five months pregnant and beginning to show. 'I don't think I feel like it,' she said. 'Anyway, I won't be able to get a dress on, I've got so big lately.'

A sudden flash of temper lit up Sparky's green eyes. 'Now,

Amy, you get going, or else go and buy another dress – one of those maternity fings. You got the money and I want you with me. I'm going to let some folk see that I am a man of substance and expecting a son.'

'Oh, all right, but I don't care about your crooked friends or what they think,' said Amy defiantly, 'I'll just go if you want me to.' The next day, New Year's Eve, Amy popped out to the market and bought a nice full flowing dress and had her hair done. She sent the little girls around to Annie's and then she and Sparky got dressed up for the party.

It was about six o'clock and she was just putting on her coat when someone whistled from down below.

Sparky went to look over the balcony. 'Wait a tick, Tommy, and I'll come down,' he yelled.

'Where are you going?' Amy asked in astonishment.

'It's just Tommy. He wants to go up the road for a quick drink. I won't be long. And I need some ciggies to take to the party anyway.'

Tears of disappointment filled Amy's eyes. 'Oh Sparky,' she said, 'don't go now, I am all ready to go out.'

'Won't be a tick,' he said, struggling into his smart jacket. 'Sit down and rest for a few minutes – it will do you good.'

Within moments, he had slipped out of the front door. Feeling very frustrated, Amy sat down heavily and wept, but in the manner of many pregnant women, she quickly dozed off in the armchair and woke up sometime later feeling extremely cold. She switched on another bar of the electric fire and looked around for Sparky. There was no sign of him. He had not returned.

Bleary-eyed, she looked at the clock on the mantelpiece. It was eleven o'clock. Surely he had not gone to the party without her, that was not like him. She went out on to the balcony just as a noisy reveller passed by underneath, singing and dancing as he celebrated the New Year.

'Oh, Sparky,' Amy cried. 'How could you have gone without me?'

She made herself some coffee and watched the New Year celebrations on the television. As she watched the film of young folk jumping into the fountains in Trafalgar Square and of the police breaking up the fights around them, she felt very glad not to be out there but safe in her own home instead, and she hoped that Sparky was not getting into trouble. The bells tolled in the New Year, one, two, three. . . . Amy listened with a heavy heart and she suddenly felt very lonely, as if a kind of emptiness had entered her heart, a coldness that never left.

At one o'clock she was just thinking about going to bed when the telephone rang. Oh, that's Sparky to say he's not coming home, she thought, I expect he is staying the night with his mates.

But it was the voice of a strange woman. 'Is that Tony Binks' wife?' she asked.

'Speaking,' said Amy.

'Well, dear, don't get too upset but I've got bad news for you.'

'Yes?' Amy's heart was thumping. Now she was sure that Sparky was in the nick.

'I am Tommy Evans' wife. He just came home in a terrible condition saying that Tony had been shot up and that three men took him off two hours ago.'

'No!' cried Amy. 'It's a joke – don't try and frighten me.'

'I am sorry, dear, but it's true. I'm in a 'phone box and must go back to my Tommy. He's in a bad way.' With that, she rang off.

'It can't be true. What shall I do.' Panic-stricken, Amy ran over to Annie's flat, but everyone was in bed and the lights were out. Then she changed her mind and went home again. Sparky would turn up, she was sure. He would get home somehow.

She sat waiting and waiting through that long, long lonely night with a strange silence all around her.

At eight o'clock in the morning she looked through the telephone book and rang round all the places and people that Sparky knew. Most of them were kind but not very helpful. 'Go to the police, Amy,' some said. Others told her to try the hospitals. It was only from the mate who had given the party that she got some positive sort of help. The lady of the house said, 'I'll send me brother Harry over to take you round to Tommy Evans' place. He knows where Tommy lives.'

Harry soon arrived in a big flash car. He was a big broad fellow who looked like a villain. 'I'm 'Arry Brahn,' he introduced himself, 'a pal o' Sparky's. We ran togevver as kids in the blitz. If 'es in trouble, mate, we will find 'im, and them bastards can settle wiff me.'

Amy didn't know if he was just trying to impress her, or what, but she was so tired and she had to hope that he could help her. He took her straight to Tommy Evans' house where they found Tommy crouched in an armchair, still shivering with fright. 'They got him,' he said in a husky voice. 'He walked right into it. You know Sparky, no one worried him.'

'Who got him? Why?' demanded Amy.

'Don't know,' replied Tommy. 'I seen a van and I dived under a parked car. I never saw their faces – just the glint of a gun.'

Harry said: 'Come on, Amy, we'll try all the 'orspitals.'

He was a kind calm man and very considerate. Amy leaned on him even although he was a complete stranger to her.

They tried five hospitals and had no luck at any of them. When they left the last one, Harry said, 'It's no good, Amy, it's ol' Bill now or nobody but I'll get aht o' the picture if yer don't mind. I ain't actually got a clean slate meself and don't want to get mixed up in this. It's a big deal and I ain't no grass.'

With her face swollen from the tears she had shed, Amy

rang the police station. 'My husband did not come home all night,' she said 'and I've heard he's been shot.'

The sergeant made a joke of it. 'Oh, he will turn up. He's probably sleeping it off somewhere.'

Then she heard a voice in the background which seemed to check him, and the more cultured voice of a detective came on the line. 'Can you give me his name and address and I'll see what I can do.'

With a sigh, she gave him the details and then put down the 'phone. She sat back and rested her head on the back of the chair feeling woe-begone and not knowing which way to turn. Suddenly there was a ring at the front door bell. She started up in shock. Outside were two men and a uniformed policeman. 'May we come in? We have news of your husband.'

Amy opened the door wide. The uniformed policeman planted himself on the doorstep but the two plainclothes men walked in. 'Do you mind having your flat searched?' they asked. 'We are in search of stolen property. Are these your husband's spectacles?' One of them placed Sparky's horn-rimmed specs on the table. They were cracked and broken. 'Is this the shirt your husband was wearing?' they asked, producing a piece of a blood-stained shirt. They put it on the table and added two spare buttons that had either fallen off or been pulled oft.

'Oh, yes!' cried Amy. 'Where is he? Where's Sparky?'

'Well,' one of them said ponderously, 'that we don't know, if you don't.' He wrapped up the items with care and put them in his pocket. 'We have a report from a witness who saw the shooting. He was in the public bar which your husband had just come out of.'

'Where was it?' she asked, feeling now numb with shock.

'In Chester Street.'

'Oh, my God!' cried Amy, 'that is Sparky's favourite pub.' She fell down in a faint.

When she came round she was in bed and a neighbour was

with her. 'Oh, Amy, we are all so sorry they got your husband last night, the bloody gangsters. Have this nice cup of tea, dear.'

Amy stared at her in disbelief but suddenly they heard tramping of feet down the hall, and men with cameras burst into the bedroom and started taking pictures of Amy sitting up in bed. Horrified she hid her face with her hands until a hefty policeman came in and turfed the newspaper men out of the flat. He bolted and barred the door and came back to assure her that they had all gone.

'Oh my God! What is going on?' Amy asked.

'Not to worry, Ma,' said the policeman. 'The news broke in the papers, that's all, that your husband has been murdered and they are looking for his body.'

Once more Amy burst into tears, and a policewoman came in to bathe her eyes and talk soothingly to her.

Amy tried to push her away. 'Get out of my house!' she cried. 'Go away!'

'Now dear, stay calm, don't get excited,' the policewoman said.

Two more detectives came and systematically searched her house, moving every ornament, opening every drawer and reading all her personal letters.

By now Amy was sitting in her armchair by the fire shivering in terror. As she watched them, she sat waiting, expecting and hoping to see Sparky come dashing in and throw all this lot out. But Sparky never came. There was no sign of him.

The newspapers had a field day. 'Small-time crook killed by East End gangsters,' they wrote. 'Body not yet found. Police appealing for witnesses.'

For thirty-six hours, Amy's flat was overrun by different people, all strangers she did not know. Than at last on Monday, Nancy arrived with Billy. They locked up the flat and took Amy round to Annie's but still the busybodies hung around staring up at the windows. The news boys prowled about talking to anyone who would talk to them, ever ready with their cameras, and each newspaper had its own version of the story. But still there was no body.

The police came back to the flat and took away what was considered evidence – all Sparky's business books and a few of his personal possessions – while Amy crouched in Annie's flat, afraid to show her face at the window.

Brother Joe came over and even the twins got special leave · and went up to Scotland Yard. But they all caused nothing but trouble telling the law how to do their job.

During those long months of waiting, the family was very supportive but only the wide boy Harry was of any real help to Amy. He had been genuinely fond of Sparky, and he talked to Amy quietly in his gruff voice, of the days when as boys they were young tearaways in the London streets, and Amy liked to listen to him.

When the time came she went into the London Hospital to have her baby and gave birth to a boy who was the spitting image of Sparky. He had the same fair complexion, and a tuft of red hair stuck up on end. Though wild with delight at getting a boy, Amy was also sad.

Harry sent her flowers and came to see the baby.

'Sparky wanted a boy so much,' Amy said to him. 'And now he will never see him.'

Harry was always optimistic. 'Don't be despondent,' he said. 'If I knows Sparky 'e will turn up like a bad penny when it's all blown over. They ain't found no body yet.'

To Amy's astonishment, down the ward one day came the small active figure of Dolly Palmer. She was still dressed in black and carried a bunch of flowers and some grapes in a basket. Amy held on to her baby and stared aggressively at her.

Dolly placed the flowers and fruit on the bed and stood

looking at the baby. 'Well, it's the image of him. My boys send their regrets,' she said.

'I don't need no sympathy from them,' replied Amy sharply.

'Well,' said the old lady, 'my boys ain't as black as they are painted, but one thing I'll tell you, gel, is that they don't know where he is, either. Well, good day to you and good luck to your bonny son.' With that, she toddled off down the ward.

Amy screwed up her brow anxiously. 'What did all this mean? Was Sparky still alive? Oh, please, God, it was true. Oh, come home, Sparky,' she wept. 'Come home to your lovely son. I'll wait for you, I'll wait for ever.'

When Amy came out of the hospital she went straight to Annie's, for she could not face that flat without Sparky. The windows had been broken and the front door latch had been forced. She had not been back long before the newspapermen came back offering her big money to tell her story of her life with this small-time crook who had reached the big headlines.

Amy could not stand it. She gathered up her baby and prepared to go down to Nancy's farm in Ashmullen where her little girls had been staying for protection. Amy was thin, white, gaunt, and very harassed and felt as if she had no true friends but her family.

Harry Brown offered to drive her down to Ashmullen to prevent her from having the strain of that long train journey. Amy was extremely grateful that this big, gruff, down-to-earth man was indeed proving to be a true friend of Sparky's. 'Don't worry, 'ave a good holiday,' he told her. 'I believe Sparky will turn up and 'e will know where ter find yer. Don't worry abaht yer flat, I'll sort aht any bastards wot comes a snoopin' arahnd.'

Amy managed a wan smile, for Harry was quite able to do what he threatened, she was very sure. The rough tough background of his youth had built into him a very strong yet curiously unaggressive character. 'I can't thank you enough, Harry,' she said when he was ready to go back to London. 'I'll try to settle down here for a while till something turns up, one way or the other.'

At the village everyone wanted to see the baby. Nancy was completely over the moon with delight. And Amy was pleased to see how well her little girls got on with Heather, their cousin.

For a space of time there was a little peace in Amy's mind, but she frequently watched the road from the farmhouse window hoping against hope that Sparky would find her. When the postman came she was always the first down the path to greet him gazing despondently at the correspondence. One letter from Letty in Canada gave her slight hope. 'We all know that Sparky was a tough, hard-living man,' she wrote. 'He will go to sea and then make his way back here and as soon as he does I'll be the one to let you know.'

It was all very pleasant, her family support, yet, in spite of the police search and her ever-watchful family, not a sign or sound of Sparky was seen or heard. He had only a few pounds in his wallet, so how could he escape? These thought she turned over and over in her mind but there were no answers.

Each day her little son, Tony, grew more and more sturdy and became increasingly spoiled. And each day she worried about Annie and Sheila, whom she had left behind. It was cosy and comfortable at Nancy's but Amy felt like a lost soul. No longer did the wide moorland impress her or the rich country scene delight her. Even the comfort of Nancy's farmhouse was lost on her. It was as if her heart had died.

CHAPTER FOURTEEN

The Wrong Man

When Sparky went out for a drink with Tommy Evans on that cold New Year's Eve, he did not notice that his friend was a little edgy. Tommy was wearing a smart pinstripe suit and a wide trilby hat. He puffed at a big cigar with nervous apprehension.

'Quiet tonight, ain't it, Sparks,' he said casually.

His tall, red-headed mate looked down at him with an amused glint in his eyes. 'It will soon liven up when the pubs open,' he told him. 'Anyway what's up?' Got a hangover or just the bleedin' creeps?'

'Nah, just a bit unsettled, that's all,' replied Tommy, looking back and to the side like some wily old rat.

'Well, cheer yer bloody self up because I am taking Amy out tonight. We'll get some cigs and have a pint and then I am goin' 'ome.'

'It's all right,' shrugged Tommy, 'might go home early meself. Let's walk to the main road and cross over to Brick Lane and have a drink in the Black Horse just for old time's sake.'

'Please yerself,' said Sparky, stretching out his long legs and walking at a quicker pace.

They went through the small alley which they knew so well, into the High Street, then across the Main Road to Chester Street, to their own local where they usually had drinks on Sunday mornings. They went in and had two drinks, treating each other. Sparky bought two packets of fags to take to the party.

Tommy Evans still seemed a little on edge, frequently watching the entrance as if expecting somebody.

'Right,' said Sparky, downing his pint and banging the glass down on the counter, 'that's me lot. I'm goin' 'ome now. Yer can stop if yer wants to. Good night guv'nor,' he said to the landlord, ' 'appy New Year, I'm orf.'

But Tommy Evans quickly finished his drink and almost gasped for breath. 'I'll come with yer,' he said urgently.

They stepped outside into the dark street. A pale moon slid in and out of the clouds making deep shadows all around. It was as silent as the grave. Suddenly a van cruised past them and a voice called out, ' 'Ere, I want yer!' There were three men inside the car, one driving and two in the back, their hats pulled well down over their faces. In that lonely street the voice echoed out, and a Cockney voice said again, ' 'Ere, we want yer, mate!'

Sparky would take no nonsense from anyone. He stared back at them. 'Well, what the bleedin' 'ell d'yer want?' He stepped forward towards the van which had pulled up at the kerb with its engine still running.

The air was suddenly split with the croak and a glint of a gun showed from the back. Without uttering a word, Tommy Evans dived under a nearby parked car. His mate Sparky spun round with a dreadful cry, his hands waving in the air, as a bullet creased his forehead, spun over his head and hit the pub window. The glass blew in with a great crash. From inside the van, a hand held the gun, and another gruff voice could be heard crying, 'Fire low, you silly sod. Get 'im in the legs.' And another two bullets whizzed out of the van and in a second Sparky was writhing in pain on the blood-spattered pavement. The van started up again and a big fellow climbed out to look at Sparky. He stepped back in surprise. 'Oh,

Christ, yer silly git, it ain't 'im. Quick, get 'im in the back before they all come out o' the pub.'

So Sparky's limp body was dumped into the back of the van which then sped away.

When they had gone Tommy Evans wriggled out from under the parked car. Getting to his feet, he started running as fast as his legs could carry him in the opposite direction.

The guv'nor came out of the pub to have a look, and the customers, who had previously been crouching down inside, too terrified to move, stood around talking excitedly. It had been just like a scene from a gangster film. They agreed, no one could believe it had happened. Outside, the guv'nor looked down at the blood-splashed pavement, at Sparky's specs that were smashed into two pieces and at the pieces of Sparky's shirt torn away as he had been dragged into the van, and knew that what had happened was serious. 'Get going,' he said to those who crept out to look. 'Don't touch anything, I'd better get old Bill.'

The sergeant was sitting having a cup of tea at Old Street nick when the guv'nor came in to report what he had seen and heard. He had been expecting trouble but not so early. He put on his jacket and came down to the pub to investigate. 'It's usually when the pubs turn out that they start,' he said, picking up Sparky's specs and wrapping them up along with the torn bits of shirt.

'Who was he? Anyone know him?'

No one answered. In this part of the town even if you knew something you never divulged it. It did not pay to know anything, the repercussions were too great.

The sergeant questioned a few bystanders who quickly disappeared and then decided that there was not much more to be done at that point. 'Oh well,' he said, 'something will turn up by morning.' And he went back to finish his cup of tea at the station.

The van careered swiftly over Southwark Bridge heading

for the south side of the Thames – Over the Water, as the Cockneys put it. Inside, the young lad with the gun shivered and vomited. 'What yer goin' to do?' he asked. 'He's bleedin' all over the place, I can't take it.'

'Dump 'im outside the 'orspital,' suggested the driver.

'Nah! too risky, they might see the number plate.'

'Well, he ain't dead, is he?'

A pathetic moan came from Sparky who was huddled on the floor of the van. 'All me effin' upholstery is goin' ter be ruined,' moaned the driver, slowing down. 'Where to nah?'

' 'Ere, turn down the next alley,' the big fellow ordered. 'It leads to the wharfs beside the river. I'll take a quick shifty at him. If 'e ain't dead we 'ad better finish 'im orf and dump 'im in the river. Then we'd better blow 'cause yer ain't done wot yer was paid ter do and they ain't goin' ter like that.'

The van turned down into a remote alley just past the bridge. It was very lonely down there – all the stores and warehouses were closed for the holidays. The river looked cold and icy as they got Sparky out of the van and dumped him down in a dark spot.

Sparky had stopped moaning now and was lying very still.

' 'E's snuffed it,' said the big fellow. 'Stiff as a bleedin' board, he'll be soon. Right, now give us an 'and and chuck 'im in. He'll float dahn on the tide.'

With a terrific heave, the driver and the big fellow threw Sparky's body into the Thames.

'Now get the effin 'ell outa 'ere down the Brighton Road. We gotta lay low for a while now.'

As they sped off into the night, the cold green river gathered Sparky up with a deep gurgle as it flowed out to sea. But predictable as the River Thames is, the tide drained out very quickly that night and washed Sparky's body up into the grey muddy banks by the underground warehouses that lined this part of the river. As the river flowed by, it rolled Sparky over and over in the thick mud until he was unrecognizable as a human being. Then with a big swoosh, it pushed him down a big hollow, and his seemingly lifeless body was rolled down into a cellar where it lay still.

At twelve o'clock the bells welcomed in the New Year. The population started to meander out of the pubs and danced in the streets, as people made their way over the bridge to get to Trafalgar Square where the celebrating was going on around the big Christmas tree. Everyone was ready to party all night. Car loads of revellers went over the bridge, youths shouted and cheered, and young lovers paused to kiss. No one noticed the pathetic mud-covered body which now rested down there in a hollow on the river bank below.

One of the last revellers was a derelict old woman. She was very short and wide because of the layers of extra clothes she wore. Shopping bags held all her possessions and bottles frequently popped out of them. She carried one bottle of booze in her hand and she would stop every now and then to take a swig at it. On her head was a battered green beret under which her grey hair stuck out around her wizened wrinkled face. But Sophia, or old Soaky, as the Cockneys called her, was feeling very happy as she sang, 'Show me the way to go home. I'm tired an I wanna go to bed,' in a cracked voice waving her bottle at the passers-by. ' 'Appy New Year,' she called and shouted, but they did not respond. Old Soaky hurled a string of four-letter oaths after them but she was such a well-known character in that part of London that no one took much notice of her. Cursing all the time Soaky climbed down the long dangerous wooden steps that led to her hideaway by the river bank. She took a few steps in the mud and then fell over the helpless body of Sparky. 'What the effin' 'ell?' she cried, putting her hand out and feeling his face. 'Oh crikey, a stiff!' Trembling, she lit a match and gazed down at him. 'Ah, the poor young sod. Too young ter chuck 'imself in the river.' Then her hand felt inside his jacket and she pulled out the mud-soaked wallet. 'Cor! seven quid,' she gloated as she counted the sodden notes. 'I'll put 'em on the pipes to dry, and I'll get a few bottles tomorrer to see me frough.'

With surprisingly agile movements she climbed up the steps to a deep recess under the bridge where the hot water pipes from the power station were situated. It was here that old Soaky slept, with just a few sacks and a bit of tarpaulin for the damp nights. Setting down her bottle, she put her loot along the pipes to dry and looked down at Sparky's lifeless, muddy shape. 'Oh, crikey,' she muttered, 'how can I look at him all night? I'll cover 'im up and let old Bill find him in the mornin'.'

She dragged down a piece of tarpaulin and rolled Sparky loosely in it, and pushed him under the place where she slept. Then with a sudden afterthought, she poured some of her whisky between the stiff blue lips. The liquor made a kind of gurgle as it went down. 'Oh well,' she said taking another swig herself, 'mustn't waste it. It won't do him no good, poor little sod, will it?'

Soaky returned to her nest and settled herself down for the night. In no time she was sleeping soundly and her drunken grunts and snores waffled across the murky, fast-flowing waters of the River Thames.

When morning dawned the tide was up and washed the sides of the warehouse. Soaky awoke feeling warm and dry in her hideaway. She lit her little oil stove and placed a big enamel mug full of water and tea leaves on it to make a 'brew up'. As the cold morning air settled in, she began to feel a bit damp and shivery.

'Never mind,' she muttered to herself, 'a nice drop of whisky in me tea will soon pull me togevver.'

As she sipped her hot tea, she was startled by a strange sound. It was a kind of dull moaning sound. Was it the wind? Or the river boats? Then she remembered that poor stiff under the bridge. She hopped down quickly to look at him. To her horror she saw that his eyes had opened, and he now stared vacantly at her. 'Oh my gawd!' she cried. 'The poor sod ain't dead.'

She went back up to get her mug and returned to hold it to Sparky's stiffened lips. He was soaking wet because the river had washed over him in the night. 'Gotta get yer outa there,' Soaky murmured. 'Wait a minute.' She pulled and pushed with all her might. She was quite strong for an elderly woman but then Soaky was not as old as she looked. Her way of life had prematurely aged her. So with much effort she managed to drag Sparky to a high dry spot, near the pipes that crossed the river. With her hand she wiped the mud from his face, and poured hot, whisky-laced tea, down his throat. There was blood on his head and a piece of his ear missing. 'Had a nasty fall, ain't yer?' she said conversationally. 'Wasn't drunk, was yer? Naughty boy.' She undid the tarpaulin and wrapped her own bedding around him talking to him all the time. 'Silly boy, fancy getting fed up with life at your age. Don't know what the world is coming to.' She explored his lower parts, and there she found a deep wound in his thigh. It was still bleeding slightly. 'Oh dear, who done that? Nearly knocked yer cock off, yer have.'

Soaky lifted up her skirt. Underneath the top dress she wore another half a dozen. For if anyone kindly gave her a dress, Soaky would wear it till it fell off her. She tore away some white material. 'Now, that's a nice calico, that is,' she said. 'I'll wet it and make a bandage. I'll soon get you fixed up, my lad, and then you can go home to your muvver. There ain't a lot of room for two dahn 'ere.' All the time, as she dressed his wound, Soaky cackled and nodded her head like some comical puppet in the theatre. She washed and bathed Sparky's body and bandaged his thigh. 'Nice looking boy,' she said. 'Real red hair, something like my Johnny. Bleedin' Germans killed my Johnny,' she said bitterly. 'Oh, the bastards!' She grabbed her bottle of whisky and began to drink. 'I'll sit right here next to yer to keep yer warm,' she said, 'but it ain't bad dahn 'ere. Look at me central 'eating . . .' she giggled, pointing to the pipes.

Sparky's eyelids flickered occasionally and his lips were now less blue. He twitched every now and then but there was no other sign of life in him. 'I'll get a nice loaf and a bottle of milk and make yer some nice sops,' she told him. 'Better get out early, in case they catches me.'

Off Soaky went, hopping along like a little dog out on a spree. First she went to the factory where the milkman left three pints for the watchman. She eyed out the land and then quickly pinched one of the bottles. 'That'll do.' Then off she went down past a little grocer's shop where the shopkeeper was so busy putting out his wares that he did not notice the quick hand that whipped away one of the wrapped bread loaves which had just been delivered.

Off went old Soaky back to her hideout, where she boiled the milk and soaked the bread in it. 'Now, some nice sops,' she cried, ramming it down Sparky's throat. He began to cough and splutter.

'That's it, luv – corf it up,' cried Soaky. 'Get all the bloody Thames outa yer lungs and this sops will do yer good.'

New Year's Day was quiet after the festivities of the night before. At midday Soaky went on the prowl again, going to different pubs where she hoped to get treated. Then she spent some of Sparky's money on a bottle of whisky. When she got back to her hideout, it was getting dark, and Sparky still lay wrapped up in the tarpaulin with a pile of sacks over him. She wiped his face with her hand, and wet his lips with the whisky. 'Come on, cock, we're gonna have a party, you and I.'

Soaky sat beside Sparky drinking from the bottle and getting very drunk as she sang all her favourite Cockney songs. She had brought some drinking straws back from the pub. Filling the mug with milk, she added some whisky and stuck the end of the straw in his mouth. 'Now, luv,' she said, putting the other end of the straw in the mug, 'sup it up, it will do you good.' Slowly, those dry lips of Sparky's began to draw down the fluid, and the colour came back into his ashen cheeks. Soaky wrapped him up warm and rolled him nearer the pipes before continuing with her drunken revelry till late into the night. Still no sound came from the body wrapped inside that bundle of sacks. He just had his eyes open and he stared vaguely about him. The warmth and the hot drink were beginning to heal his body but there was no cure for his mind; although that bullet had not penetrated his brain, it had damaged it.

Old Soaky took good care of him, and no one bothered them. The police and the watchmen were quite aware of the existence of old Soaky but they knew she would not bother them for long. For old Soaky was what was known as a 'traveller'. She came in on a bender and then would disappear to Kent for the summer, when she would work, picking fruit and such like. That had been her pattern of life since the war, when she had lost both her son and husband in a matter of weeks.

So Sparky lay in Soaky's underground cellar while the police were dragging the river and searching all around the wasteland for his body. They pulled in the three criminals but finding no corpse, they had to let them go. Someone had grassed that they had taken money from the big boys to carry out a contract but then had mucked it up. They would have felt safer in prison because the vengeance of the East End gangs was something to be avoided.

Tommy Evans sold his story of his narrow escape to the newspapers and received a large sum of money which he used to fly off to South America with his family.

But Amy, poor sad little Amy, was left with nothing. She came back from Ashmullen, to her flat with her three children, still watching and waiting for Sparky to come home.

CHAPTER FIFTEEN

Old Soaky

The Thames tide rose and fell, and the flotsam and jetsam of river rubbish piled up high on the tow path as old Soaky went back and forth, her old wellington boots squelching through the mud. She was keeping a wary eye open for anything that might be of use, that had been washed up by the tide. Occasionally she found coins or a bit of jewellery but lately her luck had been out. Added to this problem was the responsibility she had towards that poor sick lad whose body was still up under the wharf. When sober she would stare at him dejectedly wondering what on earth she should do about him. It never occurred to her that the whole country might be searching for him. For old Soaky never read newspapers, she only collected them to keep her feet warm at night.

One morning, just as she was grabbing the pint of milk off the watchman's doorstep, he opened the door swiftly and pounced on her. 'Gotcher!' he hollered. 'You wicked old cow! Stole a bottle of milk from me every day this week, yer did.'

'Owa'' Soaky yelled. 'Let me go! I'll give yer the money for it, honest, I will. Yer don't expect a poor old body like me to go chasing after the milkman, do yer?'

'Now, old Soaky, you just get yerself outa 'ere,' the watchman said. 'Yer get orf on yer travels or I'll get ol' Bill ter move yer aht.' He hovered over her, a big man in a blue uniform with silver buttons.

'Nasty old sod,' yelled Soaky, 'all the bleedin' same, yer are, when yer 'as a uniform on. I knew yer when yer didn't 'ave a pot to piss in.'

The man softened a little. 'Well, get on yer way,' he said. 'I ain't havin' you pinch me milk to feed them wild cats.'

'I only wanted a nice hot cuppa,' she whined, 'me throat gets so dry in the mornings.'

He reached inside his hut and handed her half a bottle of milk. ' 'Ere y'are, that's wot's left of yesterday's, but I warns yer, it's the last time. Yer had better get on yer way tomorro'.' With that, he disappeared into his hut and banged the door shut.

Jubilantly, Soaky lopped off very quickly back to her hidaway clutching her half a bottle of milk.

Sparky was now propped up against a brick wall. He still had a kind of twisted expression on his face but there was a little more colour in his cheeks. His eyes looked vacant as he stared around him.

'Pooh!' Soaky cried, 'wot a stink! Done it again, 'ave yer? Never mind, I'll soon clean yer up and then I'll make yer some nice sops. Does yer good that does.'

Later she sat mournfully stirring the bread and milk beside the small oil lamp, a melancholy expression on her wrinkled face. 'Pity I got to move on,' she reflected. 'Just as I was getting used to havin' a bit of company. I wish yer could speak to me, son, then I might be able to find someone who owns yer.' She patted Sparky's head as if he were a stray dog. 'Shame I got to leave yer, 'cause if they chases me outa 'ere I'll be put in an institution. Yer wouldn't like that, would yer?' she queried, but nothing came back from that expressionless face.

'If I leaves yer 'ere, yer will die. That's just as well, I suppose,' she added in a very depressed manner, 'because you, poor boy, are in a very bad way. But old Soaky ain't like that,' she said getting up and cheering up. 'Help each other, is my motto and gawd help them wot gets caught helping theirselves.' She gave a little titter and proceeded to shovel Sparky's breakfast sops down his throat. Then she wrapped him up warm and rolled him closer to the hot water pipes. 'Now yer a nice clean boy. Have a nice little snooze, old Sophia won't be long.' She spoke tenderly to him as if he were a baby. Seeing Sparky settled, she then toddled off along the riverside, walking on the tow path with her head bent, her eyes searching the ground in the hope of finding something valuable. Then she made a sudden detour up a flight of steps to an old tavern called the Tugboat, the back entrance of which led down to the river. It was here that a few remaining lightermen gathered to drink and talk among themselves. There were still some old barge owners and some descendants of the ancient watermen who ferried folk across the Thames long before they built the bridges. Yet some still plied their trade along that now almost deserted river. One such man was Jack who now sat in that sleazy bar contentedly puffing his pipe. He wore a sea cap on the back of his tousled head and beer dripped off his beard.

' 'Ow are yer, Jack?' asked Soaky sliding in beside him. 'Thought I'd find yer 'ere. I saw your old barge, the *Mary Lou* out in the river.'

'Gor blimey! Soaky, what do you want?' Jack cried. 'Thought you had passed over.'

'Naw, naw!' grinned Soaky. 'I'm still alive and kicking. Got enough to treat me? Only half of scrumpy, that will do.'

Jack beckoned the barman to bring Soaky a drink. The barman brought the cider and slammed it on to the wooden table, glancing at Soaky with the utmost suspicion.

But Soaky was unperturbed and swallowed her drink with gusto. 'I want to ask yer a favour, Jack,' she said.

'Out with it,' Jack said, giving her a shrewd glance from

under his heavy great brows. 'If it's money I ain't got any. Doing very badly these days.'

'I was goin' to ask yer to take me 'ome on yer barge,' Soaky said.

Jack guffawed. 'What, on the old *Mary Lou*? Can it, Soaky, you go home on the road, like you always do.'

'Not this time, Ben, I can't, and you often did me a favour in the past.' She nudged him with her elbow, 'And I done you a few, too.'

'Oh, blimey, Soaky, now that was twenty years ago and you was a lot different to the old bag you are today.'

'Oh, well, soon forgets, yer friends do, when yer need them,' Soaky said dropping her head gloomily.

'What's the idea of wanting to go down the river? It's miles out of yer way,' Jack said in a puzzled manner.

'I got a passenger,' Soaky explained. 'A good friend of mine, been on a big bender and got awful complications.'

'It's time you packed all that up, Soaky,' said Jack, 'at your age, too.'

'Naw, naw, nuffink like that. He's a young lad, I knows him well, I'm goin' ter take him back to his muvver,' lied Soaky.

Jack stared at her even more suspiciously. Then he said: 'All right. Six o'clock is high tide. You'd better be there, 'cause, I won't hang about.'

'Thanks, Jack,' Soaky said as she lopped away with her old wellington boots flopping against her legs and her little green beret clamped down tight over her wispy grey hair. She talked loudly to herself as she made her way back across the main road. She called in at the off-licence for a bottle of whisky and took swigs from it as she went along home to her nest under the bridge. Sparky still lay huddled by the hot pipes, wrapped in tarpaulin. Soaky poured the neat whisky down his throat, and he coughed and spluttered with some vigour.

'Good,' said Soaky. 'Now that means yer getting better. Now, we are going to the country. It's very nice down in Kent, I spent a lot of my young days down there, I did. Got me own 'ome, I 'ave, down there. I only comes up to town for a little bit of excitement. Now, yer be a good boy while I'll wrap yer up nice and warm and get yer ready.'

Buried in the debris lying around them she found a length of rope which she tied around the old overcoat and tarpaulin that Sparky was wrapped in. 'Now I got to get yer down the river,' she said. 'And I got an idea.' Off she scampered, looking this way and that like a wary stray cat. In no time at all she had found what she had in mind. It was an upright trolley that was used to carry the loads from the lorries. But it was too early to pinch it yet, while it was still light. She returned to her hideout and waited. At five o'clock, when it was dark, old Soaky made off with the trolley. She dragged poor old Sparky along by the rope tied round his middle and, with surprising strength, hoisted him on to the trolley to which she firmly tied him. The whisky seemed to have knocked Sparky out. He lay with his mouth and eyes closed. Soaky picked up her over-flowing shopping bag and hooked it over the handle of the trolley. 'Good, 'ere we go. Back to the nice countryside – that will do you the world of good, Boysie.'

Pushing and shoving, she manoeuvred the trolley down the incline to the river, and then on to the tow path and under the bridge. The tide washed around her feet, and the trolley's wheels got stuck in the mud. But she did not give up. Valiantly and with great effort, old Soaky managed to push her load towards the Tugboat tavern. At last the shadowy shape of the *Mary Lou* loomed out of the mist. A lamp shone out and a husky voice called to her: 'Is that you, old Soaky?'

'Aye, aye! Captain,' she called back jubilantly, giving the trolley a final push to get it along the gangway where the old barge lay heavily laden with cargo.

'Oh, blimey!' exclaimed Jack. 'What have you got there?' He came forward to help her, peering down at Sparky with caution. ' 'Ere, he ain't dead, is he?'

'Of course he ain't,' snapped Soaky. 'I wouldn't waste me bleedin' time 'umping 'im back 'ome if he was.'

Between them, Sparky was unloaded and carried down the gangway to a small cabin where a wood stove burned. Inside, the air was quite smoky but very warm.

'I'll put you down at the cement works in the morning. That suit you?' asked Jack.

'Right!' replied Soaky, getting out her bottle. 'Now I'll have a little kip.'

All through the night the barge chugged through the deep river mist moving with the tide towards the backwater where Soaky came from. And throughout the night, Sparky lay motionless on the bunk while Soaky dozed boozily beside him.

At dawn Jack threw an old sea boot down the gangway to wake her up. 'Stand ready,' he called 'going inshore.'

There was a loud grating sound as the *Mary Lou* rocked precariously against the sea wall. Jack hitched the barge to the bollard with a rope. 'I'll help you get him ashore,' he said, 'but gawd knows how you'll get on from there. But that's not my business. And don't you pester me any more, Soaky, I'm right fed up with yer.' He was half joking as he said this.

'All right,' Soaky said. 'Get us ashore and I'll do the rest. I ain't only a pretty face, yer know.'

Jack grinned into his beard. 'Yer a rotten old baggage now, Soaky, but you wasn't too bad when you was young and I first knew yer.'

Slowly they hauled Sparky's helpless body ashore and laid him down on the frosty grass. Then Jack untied his barge and sailed on down the Thames Estuary to a place where the Medway and the Thames joined each other in a race for the sea.

Soaky lay beside Sparky watching the red dawn streaking the sky as the sun came up over the sea. 'Soon be daylight, Boysie,' she said conversationally to the unconscious lad, 'and I'll find a way to get yer 'ome.'

Soon the world was awake. The birds sang their early morning song and over the green marsh the cattle began to low. Still Soaky sat patiently waiting for someone to turn up and transport her to that little old shack in the woods where she lived most of the summer.

Soaky's story was a sad one. She used to be known as Sophia Irene Browne, a tidy lively little Cockney woman who came down to Kent during the war with her teenage son, while her husband was out East in the army. At first, Sophia lived in a tied farm cottage with her son, Johnny, and worked in the fields and orchards. But within a year, her husband was killed out East and Johnny had left to join the navy. But he, too, was soon killed, drowned before his nineteenth birthday. After this double tragedy, Sophia went on the booze. She drank very heavily and it was not long before she was pushed out from the farmer's cottage. It was then that she packed her lot in with old Silas, a notorious boozer, who was a good deal older than she. Silas was hooked on his own homemade brew. He made wine that was extremely potent and lived in a rickety little shack in the woods. He worked his own land, paid no rates or taxes, and he made no contribution to the war effort. When Sophia from London shacked up with old Silas it became the joke of the village, but nevertheless, Silas and Sophia seemed to get on very well together. In the summer Sophia worked at the fruit picking and Silas grew his own vegetables and kept chickens. They would get drunk together on Saturday nights and could often be seen swaying home arm in arm through the country lanes.

After the war Sophia stayed on living with Silas in the old shack. Their way of life was still not all it could be. They had a hole in the ground for a lavatory and a long walk down the lane to fetch fresh water. But it was exceptionally beautiful up there on top of the hill where the emerald green forest rolled down towards the sea, away from the troubled world. There was no one to worry them, and no one to care for but each other. When Silas had sat in his old homemade chair and drank his last glass of rhubarb wine, Sophia had been devastated, but after his death she stayed on in the shack getting rather more derelict and drinking more frequently than before. There were no proper deeds to the shack or to the land around it, for Silas had dug it out of the forest and squatted on it for so many years that no one bothered. The shack stood empty whenever Sophia went off for a big booze-up in London, but the locals knew that Sophia would return in the spring like a migrating bird. Having earned the name of old Soaky, she was accepted in the neighbourhood as an eccentric.

Soaky's return this year was on the early side. A frost was still on the hedgerows as she sat on the edge of the marsh with her silent companion waiting patiently for someone to transport them both up the hill to her little shack.

She did not have to wait long. Along the lane came the crippled farmhand Jim, in a shaky old wagon, tossing out bales of hay to feed the cattle.

'Jim!' Soaky hailed him.

'Well, I'll be buggered if it's not old Soaky,' laughed Jim. 'What are you doing down here so early in the morning?'

'Trying to get up to me shack. Will you give me a lift, Jim?'

'Well, it's a bit out of me way, but I'll do it,' he replied generously.

'Got me son with me,' she said. 'I'm bringing him down for a breath of fresh air.'

'Thought he went down at sea?' asked Jim.

'Naw! Just got knocked abaht a bit, but he still ain't well. Going to look after 'im, I am.'

'Well, let's hope he will be all right,' said Jim, looking down at Sparky's lifeless body.

'I'll get 'im on 'is feet, I will,' said Soaky.

'Going to be a bit lonely up there for you in this weather,' remarked Jim.

They pulled Sparky into the wagon amongst the hay bales, and set off. 'No,' said Sophia as the shack came into view. 'I'm used to it, I've slept in a lot worse places than that, I have.'

When they reached the shack, Jim, being a very kindly lad, helped Soaky to carry Sparky into the shack. They had to fight their way down the weed-covered path and through the tangle of blackberry bushes that grew around the shack. Inside, everything was covered with cobwebs.

'Well,' said Jim as he dumped Sparky on the bed. 'I wish you luck. I'll be off now. I got a long day's work ahead.'

'Soon get a nice fire going,' said Soaky, when Jim had gone. 'Ain't it nice to be 'ome? Got plenty of logs out there to last me till the spring.'

Soaky lit the fire and in no time the wooden logs were blazing brightly. She put the ancient iron kettle on to boil and covered Sparky with lots of blankets.

'That's it, Boysie,' she said, 'sleep it orf – that's the best cure for everything.'

She settled herself in the rocking chair by the fire, pulled out her bottle and continued to take swigs from it. 'Said yer were me son, I did. That will soon go round the village,' she muttered on. 'Bloody nosey lot they are, down there, but my Johnny wouldn't mind. He'd like his mum to have a bit of company, wouldn't you, love?' She looked up at the dusty picture of a smiling sailor boy. She sighed deeply and began to doze a little.

Suddenly she woke with a jerk and sprang into action.

'Now then,' she said determinedly. 'You've got a lot of work to do, you have, Soaky.' With great vigour she began to dust down the cobwebs from the corners. She washed the cups and saucers and rummaged in the cupboards for things to eat. 'Wasn't a bad old bloke, Silas. Still got some homemade jam, he made, and honey from 'is bees and wine from 'is fruit. Always was busy, he was. I was fond of 'im, I was, so you be a good boy,' she chattered on to Sparky, 'and me and you will spend the summer 'ere in this lovely fresh air.'

She pulled back the ragged curtains to reveal the splendid view right out across the Thames Estuary. All around them the forest was quiet with just the hush of winter. The frost hung in silvery threads on the boughs and a little robin puffed himself out against the cold and hopped about on the path.

'Well, now, 'ere's that old robin, cheeky little sod, come to welcome me 'ome,' said Soaky with great satisfaction as she watched him. She was very glad to be back.

CHAPTER SIXTEEN

The Kent Woods

Slowly the beautiful spring came to that part of Kent bringing great beauty as it had done every year. Under the bushes sweet violets grew and the primroses came back to life, their green shoots poking through the moist earth with tiny golden buds about to give birth. This was the time of the year that old Soaky always looked forward to. It gave her renewed life. This year she pranced about the neglected plot pointing out to Sparky such things as the growth of the wallflowers.

Sparky now sat just inside the door of the hut, well wrapped up in a lot of old woollies.

'There y'are, Boysie,' she said. 'Them daffodils is showing through the ground. Old Silas planted them when he was young and every year they comes back up, just like me,' she would titter.

Although Sparky could not completely share the joke, there was a response from his twisted face and a kind of lightening up of his fish-like eyes.

'That's it, Boysie,' Soaky said kindly, 'get that nice fresh air in your lungs. You'll soon feel better.'

There was indeed a vast improvement in Sparky. He would point to his mouth if he wanted to eat or drink and to his lap if he wanted to urinate. Then Soaky would get out the wide-necked bottle and help him. 'Now be a good boy,' she would say. 'No bed wetting tonight, eh?'

There was also a definite change in Soaky herself. Soon

after their arrival she had said: 'Now I'll put a nice big pot of hot water on and me and you will have a wash. We're going to burn all these dirty old clothes. I got some nice frocks put away down here, and I think Silas' old clothes should fit you a treat.' She had washed Sparky and dressed him in old pyjamas and made him stay in bed. The old stone fireplace glowed all night as she had stoked it up with logs, and the high pointed roof gathered in the heat. Soaky had then washed herself and, quite unashamed, stood in the firelight naked as a jay bird. 'I'm a crooked old body now but I used to be nice and slim, I did,' she informed Sparky.

The next day she made a fire in the garden and burned all their old clothes along with the garden rubbish.

And the days were spent, when she wasn't drinking, cleaning up her little patch and making the place comfortable for her and her newly adopted son, Boysie.

With a plentiful supply of homemade wines the two of them stayed put until the spring came round. Sparky's condition continued to improve but there was no chance that he would ever really be normal. Their relationship was a good one; he was to her husband and son, and she to him a mother. They both needed each other in this wilderness, amid the dark forest overlooking the wild marshlands. They grew close and made the best of what life had left to them.

Jim the farmhand often came by to leave them cans of fresh water and occasionally milk. And Soaky went out onto the little plot that Silas cultivated and dug up potatoes, carrots and onions. 'I'll make us a nice stew tonight, Boysie,' she said to Sparky. 'Won't have no meat in it, but vegetables does yer more good.'

When spring proper came at last and the paths were clear, Soaky put Sparky in old Silas' chair and for safety's sake tied him in tight. 'Now, I'm going down the village,' she explained, 'to see if I can draw me old age pension. I do that

every year. Be a good boy and I'll bring you back some
sweets.'

A kind of nodding of Sparky's head was all she got, but it
was clear that he understood her.

Soaky pulled on Silas' old trench coat, jammed her green
beret down over her grey hair and, in her floppy wellingtons,
set off down the lane carrying an empty shopping bag. As she
made her way along the muddy woodland paths, she hummed
a little tune to herself. The birds hopped around repairing
their nests and a mating black bird sang his courting song.
There was not a sight nor sound of another human. It was
nature at its best and most wonderful high up on the green
hill overlooking the sea. Slowly down the hill she went,
noting with satisfaction the glowing patches of wild flowers
through the fresh green grass as she left the shadow of the
great oak trees and went on through the apple orchard in the
direction of the square Norman church tower, the centre of
the village.

The village was a very old settlement, situated at the end of
the marshland, which hit the Thames shore. Soaky had seen
many changes in the place since she had first discovered it –
new houses and bungalows had appeared and the population
had grown, but it had not lost that rural touch. Every year it
lay low and silent under the winter snow and every year it
would return to life when the spring came round. As she
crossed the village street, villagers who knew her called out:
'Hallo, you back, Soaky?' or 'How's tricks, Soaky? Still up in
the woods?'

To some she replied but to others she did not.

'Cheeky sods,' she would mutter. 'Knew you when you
were snotty-nosed kids, I did.'

In fact, everyone had known for some time that Soaky was
back, for Jim had quickly spread the word that she had
returned but that this time she had brought her wounded son
from the mental hospital and was looking after him.

This last fact had puzzled those of them who cared to think about it. 'I don't believe it,' said some. 'Didn't her son go down on the *Reknown*? And that was more than twenty years ago. He must be an old man now.'

'Well, I don't know who she's bloody got up there but let's help the poor old gel,' said one kind-hearted villager called Ted Hazel. 'I'll pop her in a couple of rabbits when I go up there shooting.'

Soaky was given a fairly warm welcome by the villagers who generally did not really care for the woodlanders who squatted up there in the woods.

At the Post Office, Soaky handed in her pension book. It was a tattered, dirty object that went with her on her travels.

The cashier told her: 'It's out of date, Sophia. We'll send for a new one for you. In the meantime, you can get credit if you want it.'

Soaky filled her bag with provisions, not forgetting to slip in a bottle of her favourite brand of Scotch, and then went off to the Victoria, one of the three pubs in the village. The governor took one look down his slate. 'All right, Soaky,' he said, 'on the slate then but only two, mind you.'

Soaky had her two scrumpy ciders and then trotted off to the Bull, where the same thing happened, and then on to the Evening Star. Afterwards, she wove her way down the village street, staggering a little as she humped her heavy shopping bag over the shoulders. Her old back bent but her feet were still firmly on the ground when she made her last port of call at the Merry Boys, a small inn just outside the village on the edge of the wood.

Miss Smith, the proprietor, stared at her in an unfriendly way. 'Soaky,' she said, 'I can see that you've filled yourself up in the village, and now you want to scrounge drinks from me.'

This sort of welcome always set Soaky off. She waved her fist aggressively and her language became very strong. 'I ain't no bleedin' scrounger,' she shouted. 'I pays me way, I do. Got a sick son up there, I have. Fought for the likes of you, he did.'

Miss Smith moved back as Soaky advanced belligerently.

But sitting in the corner of the pub was an old friend of Soaky's, the Donkeyman. Big, broad and red-faced, he stood up. 'Sit down, old gel,' he roared. 'I'll get you a drink. While I got a penny in me pocket, you can always have a drink off me.'

Soaky sat staring boozily at him. 'Old Donkey,' she slurred. 'It's good ter see yer still around.'

Miss Smith retired from the fray as Donkey and Soaky got together with half a dozen drinks talking of old times. 'No toffee-nosed sods around then, eh, Donkey?' laughed Soaky, knocking back another whisky.

As a boy, Donkey had looked after the string of donkeys that worked in the local quarries. The donkeys were no longer worked but the name had stuck. Now retired, Donkey, kept a few of the beasts on his plot of land and drove a little donkey cart around the village. If anyone got drunk and was unable to walk properly, Donkey was always there ready and willing to get them home through that dark wood. If by chance he was the one who was too drunk to see, it was just as well that the little donkey knew its way home.

At the end of the day, a very jolly Soaky went home singing, 'Oh, I do like to be beside the seaside,' lying on her back in the donkey cart.

The lights in the shack were not on when she arrived home. Sparky still sat tied to the chair by the fire which was almost out. Soaky very drunk and very contrite, waved the bottle at him. 'Never mind,' she muttered, 'have a little drink with me, Boysie.' She poured the neat whisky down his throat and then, after stoking up the fire, she lay down on the rug to sleep it off.

Spring gave way to summer and Jim brought up some

laying hens that someone did not want and a white rabbit for Sparky, who just sat and stared at it most of the day. Soaky went out fruit picking and was away quite a time.

Sparky was now able to move a little and could help himself to the sandwiches and drinks that Soaky left within his reach. Soaky would return every afternoon at three o'clock, loaded with cherries and blackcurrants, or whatever fruit she had been picking that particular time. In the fields they rather liked old Soaky.

'She's a good worker in spite of her boozing,' the farmer said to one of the other pickers. 'But I must say there seems to be a good improvement in her this year. She comes to work regular and she don't have the big hangovers now.'

'She's drinking much less since she had that lad up there,' said one woman.

'I'll send him some homemade cake tomorrow,' said another.

Soaky settled to a kind of regular pattern of living and made many friends who gave her little luxuries to give to her 'son' – cakes, sweets, a home-knitted pullover. They were only little things that they, being only workers, had to give. On Sundays Soaky planted the garden and tended her vegetables and tomatoes. She cleared the undergrowth around the shack and repaired the chicken house in which were two hens and a cockerel. The big apple trees produced huge green apples in the autumn and the blackberries grew in abundance. She kept herself well occupied, making fruit jellies and jam, and never worried about the outside world. There were no more trips to town, just her and Boysie and the little old shack. Occasionally she did go on a bender whenever she got fed-up and then she would go down to one of the locals to fill herself up on cider until she started singing and dancing and then the old Donkeyman would give her a ride home.

The newspapers still occasionally carried headlines of the terrible East End crime that had shocked everyone early in the New Year, of the body that was never found and of the three men accused, because someone had grassed. Then there was the news of the men's acquittal because no body had been found. None of these things bothered old Soaky. They passed her by. She simply was not interested, living her own rural life with Sparky, or Boysie, as she called him. Whenever Soaky was a little high on homemade wine, she would give Sparky a few glasses too. He would rock his head from side to side and give a kind of giggle. Soaky would hold his hand and sing. 'When Johnny comes marching home, hurrah!' and rock his hand up and down and indescribable pleasure showed in those rather lifeless eyes.

The summer had been glorious that year, with the sun beating down on them every day as they sat in the garden. Then the leaves of the trees turned, colouring the entire hill with reds and browns and greens. When winter came, it was back beside the big log fire once more. And Soaky did not feel the urge to travel up to London as she usually did. She was settled in her shack. 'You and me, Boysie, lives the life of bloody Riley up here in this lovely place,' she said. 'I'll never ever want to leave, now I've got you to look after.'

CHAPTER SEVENTEEN

The Last of Old Soaky

After five idyllic years living in the woodland shack with Soaky, Sparky had come a long way. He was now physically quite strong but still quite mentally retarded. He was able to walk a little and talk in a strange kind of gabble. He listened attentively a lot, and he was a very happy boy. He could feed the chickens and keep the fire going, and was now quite independent in his personal hygiene.

It was Soaky who got Bill Dunkley, the old blacksmith, to come up and give Sparky a hair-cut and a nice close shave every now and then. Bill was very useful to all the people like Soaky who squatted in the wood. His smithy was next door to the Merry Boys Inn, where he shod horses and often sheared the sheep in between times. He cut the small boys' hair and shaved their dads and also kept a betting book. So if anyone wanted a bet on the big race it was just next door to the pub. He also had a telephone, which was a moneyspinner for him, because he did a roaring trade with the woodlanders who were not on the phone.

Although they could not be seen easily and each was as isolated as Soaky's, there were in fact around thirty or forty little homemade shacks in that deep wood, and they carried on over the hill and all down the lane. Each one was an individual property with its own design and its own way of life. It was a secret way of living and staying away from the authorities.

The woodlanders dug into the moist earth to produce fine vegetables, and they grew wonderful roses in the clay soil. Some kept bees, others had a pig or two, and everyone had geese or hens, and lots and lots of fine apple trees.

The story was that this woodland community had begun way back after the First World War when Lord Darnley, whose family had owned all this land since the days of James I, and who was a modern and generous young lord, had bequeathed a plot of land in Parrot Wood to any soldier returning from the war on condition that he cultivated it. A fee of one pound was charged with an option to purchase a deed, though most of the old folk never bothered. They just built shacks and farmed their plots and lived happily ever after. Many children were born there and the old folk stayed on and on as other families came to the woods when the Second World War began, just to get away from the blitz, and so the woodland community was formed. After the war the younger descendants took over these shacks as weekend places and came down with droves of kids, had bonfire parties and spent their holidays wandering the woods. But they were disapproved of by the local council. The young Londoners cut the grass and went fishing and shooting for a couple of days before returning to town for the week. It was a kind of mixed group. But still the old folk clung to the derelict shacks they could no longer look after. The buildings were all very primitive. There was no running water and the shack dwellers had to walk the whole length of the lane to get water from the stand-pipe at the end of the road. Some trundled barrels to collect it, while others wore old-fashioned yokes on their shoulders with a bucket attached on each side and then staggered breathlessly back up the hill with their supply of fresh water. It was all a unique and strange way of life but quiet happiness hung in the air. When they did chance to meet the neighbours would greet each other warmly, or they would leave a little present of flowers and fruit outside your shack.

Unfortunately, like most beautiful spots, the condition of the woods came to the attention of the modern district council who had severely neglected it for many years, calling it 'unadopted land'.

For years they had ignored the old folk who had lived through the winters up there suffering so much hardship – too feeble to fetch water or chop wood – that many were found frozen stiff each spring. It was unadopted land and no business of the county council, but nevertheless, peace and beauty reigned. There was the lovely dawn chorus high up in the trees in the summer, and the nightingales always sang sweetly; the blue jay nested there and many tiny blue tits flew in and out of the clinging ivy trails. The wild life was quite prolific and the bluebells carpeted the woods in the spring. There was an indescribable beauty up there on that green hill which led down to the Thames marshland. It was there that black-and-white geese migrated from colder climates to fill the small pools. And it was here that the inhabitants were able to go out to collect their Sunday lunch. It was an idyllic way of life that had gone on for many years and, as far as the woodlanders were concerned, that would go on for ever.

But the ideas in the village were very different. Down in the Merry Boys Inn the locals talked of farming and sailing and they disapproved of the shanty farms in the woods. Then a rumour began to circulate that a compulsory purchase of the woodlands was to be made. Men wearing soft hats and carrying notebooks snooped furtively around the shacks but got little satisfaction. Then Medway newspapers started a big campaign about the woodlanders with articles about the bad conditions of the people living in the woods.

'Goin' to chuck us out the woods, Soaky,' said Donkeyman one day. 'Where will you go?'

Soaky was lolling, well-boozed, in the back of the donkey cart. 'What will I do? Me and Boysie's all right hup thar. Wot do I want an 'lectric light for? Gor a nice tilley lamp, I 'ave.'

'They say it's 'cause we ain't got a proper lavatory,' said Donkey.

'Ger away,' yelled Soaky. 'Gets a nice lot of stuff out of the old lavatory. How yer gonna grow things w'out it?'

Donkey gave a loud guffaw. 'Heryar, Soaky, back 'ome again,' he said, pulling the donkey to a halt.

Soaky staggered out of the cart. 'Let him come up here,' she roared, 'that council man, and I'll give him what for. Bloody nosey parkers, that's what they are.'

Then it happened. The council announced in the paper that they were about to place a compulsory purchase order on the eighty acres of the woods to run a new road through to the village. At the Inn that Saturday night they were all full of this news.

'Just as well,' one of them said, 'get all them old blighters out of them woods, it will.'

'It'll be good to have a bus service in to the town,' said another.

But not everyone felt that way. There were the weekenders who loved their woodland shacks and spent much time and money renovating them. Then there was those, like old Soaky, who knew no other way of living and were just content and happy to while away the seasons in that wonderful forest that ran over the hill down to the sea. Anyone who owned the land and could produce documents to prove it was instructed to contact the council but not many were forthcoming having hidden in this remote spot and resented interference from the authorities for so many years.

The council had its way and one by one they picked off the squatters and gave them a few hundred pounds and a place in the old folks' home. There were heart-rending scenes from some who had young families and tried hard to stick it out. But in the end they were defeated.

Soaky was oblivious to most of what was going on around her. She still went her merry way, and she and Boysie stayed by the fire into winter, filled up with homemade wine and kept each other company. Soaky never received letters, so when the postman puffed down the path one day and handed her a buff-coloured envelope, she waved it around in the air. 'This ain't for me, I don't have no letters,' she declared.

'Well, it's got your name on it,' replied the young postman emphatically.

'Well, you can bloody well take it back, cause I don't want it,' said Soaky.

The postman turned back down the lane and Soaky threw the unopened letter after him and it fell on the ground and got trodden into the mud and forgotten. Such incidents happened several times that winter.

In the spring when Soaky was out and about again there were a lot of old faces missing down in the Merry Boys Inn.

'Where's old Donkey?' Soaky demanded of Miss Smith.

'Gone to live in town,' replied Miss Smith. 'Him and his missus is in the old folks' home.'

'Whatever for? yelled Soaky aggressively. 'He was hail and hearty, same as me.'

'They took the money the council offered them and then the council pushed down his shack.'

'I don't believe it,' declared Soaky in horror.

'It's true, Soaky,' said Miss Smith. 'Haven't they made you an offer yet?'

'Offer? What offer?' yelled Soaky.

'Well, I'm being pushed out too,' Miss Smith said. 'They are going to pull this place down and build a school up here.'

'I don't believe yer,' sniffed Soaky, swallowing down her glass of strong cider.

'It's a fact. I'll be gone by the end of the summer,' said Bill Dunkley, the blacksmith.

Bleary-eyed, Soaky stared around the room. 'Yer havin' me on, ain't yer?' she declared.

The others knew that there was no persuading her so they

just shut up and stopped trying to convince her that what they were telling her was true.

'No one's gettin' me out of me old shack,' she declared. 'Left that to me, old Silas did. Me and Boysie is all right up there.

So Soaky ignored the warnings of the other woodlanders but each day as she went to get water the people gathered around the tap to talk of the end of the woods and as she passed them many of the old places looked desolate and empty with no children playing in the plots any more.

One day a big bulldozer arrived and pushed down most of the small shacks, uprooted all those lovely elms and left them dying in the hot sun.

Seeing what was happening Soaky started swearing revenge on everything and everybody, the lane rang with her bad language. 'Bastards!' she cried. 'Poor old trees. Leave us alone, you bleeders, we ain't goin' ter move. You go to hell!'

The workmen only laughed at her causing Soaky to swig more whisky from the bottle she had just bought.

And now it was assumed that the council had won and the woodlanders had lost. Even when Soaky went to draw her pension, they asked: 'Where are you moving to, Sophia?'

'Me? I ain't moving!' Soaky yelled. 'I'm staying in my little old shack and I'll defy anyone that tries to get me out.'

As the other shacks gradually disappeared, Soaky barred her gate and stared suspiciously at anyone who came down the path. Young men from the council got huge tufts of wet grass aimed in their faces and jugs of water thrown over their heads. 'I'll get the bleedin' gun,' Soaky would shout at them. 'I'll fix yer.'

Sparky sat outside the shack enjoying each scene with a fixed grin on his face. Soaky got very confused. She supped all that was left of the wine and forgot to cook the dinner. Having finished all the drink in the house, she went down to the village for whisky. First she went into the Victoria and then the Evening Star, and then on to the Bull, declaring to one and all that no one would budge her and Boysie from their shack. When she staggered along to the Merry Boys Inn, it was getting dark and the lights of the well-loved inn seemed so very far away that she sat down at the foot of a great oak and dozed off. The revellers came out of the inn singing as they wended their way home. The glow worms cast a strange green light; an owl hooted and the moon sank into the clouds. The woods were silent. Soaky slept on through the dark night and as the cold mist came over the marshes she tried momentarily to move but she couldn't. She lay back, still and helpless, and she gently closed her eyes and passed wearily off into a more peaceful world.

Jim found her the next morning as he went to tend the cattle. He rang for an ambulance which had to come from the nearby town. Before the ambulance arrived, Soaky was carried into the Merry Boys Inn and laid out on the old wooden table in the bar. They straightened out her old limbs but there was no sign of life left in her.

'Poor old gel,' they said. 'She was so worried about having to leave that old hut. That's what done it.'

'Here, what about her poor son?' someone said. 'He is up there all alone.'

They went up to the shack and took Sparky back to town into hospital while the ambulance took old Soaky to the mortuary.

The next week, when Soaky lay buried in the churchyard among her old friends, the council came and bulldozed down her shack, trampling over her beloved roses and uprooting her apple trees. The old shack in the woods just disappeared.

Only those who had known the woods remembered old Soaky and no one bothered about Sparky, who had been put away in that hospital for the mentally disturbed, way out of sight of the town.

CHAPTER EIGHTEEN

Still Waiting

For a long time after Sparky disappeared, Amy continued to feel in her heart that he would walk in one night, whistling a merry tune, and scoop her up into his arms in that boisterous manner he had. She suffered, long, sleepless nights and the long, lonely days and still there was no news of her man who had walked out for a quick drink and a packet of fags and never returned. Over and over in her mind she would trace the circumstances of that New Year's Eve, but she could never come up with a clear picture of what happened.

Her new baby, Tony, thrived and grew into a fat little toddler. Amy became very morose and bad tempered, dividing her time between Annie's flat and her own, always on the look-out watching and waiting.

Amy's two young girls had their own hobbies and their own friends. Her family seemed to have lost interest in her, but one good friend was always there. That was the wide boy, Harry, Sparky's old pal. It was Harry who took Amy out for drinks and repeatedly gave her advice. 'Pack it up, love,' he would say. 'Start living your own life, I'll stick by you and the kids. I promise to go straight. In fact, I have had an offer of a regular job. It's up to you, Amy, for myself I don't care. I'll remain a freelance but if you want me I am here to look after you and Sparky's family.'

Amy just could not make up her mind. She certainly liked Harry. He was common and real working class, short and with a dumpy, hairy body. He had been born and bred on the streets, just like Sparky, and he lived a dodgy sort of existence. But he always seemed to have money and was very generous with it. The baby loved him and called him Dad, but both Rachel and Tosh were resentful of him. No one on earth would ever take the place of their dad. A big enlarged photograph of their father hung on the wall in their bedroom and a book of photos of the good days in Canada was always on view.

Amy missed a man in her bed. Sparky's warm body sometimes seemed to come to her in the night, and it would seem so real that Amy would get up and look around the flat, quite expecting to find him. So she didn't succumb to Harry for a long time. When the boy was five, he was still courting her, much to the annoyance of the girls, who treated him with such scorn.

One Saturday evening when Harry called to take Amy out, he told her that his sister, with whom he lived, was emigrating to New Zealand.

'What will you do?' Amy asked.

'Find lodgings, I suppose,' he replied. 'I've got an elder brother who went out to New Zealand before the war. He's now got a meat-packing business and has done very well for himself. My sister has been thinking of going out there for a long time. It was him who got me my job in Smiffields, he does a lot of business wiff them.' For a year now Harry had held down a regular job at Hay's Wharf, his strong sturdy body humping huge carcasses of sheep. He carried good pay which he spent very generously on Amy and her children.

Amy stared solemnly at him. 'All right, Harry, everyone knows that you and I are going around together. You might as well pack in with me, but I won't marry you, not until the seven years is up. If Sparky should come back before that time then it will be finished between us.'

Harry grinned. 'It would be the finish of me too, if the old

Sparky what we used to know came back, but fair enough, Amy. I'll take good care of you. You'll have no need to work or get social welfare. I can afford to look after you and the family.'

And so began a new phase in Amy's life. Harry's strong arms went around her at night and took away those terrible nightmares. And not having to do her part-time job any longer she had more time free for Annie and Sheila. Mostly they were happy, though the girls would not take any notice of Harry. They were now almost teenagers and stayed out late going to discos. Sometimes Harry tried to give them paternal advice. 'Look 'ere,' he would say, 'you mind who you mixes wiff. In this part of town you could land plenty of trouble.'

'You are not our dad,' they would reply saucily.

Harry was a kind sort of man and this kind of talk hurt his feelings deeply. But there was nothing he could do about it. However, little Tony loved him and Harry bought him plenty of toys and played with him and enjoyed taking him outside all dressed up in smart clothes.

'Harry's a real dad to Tony,' Amy said to Annie. 'The boy worships him.'

Annie nodded her head vigorously. She still did not speak but was very alert watching everything that went on about her, and she still ruled poor Sheila with a rod of iron. Sheila had become quite thin and pathetic looking and she spent her days fetching and carrying for Annie, though she never seemed to mind. She was always in that dream world of film stars and garish magazines that she could not read but loved to look at and cut out the glamorous pictures from.

Life went on at an ordinary pace for our Amy. Now she had a man again, and he was a good man, though very homely. Harry liked to sit in and watch the television most evenings, though occasionally he would go out to watch a football match or a film. But mostly he was happy at home with the family.

Amy had never yearned for a bright life, so she mellowed in the warmth of this man's love who left her with few worries. She took less care over her appearance, growing and dressing more plainly as she tried to shift the hurt that every now and then still stabbed her like a knife in her heart. Nothing had been heard of Sparky, her true love, for seven years, and the police had stopped looking for him.

Tony went to school, Rachel went off to live in a flat with her boyfriend who worked at her office, and Tosh went off to teacher training college. Harry took on his role as head of the family with relish. 'Let's move to a nice place, Amy, and send Tony to a good school. I can afford it.'

But for Amy it was the same old reason. 'I can't leave Mother and Sheila,' she said. 'They depend on me.'

So Harry gave in but he did get Tony into a good prep school anyway, and paid for it out of his own pocket. 'I never stood a bloody dog's chance when I was a kid, so let's give the boy a good start,' he said.

So at eleven years old, Tony went to a big private school in the City. Harry took him every day and brought him home in the evenings and sat for hours trying to help him with his homework, while Amy passed away her time with Annie and Sheila.

Annie had spent some time lately in and out of hospital. She had a chest complaint which caused her a lot of trouble in the winter months. During this time, Sheila spent many hours going back and forth to the hospital carrying bunches of flowers or bags of sweets, scurrying along on her thin, spindly legs. During Sheila's visits she often noticed another person at the hospital, a small, black-clad figure who seemed to carry the weight of the world on her shoulders. It was old Dolly Palmer whose husband was dying of cancer. All her three boys were now away in prison, and she looked a tragic little figure as she trotted from prison to prison and then to the hospital. Everyone respected her, and all past crimes were forgotten, because that is the way of the East Enders. They would ask her: 'How are you, Dolly? How is the old man?'

'Oh, he is still lingering,' she would reply. 'Not much hope, I'm afraid.' She would stop by to say a word or two to Annie who sat up in bed gasping for her breath and pointing out of the window at the old church tower which was the only remaining structure still standing from the old days. She would turn to Dolly and give her a big smile.

'I know, Annie,' Dolly would say. 'There's not much left of the old place, is there?'

It was while she was watching that window that Annie passed on. A peaceful smile spread across her face and miraculously at the last moment her voice came back as she said, quite clearly: 'Hello, Emily.'

Amy was standing beside the bed cuddling the weeping Sheila and could scarcely believe what she heard, for Emily was that lost eldest daughter who had been killed with her children by the bombs.

Annie's funeral was a big East End affair and all the family came. Letty and Lily came with their families as did the twins, and Joe and Billy. Thus all the Flanagans gathered together for the first time in many years to see their mother given a splendid send-off. The long line of carriages and all the market traders stood still to Annie's memory and many remarked on how that nice big well-dressed family that represented her now had once been the poorest lot of kids in the district.

After the funeral they all went home, back to their nice respectable lives, leaving only Amy and poor Sheila still in this slum place.

Sheila was completely lost without her mother who had ruled her life; she had very little left of herself. As far as Amy was concerned, there was only one thing to do. 'Sheila will have to come and live with us,' she told Harry. 'She won't be happy with anyone else.'

Harry gave a deep sigh but gave in graciously.

So Sheila moved in and certainly was a problem. One thing she liked was to keep busy, so she would constantly fiddle around washing the dishes, and not very well either. Harry, who had been the dishwasher for quite a time, was thoroughly put out.

Sheila's humming also annoyed him intensely. It was a continuous, tuneless hum, that Sheila sang all the time when she was happy, and it interfered considerably with Harry's television viewing. In no way were Sheila and Harry compatible; they were at cross purposes all the time.

Amy always sided with her sister during any of these confrontations, another fact that made Harry exceedingly cross. But Amy was not going to give way. Harry was not going to rule her life, particularly when he was not even her husband. Amy and Harry began to pull apart and he spent more time and effort on the boy, Tony, taking him on Saturdays and Sundays to films and football or down Petticoat Lane. Tony was growing into a tall slim lad, so much like his own dad. And he also had that quiet humour that Sparky had possessed.

The area had quietened down a little but was still a dangerous place to be after dark, for young unemployed boys hung around in gangs and fought each other viciously. It seemed that a new kind of criminal was replacing the old heavies, most of whom had died in the nick. The police had formed a vice squad a few years back with which they had really cleaned up the town. The Palmer brothers and their associates had all gone on down with long sentences for various crimes.

When Tony was about thirteen and doing very well at school, something suddenly happened to shake that East End community. Some fellow in the nick had turned Queen's evidence and crimes previously unsolved had come to light. One was the story behind the disappearance of Tony Binks, known to the underworld as Sparks. The news hit the newspapers and television screens. So, one evening, as some big shot expounded his theory on the old crime, young Tony sat looking at the photographs of his real dad as they were displayed in bright colour on the telly.

Amy got up and turned the television off but Tony stopped her. 'Hey, Mum,' he said. 'That's the same photo that's in Rachel's photo album and he's got the same name as mine. Who is that man?' he demanded.

'I don't know,' said Amy as tears welled up in her eyes. 'Go to bed now. You need to get up for school in the morning.'

He obeyed, good boy that he was, but he was no fool. He was a studious lad with a good education, and he knew how to do research. He read the newspapers and the old newspaper cuttings which he found in an old suitcase belonging to Tosh. He even confronted Harry one day. 'Are you my father?' he demanded, 'or is it that bloke who's supposed to have been murdered by these gangsters?'

Harry could not lie but he held down the situation very well. 'No, lad,' he said. 'That was your real dad and he was my best mate. If he is still alive somewhere I know he would want me to take care of you.'

Tony put his arms around Harry's neck warmly. 'You are the only dad I know,' he said, 'and that is all right with me.'

From then on there seemed to exist a barrier of coldness between Amy and her son. It puzzled her. She could not define it but she always felt it was there.

This led to more trouble with Sheila, who liked to go to bingo on Friday nights with Amy, but Harry was now insisting that Amy stayed home with him and Tony to help improve the situation between mother and son.

Amy was between two fires: her fondness for Sheila and her allegiance to her lover and son.

'Let Sheila go alone,' said Harry, 'she knows the way.'

Uneasily, Amy gave Sheila money on Friday evening to go to bingo which she did manage to do perfectly well. Amy went to meet her on the way home when it got dark. One night when she met her, Sheila said, 'I'll get the fish and chips.' They usually bought fish and chips after a night at bingo.

'Are you sure? Will you be all right?' asked Amy, half delighted and half alarmed by Sheila's sudden assertion of independence.

Sheila nodded vigorously.

'Then I'll go home and put the kettle on.'

Back at the house, Amy waited for quite a while and Sheila did not return. Tony and Harry were deeply engrossed in the football match on television, and she did not like to disturb them, but she began to get very worried. Eventually, she said timidly, while looking out of the window, 'Sheila's a long time. I'll go and see if she is all right.'

'No, I'll go,' said Harry with a sigh, getting up and putting on his jacket before going outside into the cold night air. There was no sign of Sheila in the fish-and-chip shop where they said she had been in and out half an hour or more before. Harry stood bewildered looking out over the darkened park. Suddenly he heard a little groan and stumbled quickly towards it. There he found poor Sheila lying half-unconscious on the grass, her clothes ripped and her body covered with blood.

Harry picked her up and, as he ran with her towards the house, she came round and started to scream hysterically at him, hitting out at his face. In her confusion, she did not know him. Harry ran into the house, where he laid her down. 'Ring for the police,' he said to Amy. 'God knows what they have done to her, poor soul.'

Amy tried to calm Sheila, but she just uttered those dreadful piercing shrieks. It was only the hypodermic needle of the doctor that finally silenced her.

The police arrived and examined the spot where she had been attacked. Her handbag had been turned inside out, and the fish and chips were scattered all around. Someone had heard her screams and seen three youths running away. But if they were the culprits and what they did to her only Sheila could tell, and her poor distressed mind could not cope any more.

So once more the newshounds came down on Amy. Harry chased them off and little articles appeared in the papers raking up old sores and the past including all the details about her husband's disappearance and the fact that she was now living with another man. Sheila's attackers were never caught and she stayed in the hospital for a long time. And in that time she became very withdrawn.

As much as she wanted Sheila home, Amy knew that it would be hopeless because every time she saw Harry, she started to scream. For some reason the sight of him brought that terrible nightmare flooding back.

'Oh, my God,' cried Amy, 'what else can happen to me?'

'Let's get married, Amy,' Harry said one day. 'Even if only for the lad's sake – he knows it all now.'

'I'll think about it, Harry, but I have enough to worry me at the moment,' replied Amy.

Harry looked sad but in his kind, steady, gentle manner he did not push the subject.

The problem of Sheila was uppermost in Amy's mind. She had promised her mother that she would take care of Sheila, so she could not leave her in the hospital and in no way would she settle down with Harry!

For a year Sheila stayed in the mental home and Amy visited her regularly. She would weep so many tears over her sister that even young Tony got a little fed-up with it all.

Then Harry said: 'Amy, this is the last time I'll ask you, but if we get wed we can go out to stay with my sister Marge in

New Zealand. She is doing very well out there. It'd be just you and me and the boy.'

Amy stared at him aghast. 'But what about Sheila?' she asked in horror.

Mild generous Harry suddenly lost his temper and they started to quarrel violently. 'Fuck Sheila!' Harry cried out loud.

Amy hated bad language. 'There's no need for that,' she replied frostily.

Then Harry let loose his feelings. 'For Christ's sake, Amy. What am I here? I have worked my fingers off to look after you for ten years now, and you still treat me like the flaming lodger.'

'Well, if you don't like it, you know what you can do,' she retorted, her temper welling up inside.

'Yes, I do and from now on it's time to make a decision, I'll take that job in New Zealand and if you won't come, you can stay here.'

'My son stays with me,' she challenged him.

'Okay, you know how I love that boy, so chuck dirt at me. But I warn you, Amy, I am off in the New Year whatever you do.'

'Oh, go and leave me alone,' yelled Amy. The very mention of New Year always had a bad effect on her.

Amy went off to bed to weep her heart out. 'Oh, Sparky,' she sobbed into the pillow, 'if you are alive, come back to me. I love you, and no one will ever replace you.'

But only the silence of the night answered her, because for the first time in ten years Harry had got drunk and lay sleeping on the sitting-room floor. Tony had got up in the middle of the night and covered him with a rug.

Amy's sister Nancy, now a plump, contented woman, visited Amy just before Christmas, and when she heard Amy's tale of woe she said: 'Why don't you just forget Sparky and marry Harry? He is a good man and good for you.'

'He still wants to go to New Zealand,' Amy snivelled, 'and I had enough of going to Canada. Why should I leave everything behind for him? And besides, if Sparky ever came home he would not know where to find me.'

'Oh, don't be so ridiculous,' cried Nancy impatiently. After that, she gave up on Amy and returned to her comfortable home.

On Christmas Eve it was Lily who visited. She was big and husky, unmarried and sort of mannish. 'You must be mad, Amy,' Lily said, when she heard what had been going on. 'Why not go away? It will be a new life for you out in New Zealand, and that's the best way to forget.'

'Well, I have still got Sheila to worry about,' insisted Amy.

'Oh, shut up!' said Lily impatiently. 'Sheila will never be normal, and you and I know that, just as Mother did.'

'Well, she is still our sister,' said Amy.

'Look here,' said Lily with authority, 'if you like, I'll have her down with me. I am matron at the home now and those kids of mine would be company for her. It'll bring her out of herself.'

'Oh, no, not disturbed children,' said Amy.

'Amy, my kids are deaf and some are dumb but they are deprived in the way that we were. It will be good for Sheila. I'll send a note to the hospital and have her there for Christmas.'

In the end Amy agreed, so she had a very quiet Christmas with just Harry and Tony.

Tony was becoming quite a radio addict. For Christmas Harry had bought him a shortwave radio and some radio equipment, including a set of headphones. This headphone set Tony wore a lot, walking around with them on so as not to hear Amy and Harry bickering with one another.

At New Year, Amy got moody, as she always did, and started to moon over Sparky's photo with big tears in her eyes. Earlier that evening she and Harry had had another argument about going to New Zealand, and Harry was fed up. 'I must be bleeding crazy,' he said, 'ten years now I've lived with Sparky's sodding ghost.' With that he had flounced out of the house.

Amy picked up a novel to read, in an effort to occupy her mind and show that she did not care, while Harry walked the deserted streets outside thinking of the days long gone when he had romped the streets with Sparky. He realized that it was in the street he now walked that Sparky had been gunned down, never to be seen alive again. It was quiet and he felt a little creepy but his footsteps guided him along the same route. It was eight o'clock and the lights of the pub, where they used to drink, shone out in front of him. He pushed open the door and went in. It was very quiet in there, for this had once been the haunt of gangland but now it had changed hands and had become deserted as the Asians, who didn't drink, moved into the area. Then three men entered the bar. They were a little drunk. They ordered drinks and sat down shouting at one another.

Idly Harry stood up at the bar listening to them. One was a portly fellow dressed in good clothes and smoking a cigar. He swaggered up to the bar and ordered brandies in a loud voice. The other two were typical East End youths. They were dressed in leather jackets and jeans and had strange haircuts. Their leader's voice rang out across the room boastfully. 'This is the pub I used to use when I was one of the lads,' he declared. Then he lowered his voice. 'As a matter of fact,' he continued, 'this is where I had a last drink, me and me mate Sparky, before they got him.'

Harry could not believe what he was hearing as that loud voice continued in its boastful manner. 'Oh, those were the days, bang! bang! And that was yer lot. After me, they was, but gets old Sparky and he's never been seen since. Them what done it are all inside now. That was fourteen years ago but it don't seem that long,' he added in his raucous voice.

'You mean they did a murder here?' asked one lad.

'Just outside this bloody door, mate,' declared the fellow in a loud manner.

Harry stared straight at him. Of course, it was that bastard Tommy Evans who had set Sparky up. He was supposed to be in South America. A wave of red hot temper suffused Harry. There he was, the fat sod sitting down there boasting about what he had done to Sparky. It was because of that fat sod that Amy had such an unhappy life. Without a word, Harry leapt forward and grabbed the fat man by the throat.

Tommy Evans was taken by surprise, as Harry jolted his head back straight through the plate glass window. All hell was let loose as the young lads jumped into the fray attacking Harry.

Tommy Evans rolled about on the floor gasping for his breath with a huge gash in his neck while Harry fought off the other two ruffians. Harry was strong but eventually they knocked him down and out, and were still busy kicking his ribs when the old Bill burst in upon the scene.

Amy had put down her novel and began to think about going to bed. There was not much to stay up for. Young Tony sat idly watching television when the phone rang. He answered it eagerly for he was missing Harry who did not often go out and leave them like that.

Amy was yawning and about to rise to go to bed when Tony returned from answering the phone his face very white and set. 'Mum,' he said, 'our Dad's got himself in trouble. That was the station sergeant. Dad is under arrest and said to go down in the morning to Old Street Station.'

Tony looked so forlorn that Amy rushed to him and held him tight. 'Oh, the silly great sod,' she said. 'Got himself drunk, I suppose. Wasn't in his car, was he?'

Tony shook his head. 'No, I saw him walking towards the main road. He was ever so fed-up, Mum. Poor old Dad.'

Tears were about to fall from those greeny grey eyes, so like Sparky's.

But Amy's courage came to the fore. 'Serve him right,' she declared. 'It won't hurt him to spend a night in the nick. We'll bail him out in the morning. In the meantime I'll make a nice cup of cocoa and we'll turn in for the night.'

Early the next morning she was down at Old Street Police Station. She was on her own, having told Tony to stay in bed. 'I'm used to this,' she said. 'But I don't want you mixed up with all those drunks down there.'

When Amy saw Harry she was very dismayed. His head was bandaged and there were bruises all over his face. A large copper hovered over him as he sat looking very sorry for himself.

'Why won't they let me bail you out?' demanded Amy. 'What on earth have you done?'

'I duffed up Tommy Evans,' he said in a whisper. 'Sorry, love.'

Amy's face went deathly white. 'But I thought he had gone abroad.'

'So did I till I heard him boasting that he set Sparky up. Then I couldn't control myself,' said Harry.

Amy stared morosely at him. 'Oh, here we go, it's going on forever.'

'They won't let me out because Tommy's in a bad way. You see I pushed his head through the pub window.' Harry looked both proud and sheepish about what he had done.

'Oh, my God!' cried Amy, holding her head in her hands in alarm.

'Look, try not to worry, love, and make it all right for me with Tony. Reassure him. I'll get by and there's money in my post office book if you need it. Just bring it in and I'll sign it. I expect I'll go on remand to the Scrubbs but try not to let it get you down.'

Amy walked out of the police station with her head in a

whirl. When would all this end? Was there no place to hide? It was bound to get in the papers and what with Tony at that posh school, it did not bear thinking about.

The next six weeks were hell on earth for Amy and no one came forward to help. A snide little reporter who was at Harry's hearing followed Amy home and tried to put his foot in the door. 'Tell me your story,' he said. 'You are Mrs Binks, aren't you, the wife of the notorious criminal who disappeared and whose body has never been found?'

'Go away!' screeched Amy hysterically trying to jam the door against him.

As they struggled over the door, Amy suddenly heard a yell from the reporter as Tony, arriving home, swung his foot up and hit the little fellow where he felt it most, causing him to drop his notebook and send the camera spinning. Tony's face was flushed with rage as he cried out: 'Now piss off and leave us alone!'

Amy was astounded. Here was Sparky reincarnated in young Tony with his red hair and glaring eyes. As the reporter retreated, they bolted and barred the door and windows and took the phone off the hook. But it was too late. The daily papers had published an article about her and Sparky and the Sundays collected up a lot of old dirt.

Amy and her fourteen-year-old son clung together in their trouble. He told her that he was not going back to school after the holiday however hard she tried to make him go.

'Mother,' he said, 'you just don't know those toffee-nosed sods. They will never let me live it down. No, thanks. When it's all blown over I'll get a job but in the meantime I'm here to look after you and stand by our Dad, because if that bloke Tommy Evans dies, he will go away for a long time.'

'Oh,' sobbed Amy, 'what have I done to deserve all this?'

'All I can say, is that you are a born bloody loser,' said Tony in a hard voice.

Amy looked at him in shocked surprise but then a tiny grin

spread across her face. 'Well, I suppose you would call it that.'

Harry came up for trial and Tommy Evans appeared in a wheelchair, his head all bandaged and his neck plastered. He had a top lawyer working for him. Evans, the lawyer said, had been having a peaceful drink when he had been viciously attacked without warning.

The defending lawyer brought forth the mitigating circumstances and Amy's life was tossed back and forth across the court by these hard legal minds. The fact that Harry and Amy were only living together and not married, and that there was no evidence that Tommy Evans had done anything outside the law meant that Harry ended up with two years inside for breach of the peace, causing damage to the pub and causing grievous bodily harm to Evans. He got only two years because he had not been in any trouble for ten years and he was sent to an open prison.

As they listened to the sentence, Tony sat beside his Mum, his face hard, white and bitter. Harry cast a long look at him and winked in his direction.

Amy was allowed to say goodbye to Harry before they sent him down. Peering at her through a window covered with wire mesh, Harry's eyes were red as if he had been weeping. 'Take care of yourself, love,' he said. 'Don't waste your life on me, but whoever you get let them be good to Tony.'

'Don't be silly,' snivelled Amy. 'I'll wait for you. Both Tony and I, we said we would and we mean it.'

CHAPTER NINETEEN

The Awakening

It was not easy to take the fact that Harry was in prison, but life had to go on. Amy still had her fine son to consider. He came first before everything else. She had clung to him and brought him up with love and care. Harry never came between them. Her girls could look after themselves now but there was still poor Sheila. Amy had promised her mother that she would look after her afflicted sister, and she would never go back on her word. She wondered if she had done the right thing in allowing Sheila to stay so long with Lily at the home for disturbed children. Now that she was alone again she would go and bring Sheila back home to live. Tony had taken this news fairly casually when she had mentioned it to him, as is the way of the young folk.

Tony now had a job with an electrical firm and doing very nicely, and he was also going to evening classes to finish his studies.

Harry wrote to them regularly from prison. He was allowed to write one letter a month. 'Please don't bother to visit me, Amy,' he often wrote. 'It is a long way to come. But if you do, don't ever bring the boy because I don't think I could bear to have him see me cooped up here in the nick. So let's leave it for a while, shall we?'

Amy would have happily gone down to see Harry, just as she had done for poor Siddy, but she respected Harry's wishes and just wrote to him and sent him the little extras that he was allowed. She felt quite lonely and bored, and began to think about getting herself a job, as money was running low. She was still getting offers from the newspapers to tell her side of her story but she hated them so much that she did not succumb. The first thing she had to do was get Sheila back, but when she set about doing that she received a very rude shock.

It had been four months since she had seen Sheila and now the spring time had come. Lily had often telephoned Amy to say that Sheila was doing very well and was being a great help in the children's home. But when Lily told Amy that she had also arranged with the mental hospital to let Sheila stay permanently, Amy was not at all pleased. She got herself ready and went down to Sussex to see for herself. She found the journey tiring. She had travelled very little of late and, now turned forty, she was beginning to feel her age.

Lily's children's home was a big white house with a lovely garden. Small children played outside on swings and round-abouts while others sat very still on a big long balcony.

Amy found Lily in her office. Her sister was as big and busy as ever. 'Nice to see you, Amy,' she said. 'Sorry about our little bit of trouble.'

'Trouble is my middle name,' said Amy dryly.

'I'll send for some tea,' replied Lily without a trace of a smile. That close family feeling they had once shared had gone. It had faded away with the years.

Sister Lily had always been a bit of a bully, and Amy had always preferred her sister Emily, and this well-built, well-spoken lady in the stiff starchy uniform seemed quite unfamiliar to her.

Lily sat back at her desk busily writing reports. 'Sorry,' she said. 'But I must dash these off quickly. Then we will have our cup of tea.'

Feeling very depressed, Amy sipped her tea. 'How's Sheila?' she ventured.

'Oh, she is fine,' beamed Lily. 'You won't know her. She spends her time helping me with the younger children, and

I got her on a course of tablets which are stopping those convulsions. We'll go out and find her, shall we?'

Amy sat there feeling a little confused. She did not want to share Sheila with Lily like this. Sheila had been the little lame duck that she, Amy, had always looked after. Sheila was part of Amy's very own existence. But she did not say anything.

After tea they strolled around the grounds and came upon Sheila sitting under a big oak tree. She was dressed in a pretty blue summer dress and was cuddling a fair little child close to her side. They both sat listening to a young woman who wore horn-rimmed glasses and whose hair hung in long pigtails.

'Oh, there they are,' declared Lily, 'and that is our therapy teacher with her. Sheila adores her. It's a strange coincidence, but her name is Amy, just like yours.'

Seeing her afflicted sister Amy advanced eagerly towards her but Sheila looked up and seemed afraid. 'No, no!' she cried, putting up her hands to shield her face.

'It is Amy, darling,' Lily said. 'Amy's come to visit you.'

But Sheila did not respond, and Amy almost sobbed with grief.

Sheila got up and ran towards the therapy teacher who put her arms around her. 'There's nothing to be afraid of, Sheila,' she said. 'It's your sister Amy come to see you.'

But Sheila clung to her frantically, grabbing her tightly with her fingers. Amy, the teacher, moved towards the house. 'I think I'd better take her inside,' she said. 'It's too much of a shock for her to see you again, I'm afraid.'

'Sheila!' roared Lily. 'Stop being so silly! This is our Amy.'

But Sheila just covered her face with her hands and clung to the teacher.

Tears were now pouring down Amy's cheeks. She could not believe that Sheila did not recognize her. 'But I thought you said she was getting better,' she gasped, staring at Lily.

Lily shrugged nonchalantly. 'Well, she is, but you don't

understand, this is her world now and the other Amy has taken your place in her disturbed mind.'

'Oh, no, I can't believe it,' wept Amy.

Lily gave her a good thump on the back. 'Now cheer up, Amy,' she said. 'You don't have to worry about Sheila any more now that she has found peace of mind, so why disturb it? Come, let's go in and have a drink, my dear. I deal with these cases all the time and the mind is a very strange thing.'

'Do you think she will ever come home to me?' asked Amy with anguish in her voice.

'No, my love,' said Lily. 'Leave her here. It's the best and kindest thing to do. These things take their own direction and all that slosh and sentiment we were brought up with does not help. When she lost Mum she clung to you, but then Harry came along and she lost you to him. So now you had better leave her alone. Come on, let's have that drink,' she said more gently, now acknowledging Amy's sad face.

In Lily's office they sat drinking a couple of gins. 'Stay for dinner,' Lily urged her.

'No,' said Amy. 'Please ring for a cab. I want to go home.'

As she travelled home in the train, Amy turned the day's events over and over in her mind. Was she sorry that Sheila did not want to see her any more? She could not decide. But she did know that Lily had turned into a hard-hearted bitch. She made her mind up there and then that she did not want to see her sister, Lily, for a very long time to come. She would tell Tony of this meeting with Lily but she would not tell Harry, for she knew without a doubt that he would only laugh at her. She was sorry that Sheila did not need her any more and really could not believe it still, but, looking on the bright side, at least she would not have to worry about Sheila's welfare any more. She was basically having good treatment and she certainly seemed happy. What had happened would have to remain her own private sorrow, tucked away in her heart with the rest of her sadness.

Now ahead of her she had two years of comparative

freedom. There had to be some reason for struggling on, and she supposed she had better find it. Tony was trying to grow up fast, and detaching himself from her increasingly. The two girls did not even bother to write to her. Rachel was too busy with her own family and Tosh – well, God knows where she went when she left university. How strange and lonely Amy felt. She was very glad to be home, to dream around the fire.

That night was strange and restless. She lay half asleep and tossing, when suddenly she heard whispering in her ear and there was Annie, her mother. Annie was young again, and wearing a bright scarf over her dark hair. And then poor Siddy appeared, just as she had seen him dead. And then came the tall, ginger-haired Sparky. Amy tried to move but her limbs seemed paralysed. She tried hard to get up but still could not move; she tried to call out but no sound came. She lay in her bed, sweating with fear, but after a while her muscles relaxed and she returned to normal. She switched on the light and from then on felt too frightened to go back to sleep.

'Oh dear,' she sighed, 'what is happening to me? I'd better go to the doctor in the morning.'

The next day the local doctor gave her some pills. 'It's nervous strain,' he said. 'You must keep occupied. Why don't you go out to work? Then you will get a sound night's sleep. Your problem is caused by worry, and you have certainly had your share of that.'

So Amy began to write after jobs, but there were many young folk out of work and it was not easy for a person of her age to find employment. One day she saw an advertisement in the paper for women who could sell and work on commission. At the interview they explained that it was promotional work and that after training she would move around with a team. She would need to be able to drive a car, they told her, but while training it was not necessary.

'It sounds exciting,' said Tony when Amy informed him

that she was on the short list for this job. 'Why don't you take Harry's car and learn to drive?' he suggested. 'Take driving lessons right away. I'll treat you.'

Amy smiled. 'It's all right, son, I can still afford that,' she said, touched by his offer.

Amy got the job, and so it was that she pulled her socks up. She got her hair cut and permed in a nice short style, bought a smart suit and went daily to the city by tube to do her training. In the evening she had her driving lessons. The effect on her spirits was marvellous. She made friends with other young women and slowly regained confidence in herself. The smart slim woman who walked briskly to the station each morning was more like the old Amy but with a quiet poise she kept her past to herself. She was like the survivor of a great battle, living only for her son, and still in her heart for the day when Sparky would return to her. But in the meantime there was poor Harry stuck in the nick. She felt guilty about him. In some ways it was her fault, she believed. She should never have involved him in her life. That was the heavy feeling of guilt she carried so she must not desert him. Occasionally she did go to visit him down on the island where many East Enders had resided in the past. These trips to the Isle of Wight were often the highlight of her social life.

Harry was a tough little man and prison life had made little difference to him. He joked with her on these visits and sent his love to Tony saying, 'Tell the boy to keep his nose clean and not get tangled up with the law. They've got some vicious little sods down here these days.'

Amy brought him all the news and gossip of the East End. He loved to hear it all. 'They buried old Dolly Palmer last week,' she told him one day.

'Go on!' exclaimed Harry. 'Some blokes are going to miss her. She must have visited every nick in the country chasing after them twins of hers.'

'Yes, she wasn't a bad old girl,' agreed Amy. 'They say she

was very generous to the wives of the boys in prison – not that she was short of a few bob. Those villains she brought up took good care of her.'

'Ah, well,' said Harry philosophically, 'even us tough boys remember and love our mums.'

'Buried her in style, they did,' said Amy. 'TV cameras and film stars were there and her boy Terry was even allowed to attend – with the cuffs on, mind you, and old Bill in attendance.'

This amused Harry; he roared with laughter. 'Well, who would have thought our street would get so famous?'

Amy suddenly turned serious. 'Will you get pardoned next year, do you think?'

'I bloody hope so,' said Harry. Wistfully he added. 'Do you really want me back home, Amy?'

'You know I do,' she told him warmly.

Harry gave her a big grin. 'I'd kiss you,' he said, 'but that bloody screw is looking at us.'

The prisoners and their visitors were allowed to sit and chat but were absolutely forbidden to touch each other in case a visitor slipped something to a prisoner.

With Harry being so chirpy she enjoyed her visits to him. Now she was visiting him once a month, going down on the train, where she met other prisoners' wives. Some brought young children with them. It seemed to Amy that each time she visited, the wives were younger and there were more and more children who screamed blue murder when it was time to leave their dads behind. It was such a pity, she thought, that this army of young men was locked away like this when in her young days they would have all been in the forces fighting for survival. Now, in this open prison, they stood in bored, pathetic droves, dotted along the pathway, standing with brooms and shovels in hand as they pretended to keep busy with one eye on the visitors arriving, in the hope of seeing someone they knew.

Amy would look at them and sigh. Was there no other way

of punishing these offenders? This way only punished their families as well. The young women had to be mother and father to their babes and struggle along on the money they received from the welfare state. Amy's sad brown eyes would watch the young girls talking to their husbands and bouncing their young babies on their laps as they pretended to be cheerful so as not to depress their caged men. Amy, *she* knew their heartbreak, for she felt as if she had spent all her life waiting in one way or another – first for Sparky, now for Harry. She supposed she must be raving mad, but this was all life had given her, so she had better make the best of it.

In her new job she was now 'out on the road', as they termed it. She had passed her driving test and drove herself around the suburbs selling various commodities to the shops working on a good commission basis. She had great confidence in herself now.

Tony was doing a part-time course in electronics, like his dad. He was a wizard at this kind of thing. He had become very interested in computers and now had his room rigged up like a miniature radio station.

Now that she was happier and more satisfied, time passed quickly for Amy, and her terrible past began to fade. Harry would be home soom after the New Year, so she did not mind having to wait to pick up the threads of their life once more. But to her dismay Harry seemed to have had other ideas. In his last letter he had written to say that his sister Marge had written to him and asked them to go out to New Zealand when he got out of the nick. 'I think it will be a good idea, Amy,' he wrote. 'New Zealand is a fine country with plenty of opportunities. I will not get my job back and don't fancy being out of work.'

Amy was very angry when she read this letter. 'Well, after sticking by him while he was in the nick,' she raged, 'now he wants to go off to some forgotten land.' Canada had been enough for her. No way would she pull up her roots again. It was the East End for her till the day she died. She wrote a letter back to Harry. Her tone was cool. 'No, Harry, definitely not. I now have a good job and in no way will I jeopardize that. My home is here.'

When Harry read her letter he sighed a deep sigh, but he did not mention New Zealand again to Amy in any of his letters. But as the year rolled on, he became keener and keener on the idea as his sister's encouraging letters continued to arrive. In every letter Marge would point out the advantages of emigrating to New Zealand. She wrote that her husband was now the overseer of a big meat packers and would welcome his skill and give him a good job anytime. 'Leave it all behind, Harry,' she wrote. 'The East End has not been all that good to us. We lost Mum and Dad and our sister, and now you have been towed into trouble. Come out here with me and make a new start.'

This last letter decided Harry. If Amy would not come with him, he would just have to go alone to New Zealand. Maybe Amy would get wise afterwards and follow him out there later.

It was a terrible blow to Amy when Harry told her of this decision but in no way would she give in and leave Tony. 'Do me a favour,' she said. 'I won't go. I had enough of being abroad in Canada with Sparky. I was so homesick then that I nearly went mad.'

'Oh, grow up, Amy,' Harry said gently, 'that was a long time ago.'

But Amy was quite adamant and very annoyed. She even missed a visit deliberately to the prison just to make him change his mind, but Harry's mind was made up.

'My sister and brother-in-law will pay our passage out and find me a job,' he told her. 'What chance do I stand out there?'

He pointed at the prison gates. 'When I get my release I'll just be standing on the bleeding corner all day with all the other out-of-work hoodlums.'

'Oh, well, Harry, please yourself,' shrugged Amy. 'I'll get by.'

CHAPTER TWENTY

The Return

Greatstone is a busy little town with narrow roads and plenty of heavy traffic making its way to the coast. Amy was always a little nervous in strange places, her grass roots feelings were so strong that when she was a mile or so away from the East End she would begin to panic. This was her last visit to Harry, for he would be out in January.

The Welfare for Prisoners' Wives organization ran a coach from the train station which deposited them all outside the prison gates but this time Amy had declined the coach. For once she just could not bear to watch the young mothers and their whining children, and she wanted to make her own way there alone this time as she gathered her strength to give him her final and definite answer for the New Zealand plan. She had to make it clear once and for all because the last thing she wanted was to have him secretly hoping that she would change her mind.

As she came out of the station her head ached with the tension of travelling and the worry about this ultimatum. She had to wait some time for a bus out to the open prison, so she decided to go and get a cup of tea in the meantime. She crossed the road and headed for the big Army and Navy store. It was a lovely big shop and reminded her of her first job she had as a sales lady. It was then that she had first met Sparky. She sat in the shop's cafe sipping her tea and dreaming of those days long gone. It was many years now since Sparky had disappeared. She accepted at last that he would never come back to her now, but she still mourned him deep in her heart. His memory was like a knife left sticking there; and in no way could Harry have replaced him.

Today she decided she would reorganize her life. Let Harry go out to New Zealand. She had a good job now and could well support herself. It had not really been an easy decision because Harry had been so good to her and Tony. There was a nervous sweat on her brow as she clutched her hands around the cup, but she collected herself, placed the cup in the saucer and swept off through the store, her tall slim figure passing on to the store's gaily decorated counters.

In two weeks it would be Christmas. Balloons and streamers swung from the ceiling, and everywhere there were dainty Christmas lights. A large and beautifully decorated Christmas tree was on display in the centre of the main hallway and the sight of it comforted her. She would be lonely this Christmas but she might visit one of the family. She began to look at the presents on the well-laden counters and came upon a display of pretty silk scarves. She fingered the soft silk and again her mind went back to that special day twenty years back when she had sold silk scarves at her first department store. She then noticed a little bit of confusion going on around her, as a large crowd of disabled men and boys went through the shop, accompanied by a couple of uniformed nurses and minders. They were out on their annual Christmas shopping spree, and were all very noisy and excited about it. With their bent crooked legs and misshapen heads, they milled around her and the counter, and she stood back nervously. Then along came a retinue of bathchair patients – poor unfortunates who were unable to walk at all. Amy tried not to look and stood still fingering that silk scarf.

Suddenly there was a strange animal-like wail and a long thin skeleton of a man with sparse red hair almost fell out of the bathchair and grabbed hold of her legs. His red-rimmed eyes rolled as if in a fit, and he jabbered excitedly like a monkey. His grasping hands dug deeply into her flesh and held on to her as she tried to pull away. Horrified, she looked down at this twisted man in a bathchair, and the world suddenly swirled before her. For a brief second she thought this creature was Sparky, and she gave a frightened gasp and fell sideways, almost collapsing on top of this horrible thing who still clutched desperately at her skirt.

The nurse and shop assistants ran to her aid and she was carried half-unconscious into the staff room, while Sparky was slapped and put back upright in his bathchair. Then the party of patients went hurriedly on its way.

When Amy came round, the nurse was offering her a drink. She was very apologetic and asked if they should get her a doctor. Was she all right? Did she know why she fainted? They fired questions at her but all Amy could see was those red-rimmed rolling eyes of the mentally disabled man.

'We do not understand what happened. Boysie is usually so good, and well-behaved,' said the young woman in uniform trying to explain her patient's behaviour. 'We wondered if it's possible that he recognized you or something, or did he have a fit and cling onto the first thing handy? They do, you know.'

Unable to speak, Amy looked up at the nurse in dismay and just shook her head.

'Well, we have sent him back home to the hospital. He has been with us for a very long time,' said the nurse.

'Who is he?' Amy stammered out at last.

'No one knows very much about him. All we know is that his mother always looked after him and he came to us when she died. Here's the address of the hospital to write to if you wish to make a complaint.'

Amy gazed at the card in a daze. She turned and said: 'Please, will someone get me a taxi? I have to visit someone.'

As the old taxi rattled along the country road, she tried to collect her wits. No, it was not possible, it had been her own imagination, she told herself. That poor devil had just fallen out of his bathchair on his own. He had a fit. She had to put it from her mind. Perhaps the strain of all she had been through of late had been too much for her. Now she began to cry and heavy tears poured down her cheeks. What should she do? 'Oh my God,' she wailed, 'how much more can a heart and brain stand?' She had to escape, and there was only one way – into the arms of the warm, comfortable, caring Harry.

Harry was very pleased to see her. They walked about the prison grounds together, wrapped up against the cold. Under his coat, Harry wore a faded blue shirt and jeans. He looked very fit. He put a finger close to her eyes and wiped her cheek. 'You have been crying, matey,' he said. 'What's wrong? Tell Harry.'

Amy clung to him. 'Oh, it's all right,' she said. 'I'm depressed about you going away, that's all. And I shall be so lonely at Christmas this year – that is the worst time.'

'Well, my love, I have got news for you,' he cried jubilantly. 'I'll be home the day after tomorrow and we will be able to have Christmas together. I got me remission so at last I'll be free of this place. And there'll be no more bird for me, I'm definitely going to New Zealand. Oh, Amy,' he said, clasping her hand, 'say you will come with me and I'll be the happiest man alive.'

Amy held his roughened workingman's hand and closed her eyes to try to forget the nightmarish incident. 'Oh, Harry,' she said. 'I feel safe with you, and I can't live alone any longer. I'll sell the furniture to pay for my fare and come to New Zealand with you.'

Harry hugged her with delight and swung her round. 'You've changed your mind somewhat. Ever since I mentioned the idea you've said you'd die rather than live anywhere outside the East End.' He chuckled loudly, and his eyes twinkled.

'Oh, Harry, please don't laugh at me. My mind is made up. Even if Tony will not come with us, I'll still go. I've had enough of this country, after all, and I want to leave it all behind.'

'That's me gel,' said Harry giving her a rough kiss.

Once Harry was home from prison, he and Amy got busy packing up and putting all the furniture up for sale. Amy was surprised to discover that she had no regrets now. All of a sudden she could not bear to think back to the past, and she had a strong and sudden urge to go forward.

To her surprise and pleasure, Tony wanted to join them. 'I might as well,' he said. 'After all, Harry is the only father I've ever known and I would miss him. And there are good prospects out there and times are getting very bad here in England. Even a good education is no guarantee that I would get a job.'

All packed and ready, Amy took a last look from the balcony of her flat, looking away over the roof tops towards the tower of the old church. 'Goodbye, Mum,' she murmured. 'It's all changed now. You would not like it here now, either, so I am going to a new life.'

And so in March, Amy, Harry and Tony sailed away on a ship to the other side of the world, never to return to the East End again.

CHAPTER TWENTY-ONE

Boysie

The hospital staff were all very concerned about Boysie, who was a general favourite with staff and patients alike. He had been with them now for four years and had gradually improved enough to make friends with the other patients and do little tasks to help the nurses.

Nurse Helen was particularly attached to him and had tried patiently to teach him to write his own name, but so far she had not accomplished much. But she did have quite a warm feeling for this poor unwanted man who needed friendship so much. They all called him Boysie because the local folk in the woods had told them that was what he had been called by the wretched old woman who claimed him as her son. Nurse Helen knew his story quite well and whenever she was on night duty and he was unable to sleep, she would sit by his bed and talk to him. 'I am from Kent,' she would say. 'I know those lovely woods where you came from. I used to go up there on my bike when I was at school.'

Boysie would grimace in reply and a sudden glint in his rolling eyes would tell her that he understood what she had said.

Helen had been brought up in the medical profession. Her father was a country doctor and her mother an ex-nurse. Helen herself never made the grade at the school because she hated to study and loved the free fresh air, preferring pony riding and biking in the woods to books. So she neglected her school work and did not obtain the medical degree her parents had wished for her. Yet Helen was content. First she did child nursing and had then progressed in stages to the psychiatric hospital where she was now. She did not mind in the least that she was not a doctor. The pain and suffering of these disturbed patients were to her like that of little puppies or kittens. She had to fuss and care for them. At twenty-two years old, she was a fair-haired, good-looking young woman and so full of happiness that a peaceful halo seemed to surround her. There was no doubt that she had found her rightful place in life. For the two years she had been in Greatstone she had got very attached to Boysie and he had improved under her care. But now, after his outing to the town, he lay in a coma. After seeing Amy, he had gone into a fit and had never recovered from it. But no one seemed particularly concerned about him now. The doctor's attitude was callous. 'He will never be cured,' he said. 'It might be the best thing just to let him slowly fade out.'

Helen was incensed about this attitude. She quarrelled with the other nurses and was in trouble with the sister. She tried to rouse Boysie and refused to keep giving him the sedatives prescribed for him. Eventually she was pulled up before the matron for disobedience of the hospital rules. The matron tore her off a strip and fined her. The meeting became so heated that in the end Helen announced that she wanted to leave. She left matron's room and was crying in the corridor when Dr Macgregor came by. They had trained in the same hospital but he was now an up-and-coming neurologist at a big London hospital. As Helen sobbed loudly outside matron's office, Dr Macgregor came up close to her. 'Tears?' he exclaimed. 'Not our Helen, our little sunshine girl? Who has upset you?'

Helen motioned towards matron's office door.

Dr Macgregor's eyebrows were raised. 'Oh, and what have you been up to?'

Helen liked him and was soon unburdening her soul to him. 'It's Boysie,' she said. 'He is in a coma and no one's doing anything to help him.'

'Oh, I see, you mean the young ginger lad?'

'Honestly, Dr Macgregor, I know he understands me, I am sure he does. I realize it is wrong to get personally involved with a patient but I can't help myself this time.'

Dr Macgregor patted her shoulder. 'Dry your tears and I will have a talk with matron to see if I can get some idea of the case. Now, cheer up, Helen, you are a wonderful nurse, and I'm sure they would hate to lose you.'

The next morning Helen was more her old self. She had been taken off Boysie's case and was in another ward but she noticed with satisfaction that Boysie was getting a thorough examination by Dr Macgregor, as well as the hospital's medical officer. And she was delighted to learn that he had been taken off all the drugs.

One evening she crept in to see Boysie. He just stared in front of him, his eyes glazed, and he obviously did not recognize her. The nurse on duty told Helen that he was at least sleeping more peacefully than he had before and 'he is going off to London tomorrow,' she added.

'Oh?' cried Helen, a little dismayed. 'Why?'

'They think they can operate on his brain. There seems to be some pressure there. They might even cure him and then he will be almost normal again.'

'Oh, how wonderful,' cried Helen.

'Of course,' said the nurse, 'it's a chance in a thousand. It's more likely to finish him off at the start.'

Helen dashed off to the lavatory to have another weep but in her heart she felt lighter. At least the doctors were going to try to do something about him, she thought, and not just let him lie there and die.

The next day, Boysie was taken away to the Brook Hospital, the most famous place in London for brain surgery.

While he was away, Helen moped around and rang the hospital twice a day, but she never got much information out of them because it was a new kind of treatment and the results would not be clear for some time.

Six weeks later Boysie came back to his old hospital. He looked quite different but he was still very confused.

Helen had wept many tears over him but the doctors were confident. Apparently they had taken part of a bullet out of his brain and were amazed that it had remained there for so long. No one could enlighten them as to how the bullet got there in the first place but they guessed that it was from some sort of shooting accident in his youth. There was no one able to tell and no one to care – only Helen, who was more determined than ever to get through to him. The matron was more sympathetic to her now and left her alone.

Slowly as the spring came round, Boysie improved. He sat up and grinned at her, and when she pushed him around the gardens to show him the first primroses, he seemed very pleased. He even tried to say something. As he struggled to get out the words, Helen put her ear close to his mouth. To her amazement and delight, she heard him whisper: 'Soaky. Woods. Flowers.'

Each day Boysie managed a few more words. Soon he was having speech therapy classes and physiotherapy, and gradually he learned to walk again. Tall, thin and stooping forward on a frame, he soon learned and before the next Christmas had come around, the improvement in him was amazing. He had put on weight and with the help of a pair of large spectacles he managed to focus his eyes. Helen was so happy for him. She bought him sweets and knitted him a pullover and she protected him from the more violent patients. She felt that he was hers; if it had not been for her interference they would have let him die. No mother could have been prouder of her boy than Helen was of her patient Boysie. He now would sit in the recreation room nodding his head to the music on the radio and trying, in an odd strangulated manner, to sing a song.

'Oh, look at him,' said Helen. 'He can hear the music and is really enjoying himself.'

But still in her heart she was worried. For if Boysie continued to improve at such a rate they would send him away to some other place – a permanent home for the disabled. She was not sure she could face losing him, she had become so attached to Boysie. Despite that concern, Helen was very happy. The following year she worked very hard for her sister's cap and obtained it. Her parents were rather surprised at her success for she had always been such a happy-go-lucky child but now had become very serious minded. Helen went home to Sussex occasionally to see them and always talked of this hospital and the marvellous recovery of one patient known as Boysie who now worked as a part-time porter and lived in the hospital.

'Daddy,' she said, 'it is nothing short of a miracle. You would never recognize him from what he was like. He has developed so well. He still has trouble with his speech and does not recall his past but we are great friends and he is very attached to me. I do feel very responsible for him.'

Her father pulled a long face. 'You are twenty-three years old, Helen,' he said, 'and it's time you found yourself a partner, but I'd rather you didn't fall for one of your lame ducks, one of your mental patients.'

'Now, that is very unkind,' Helen replied as her face flushed indignantly. 'I will bring Boysie down to meet you.'

'Don't bother,' her father replied sarcastically. 'I have plenty of disturbed patients of my own.'

Weeping tears of anger, she later told her mother about this conversation. 'Take no notice,' her mother said gently. 'He just works too hard. Bring your friend to visit us if you want to.'

'No, I won't,' said Helen, 'for if Daddy is unkind to him, it will undo all the good we have done.'

Helen put a stop to her visits home on her Sundays off, and instead she went walking in the country with Boysie. He had now put on weight and had grown into a fine figure of a man, with broad shoulders and a mop of bright red hair. He wore a nice tweed suit but he still dragged one leg a little when he walked. Helen soon corrected this drag with a good walking stick she bought him.

'For your birthday,' she said, holding it up towards him.

He grinned and shook his head, indicating that he did not have a birthday.

'Yes, you have,' said Helen, 'it is a certain day a year ago when you were very ill and then came back to life.'

They sat on the park seat and he shyly put an arm around her. Helen leaned her head on his shoulder. They were so happy and peaceful together.

'Don't you remember anything about your past life?' she asked him.

'Yes,' he nodded, pointing to his head and then his mouth, as if to say, 'I do but cannot say.'

'Oh, poor darling,' Helen kissed and fussed him. 'Next Sunday we will go on the bus to those woods where you came from. Would you like that? And if you remember anything you will tell me. All right?'

Boysie took her hand to his moist lips and kissed it.

'Oh, Boysie,' Helen giggled. 'You are becoming a real Romeo. Come on, let's get home to tea.'

Hand in hand they strolled back to the hospital as happy as any two people could possibly be.

Boysie had his own little room at the hospital and a light job as a porter plus three meals a day. Everyone seemed to have forgotten that he was once a patient. He was now big and strong and a great help with the more disabled patients. As far as the hospital authorities were concerned, Boysie had become part of the fittings, that is, to all except Helen, who fell more in love with him each day.

The next weekend, Helen kept her promise. They packed a picnic basket, and caught the bus into town to take them out to the woods where Sparky had come from. They got off at the end of the road, it was a lovely summer's day. Flowers bloomed everywhere, and birds sang a song of welcome as they strolled up the hill to the woods. On one side of the road were some brand new bungalows, and Boysie shook his stick at them.

'Oh, dear!' said Helen, 'they have started to build on the land. What a pity, it was so lovely up here when I was at school.'

They continued up the long lane to the top of the hill where there was a wonderful view of the point at which the Thames and Medway met. The two rivers gleamed in the sunlight and ships sailing up the river to London or out to the wild empty sea looked like tiny toys.

'Oh, it is lovely up here in spite of the building going on,' exclaimed Helen. 'Do you see anything that you can remember, Boysie?'

Boysie just shook his head and began to investigate the picnic basket.

After they had eaten they lay down side by side and looked up at the swallows flying around overhead in the lovely blue sky. Most of that lovely green forest had been destroyed. Great oak trees lay still on the ground dry and perishing in the hot sun and there were large gaps in the woodland where it had been cleared.

'Oh, what a shame,' said Helen but Boysie had got excited and was pointing to a piece of old rope attached to a fallen tree.

'You remember this?' It *did* mean something. 'Oh, it is so exciting, darling, tell me about it?' Helen cried.

They sat on the fallen oak and kissed as lovers. Then Boysie showed her that this piece of rope had once been Soaky's washing line. That much he recalled.

'Was she your mother?' enquired Helen gently.

He shook his head.

'You are a good bit older than I am,' she ventured. 'I often wonder if you had a wife and family?'

Boysie suddenly looked sad and then said in pure Cockney: 'Yus, I did.'

Helen smiled. 'Oh, Boysie, what English you speak! It is not very good.'

But Boysie had got very excited and was now pointing towards the river. Helen stood beside him and held his hand, a puzzled frown on her brow as she tried to work out what he meant. Suddenly she knew. 'Down the river to the town, to London town!' She turned to him, her eyes lit up with excitement.

Boysie grabbed her hand and held her close. He was getting very agitated.

'So that's it, darling,' said Helen. 'You are not from Kent woods but London. Well, that is marvellous, but it will have to do for today.'

But Boysie wanted to continue holding her. He kissed her repeatedly on the lips and would not release her. Helen moulded her body to his for a moment as she realized that he was now a true man and that he obviously wanted to make love to her. She held him close in return. 'No, darling,' she said gently. 'I have not done that yet, but if I do it will be with you. But not now. Be a good boy and let us go home.'

Boysie smiled happily. 'I . . . love . . . you,' he said slowly but very clearly.

As they went down the hill he whistled a catchy tune which Helen recognized. 'Maybe it's because I'm a Londoner that I love London so.'

'Oh, it is so marvellous,' she cried. 'It's all slowly coming back to you.'

As time went by their relationship became more intimate. Boysie improved with each passing day, but Helen discovered that he had a perverse kind of humour and could also be very jealous and have bad temper moods. But normally he was just very happy and very willing to help anyone who needed it.

The doctors were delighted with his improvement, and one even expressed the opinion that he thought Boysie might one day remember very clearly who he was and where he came from.

After this good report Helen was slightly worried. The two of them were now very involved and very much in love. She had once even mentioned marriage and Boysie had smiled a really nice smile as if to say that as long as she stayed with him he would do what ever she wanted. His sentences were short but to the point, so they had no difficulty now in communicating. But he was still shy and awkward with others. Helen continued to worry. Suppose he suddenly found out who he was? He must have had some background. The doctor had stated that he was well past thirty-five or might even be forty, and she was just twenty-four. He must have lived with someone somewhere. Worried, she turned it all over in her mind, hoping that the truth would never be revealed. It would not bring pain and trouble.

'Boom' 'Boom!' Boysie suddenly said one day. 'That's it, bombed, my mother down our street.'

'Was she killed in the war? Is that what you are trying to tell me, Boysie?' Helen asked cautiously.

He nodded emphatically.

'So you definitely came from London,' she said. 'Perhaps we had better continue our search for your identity,' she said without enthusiasm.

Boysie stared at her thoughtfully and then took off his big specs. 'No, no,' he cried, 'I stay with you.'

'All right, my love,' she said, fondling his mop of hair, 'if that is what you want, I'll leave the hospital and we will get a flat and live together.'

This pleased him. He said, 'I am strong, I'll work for you.'

'I am sure you will but in the meantime we will lay our plans and go away together.'

No one was surprised when Helen left the hospital. She had been very lucky and landed a position as district nurse with a cottage thrown in with the job. It was in a remote village way down in Surrey.

A week later Boysie suddenly discharged himself from the hospital. Helen met him in town and they travelled down together to their cosy love nest. And as far as the population of the village was concerned, Boysie was the district nurse's husband.

The roses around the door and the pretty garden in front of their new home soon became Boysie's pride and joy. It gave them great happiness and they felt that they had left the tumult and the cares of the outside world behind.

The years passed very quickly in that remote country cottage which they had called Shady Nook. It was now a real home. Helen had two children and had become rather plump but her nature was still very sunny. She rode her bike leisurely around the country village in her neat nurse's uniform with her big black bag strapped to the handlebars. She visited the old and the sick and often the poor just to bring a smile, sustenance and words of comfort. Sister Helen was well known for her generosity and was very popular in the village.

'Strange man, that husband of hers,' the gossips in the pub would comment. 'Never holds a complete conversation. If you ask him anything he just says, "Ask the wife". Mind you, he's a nice quiet man, and good looking, too, but a lot older than her.'

Peace and contentment seemed to exude from Shady Nook. The roses round the door flourished and the flowers in the front garden bloomed in profusion. Boysie, the withdrawn, ginger-headed man tended them with love and care, and he also grew vegetables out in the back garden. Quietly he went about his work. His red hair shone bright in the sunshine and a nice bushy moustache gave him a sober appearance. The world outside did not bother him for he had found complete happiness in these late years. He also did little electrical jobs and was getting very good at them.

Helen was impressed by his skill. 'I often wonder if you once studied electronics somewhere,' she said, 'you are so good at that kind of work.'

'Oh well,' said Boysie. 'I don't remember, so what does it matter?'

Helen put a big notice on a board at the front gate outside. It read: 'Electrical repairs done. Plants for sale, and seasonal fruits.' Thus with her own salary on top they fared very well. John and Jennifer, their two children, grew up strong and carefree. They fished in the stream and went for long walks over the hills with Daddy. He was the be all and end all of their young lives. He was always at home while Mum was often busy and out of the house at odd hours.

Boysie had forgotten the bad days and was now living a full life. There were still times when he was very slow and stood staring into space as if there was something on his mind which he could not recall. But Helen was the bright and breezy one, doctoring him up and saying, 'No, my love, no looking back, only forwards.'

Then one day when Johnnie was six and Jennifer four, Helen suggested an outing. 'It would be so nice to give the children a day out. Let's go up to London for the day.' They rarely left the village, so this was a real treat.

There had been a royal wedding recently and the town was still flood-lit. The West End was a gay land bright with decorations, and quite a sight to see.

'London?' said Boysie, a little amazed.

'Well, it will be nice for the children to see it,' replied Helen. 'Most of the villagers have been up there.'

'As you wish, dear,' he said.

On Sunday morning they set off. They caught the excursion train to Victoria Station, and the kids were extremely happy and excited. Helen and Boysie were nicely dressed and looked like a very handsome respectable couple from the country.

They walked to Trafalgar Square where they fed the pigeons and Boysie carried Jennifer shoulder high down Oxford Street mingling with the tourists. It was fairly quiet because all the shops were closed.

Suddenly Boysie said brightly. 'It's Sunday, let's go down the Lane.'

'What lane?' asked Helen in her ignorance of London.

'Petticoat Lane,' he said decidedly. 'Come on, kids, we'll go down the tube.'

The escalators and the underground trains were an added thrill for the children.

'It's nice in the smoke, ain't it kids?' said Boysie with a laugh.

As they went out into the East End streets, a strange mood seemed to have possessed him. They milled among the crowds in the busy market. Helen felt a little nervous and held firmly on to her purse in case it got stolen. They hung about the stalls laughing at the Jewish traders and their Sunday patter. When the kids bought coloured balloons from a wizened old man, Boysie called to him, 'Hullo, mate, how's tricks.'

Helen looked concerned. 'Do you know him' she asked.

'No,' said Boysie, 'but I just felt like saying hello.'

'Did you used to live here, Daddy?' asked John, staring in wide-eyed wonder at the stall full of toys.

'No, but I used to play about down here on Sundays with me mate Harry and we used to get two bob each for helping to pack the stalls up when the market closed.'

'How funny,' giggled the kids. They were certainly enjoying themselves.

But Helen looked a little pale. Inside she felt sick. It had not been a very good idea, this East End trip, she thought. Boysie might recall his past life and she might lose him.

But Boysie seemed so full of beans and it was hard not to be happy for him, and he strode through the back streets holding himself upright and very alert. He stopped in front of an old pub that was now closed down. The windows were barred up, and Boysie stared at it in a puzzled way. Then he turned and said: 'Come on kids, I'll find the place where I used to live.'

With Helen trailing slowly along behind, and holding his kids' hands, Boysie strode along through the maze of odd little streets, alleys and high-rise flats. He looked around very intently until they came to another smaller market. Here the road ran over a small rise with an island in the centre of the road. 'Look,' he said, 'this is it, Whitmore Road. We used to run races down there to the old church and back again when I was a kid.' Again he stood still and looked solemnly around him. There was no trace whatsoever of the old street. There was not one house or person left to reassure him. Tears flooded his eyes as he put his hand to his head. 'It's no good,' he said miserably. 'It's all a blank void, but I am sure this is the place.' He shook his head in grief.

Helen put her arms around him. 'Hush, darling, don't look back. Let's only go forwards. I'll call a taxi and we will go home to Shady Nook.'

Boysie nodded and smiled at her. Then hand-in-hand, they turned and walked back slowly towards the tube station.